BEHIND A CLOSED DOOR

MEL SHERRATT

ISBN-13: 978-1493641802
ISBN-10: 1493641808

Also in The Estate Series

Somewhere to Hide (Book 1)
Fighting for Survival (Book 3)

PROLOGUE

Of all the shenanigans that occurred on the estate, nothing sent shivers down Josie Mellor's spine more than a no-response call.

'Josie, it's Trevor. The alarm's going off at five Nursery Lane. No one's answering.'

'But that's Edie Rutter!' Josie grabbed her car keys, the phone still against her ear.

'Her son can't get there for about an hour,' Trevor continued. 'Any chance of you checking on her for me?'

'I'm already on my way.'

It took Josie less than five minutes to drive to Edie's home. She banged on the front door and lifted up the letterbox to shout through.

'Edie! It's Josie. Are you there?'

She looked through the window but could see no one in the front room. She raced around to the back and stood on her toes to look through the kitchen window. There didn't seem anything amiss, although she couldn't see the floor from where she was standing. She moved to the bedroom window, took off a woollen glove, and gave it a firm rap.

'Edie?'

Cursing her short legs, Josie moved aside a terracotta plant pot, jumped up onto the low wall and looked inside. Screwing up her eyes, she tried to focus through the pattern of the netting.

In desperation, she began to lift up some of the pots around the tiny patio area. At her third attempt, she found what she was looking for. Moments later, she unlocked Edie's front door and stepped in. Please God, she prayed, don't let it be gruesome. Let her be asleep.

The television was on low as she stepped into the tiny porch. Through the slightly open door, she could see a foot in a pink slipper. Pushing it open, her hand shot to her mouth. Wide eyes stared straight at her. Edie was lying on her back, her head turned towards the door. There was a pool of blood around her ear.

Josie gagged. There was no life in Edie's eyes but she looked terrified. The buzzer for the lifeline system still hung round her neck; Josie had fitted it when Edie's husband had died. Alfred Rutter had left Edie broken-hearted and distraught – leaving Josie with the job of visiting her regularly to see that she was coping.

'God bless you, Edie Rutter,' Josie whispered into the silence of the room. It was then that she noticed the mess. The living room was littered with Edie's possessions; the lamp and its occasional table lay on its side, photographs were ripped from their frames and discarded, glass shards sprinkled like confetti, and the mahogany sideboard stood with its doors wide open, its contents slung across the carpet. And what was that on the poker? She shuddered.

A noise behind her made her jump.

'Fucking hell, Andy, you scared the shit out of me! Couldn't you have knocked to let me know you're here?'

'Sorry, the door was open. I heard the call and then I saw your car outside.'

Tears streamed down Josie's cheeks. Her hand shook as she pointed at Edie. 'She's dead. And I don't think it was an accident.'

Andy took off his police helmet and a glove. He checked Edie's neck for a pulse. Then he held his palm in front of her mouth. But there was no sign of life.

'What the hell happened in here, Andy?' Josie asked. 'It's one thing to rob the old dears but another to take their lives as they try to defend what's theirs.'

'There are some nasty bastards out there. We can't protect everyone, no matter how hard we try.'

'How long do you think she's been there?' Josie glanced at the clock on the mantel piece. It was only nine thirty-two. 'All night, maybe?'

'Early hours, I suspect. She must have come round enough to raise the alarm before she died.'

Josie pointed to the poker lying on the rug, knowing better than to touch it. 'There's blood on that.'

Andy nodded before reaching for his radio. 'I'll get the team out, set the wheels in motion.'

When Josie didn't move, Andy placed a hand on her shoulder. She looked up at him with tears in her eyes.

'How can anyone do that?' she asked. 'Even if it was an accident, someone left her there to die. That's beyond belief. It's so cruel.'

Andy sighed. 'Aren't you forgetting something?'

'What?'

'This is the Mitchell Estate.'

CHAPTER ONE

Josie Mellor threw her car keys onto her desk and collapsed in a huddle on her chair.

'What is it with me and the Bradley family? That's five more complaints I've received in as many days. I was hoping after I'd been to visit Gina last week that the twins would behave themselves.'

'Your three-fifteen's here,' Debbie Wilkins shouted over. 'I've put her in interview cubicle one. She seems a bit stressed.'

'A bit stressed?' Josie retorted. 'She ought to try finding dead people and dealing with the aftermath like I did with Mrs Rutter last month. And before I can take a minute to catch my breath this afternoon, I've got to deal with all *this*.' She pushed aside the pile of phone messages on her desk that had grown considerably since she'd left it two hours ago. 'I'm sure our tenants think I have the answers to all their problems.'

'Poor Edie,' Debbie said as she joined her.

'I really liked her. She was a lovely old sort.'

Josie had been distraught when Edie had been found dead with head injuries in her bungalow a few weeks ago. The place had been trashed and a huge sum of money, among other things, had been stolen. But Mrs Rutter's daughter had been particularly upset that a pearl necklace with a clasp in the shape of a butterfly was missing. It had been a family heirloom for years. There had been no leads at all, not even with the press coverage it had received for a couple of weeks afterwards.

'It doesn't seem fair, does it?' Josie could feel tears forming again. 'People shouldn't die all alone. I met her son at Mr Barber's funeral. He thought a lot of his parents, not like some of the families on the estate.'

'Cluck, cluck, Mother Hen,' Ray Harman chirped up. 'It's a good job everyone has Josie Mellor.'

Josie pulled a face at Ray. 'Yes, it is, because if it was up to you, there would be no Mitchell Estate, right?'

Ray nodded, pushing his glasses back up his nose. 'You got me.'

'Yes, I got you a long time ago, you smarmy git,' she muttered under her breath.

'You've only yourself to blame, though. If you would insist on spoon-feeding the morons, then what do you expect?'

Josie ignored him. She'd known a lot of people like Ray during her eighteen years working for Mitchell Housing Association. Ray was in his late forties and had been a housing officer for longer than Josie, yet he didn't mince his words when it came to job dissatisfaction. Between the two of them, they covered the sprawling estate, along with Doug Pattison, the maintenance officer. Doug looked after reporting all the repairs needed at the properties, but would always offer to help out if Josie didn't feel safe going to a visit alone. Ray, however, would be far too busy checking if garden hedges were an inch higher than they should be or whether Ms-Anderson-at-number-fifty-two's skirt needed to be an inch higher than it was.

Josie picked up two folders from her desk and wiped her eyes again. 'Right, then, I'd better get started on the next one. As the saying goes, no rest for the wicked.'

She put on her broadest smile as she walked into the glass-walled cubicle a few minutes later. 'Hello, Kelly.'

Kelly Winterton's face scrunched up with indignation.

'And, you,' Josie turned her attention to the young child sitting next to her, 'you must be Emily. Am I right?'

Emily nodded shyly.

'Do you remember me? I've met you before, at your house, and it's very nice to see you again. Now, if I give you some pens and a colouring book, do you think you can choose a picture to fill in with some bright colours while I speak to your mummy?'

'Have you got a red one?' asked Emily, wide brown eyes looking up expectantly. 'Please.'

Josie gave her one of the folders and watched her face light up when she saw the packet containing felt-tipped pens of every colour. Along with her mittens, her coat and scarf came off in a flash as she got down to it.

'Now then, it's your turn.' Josie pushed a thick form across the table towards Kelly. 'You'll need to fill in the bits I've marked with a cross while I go through your options.'

Kelly remained silent while she chewed on her nails.

'As the tenancy is in Mr Johnstone's name only, and due to his recent trip to Her Majesty's Services, the number one priority is to stay where you are now – at Patrick Street – while we set eviction proceedings in motion.'

'Eviction proceedings!' Kelly cried. 'What do you mean? He's only been sent down for six months!'

Josie flicked over a page and pointed to a box. 'Mr Johnstone isn't entitled to housing benefit if he's in prison for longer than thirteen weeks, and as he won't be able to pay the rent himself, we'll try and get him to give up his tenancy. Six months will give him a bill of at least two thousand pounds to pay when he gets released. And he'll have a criminal record – which will work in our favour. We don't do evictions willy-nilly. We feel we have a duty of care to offer you something else, and we have to follow procedures – take Mr Johnstone to court first, sign paperwork, so it's likely to take a while. You can stay at Patrick Street until that date, if you wish.'

Josie had Kelly's full attention now. 'But what if he only serves three months, half his time? Scott'll keep his nose clean, you know him.'

'Not my rulings, I'm afraid. And if he doesn't assign the property straight back to us, for every week he's inside, he'll be liable to pay when he does get out.'

Kelly sat forward. 'I'll claim benefits, then. I live there too.'

'Are there any bills in your name?'

'How the hell should I know?' They sat in silence until Kelly sighed loudly.

'I don't think so,' she replied.

'In that case, you have no proof that you've been living there. You're registered for benefits at 18 Christopher Avenue.'

Kelly frowned. 'No, that's my mum's address. I left there five years ago when I shacked up with Scott.'

'Not according to our records.'

'But he filled the forms in for me!'

Josie raised her eyebrows questioningly.

'I had my money paid into my own account,' Kelly snapped. 'I didn't have to ask him for it if that's what you're getting at!'

'No, what I'm trying to tell you is that he lived at Patrick Street claiming as a single man. You were – unbeknownst to you, maybe – claiming as a single mother.'

'But why would he do that?'

'To get more money. Lots of couples scam that way.'

Kelly shook her head. 'He wouldn't do that, not to us.'

'Oh, he would,' Josie told her. 'And he has.'

For a moment, Kelly sat quietly while her brain tried to work out the logistics of the conversation. She wondered how long the eviction process took but didn't dare ask. Even she realised that the rights must be different when a prison sentence got handed out.

'Mummy, look at my picture,' said Emily, thrusting the drawing book at Kelly.

'It's very good.' Kelly glanced at it quickly. 'Can you do another one while I finish off? There's a good girl.' She looked at Josie and spoke quietly. 'And my other option?'

Josie pointed to another box. 'You could have your own tenancy. It would have to be another property, though – it couldn't be Patrick Street because that's in Mr Johnstone's name.'

Kelly quickly wrote down her national insurance number. 'Would Scott be able to move in with me when he gets out?'

'Yes, but you'll have to declare it to the benefits agency. No more single living.'

'*I* didn't know that I was.'

Josie turned the form over to the back page. 'If you do decide to have your own tenancy, there are two flats ready to view.'

Kelly narrowed her eyes. 'You never said nowt about moving into a flat!' she hissed.

'There are only the two of you, and with you being classed as homeless now, you don't have much of a choice, I'm afraid.'

'But I'm not homeless – you're forcing me to leave my house! And there are three of us. You're forgetting Scott.'

Josie leaned forward, aware how vital it was that she gained Kelly's trust. 'I don't feel good about doing this but Mr Johnstone played things really clever. By keeping your name off any of the household bills, as well as the tenancy agreement, it means that you can't prove you've been living there for the past twelve months. Therefore, you're not entitled to stay. If he won't sign the forms, we'll start eviction proceedings for non-payment of rent. Eventually, the property will come back to us.'

'But you know how long I've been living there!' Kelly's eyes pleaded to Josie. 'You could vouch for me!'

'It's not that simple. For all I know, you could have been staying over for a couple of nights whenever I've visited.'

Kelly sat back in her chair again and folded her arms. 'So I'm fucked, whichever way I look at things?'

Josie was used to tenants swearing at her when she told them something they didn't want to hear. Unlike some of the violent ones who'd come within an inch of her face to do so, she sensed that Kelly wasn't using it for the benefit of annoying her. Her anger seemed to be directed at the system.

'The other thing I need to tell you is that both flats are on the top of the estate.'

'You mean on the 'hell'? Jesus Christ! It gets fucking worse!' Kelly kicked the table leg in temper. Emily jumped but with a quick, reassuring smile from her mum, continued to draw.

'It's only just off Davy Road,' explained Josie. 'Much better than being right at the top. And watch your language, please.'

Kelly could feel herself breaking. The Mitchell Estate was mostly made up of rented accommodation, some properties owned by the local authority and the majority of the remainder belonged to Mitchell Housing Association. It was split down the middle by a main road. Everyone knew that the top of the estate was the worst place in the city to live. 'Living on the hell', it was known as: the bottom of the estate, The Mitch, wasn't much better, but was definitely the lesser evil of the two.

As Kelly's head fell into her hands, Josie's heart went out to her.

The application form told her that she was twenty-four and Emily was four. From her appearance, Josie could see that Kelly was capable of looking after herself. She could spot no obvious indications of self-neglect; no dark bags under her eyes, no sallow, spotty skin, so she wasn't doing drugs – always a good sign. Kelly's dark brown hair was cut in a short and spiky style, and her iconic elfin face wore just the right amount of make-up to make Josie feel fifty-seven instead of thirty-seven. She wore stylish clothes, all clean and pressed, and her daughter was spotless.

'Both flats need decorating,' Josie forged ahead, regardless of Kelly's silence. 'Which we will give you an allowance for, but it probably won't cover the cost of all you'll need. I take it from your earlier comment that you'll be claiming benefits?'

Kelly slapped her hand down hard on the table top. 'Don't you look down your nose at me, you snotty cow, with your high and mighty attitude! Just because you work here doesn't mean that you're better than me. I used to have a job before I had Emily, but Scott wanted me to stay at home with her when she was little. What's wrong with that? Don't you think bringing up a kid is worthy of a job title?'

'You need to calm down, Kelly.'

'If you must know, I hate living off handouts. It makes me feel like crap.' She looked up again with a glare. 'Don't you think I wish I could get a job again? But it's been too long – who'd take me on? I've got no one to look after Emily. And if I did, I'd get a pittance that won't be worth getting out of bed for.'

'Don't knock yourself too much. You have as much chance as anyone.'

'But what can I do?'

'Lots, if you put your mind to it.'

Kelly stared at Josie, ready to protest again, but realised that she wasn't patronising her.

Josie pointed to the last empty box. 'You need to sign here as well. I also need to do a property inspection.'

'But I don't want to move out!'

'You don't have to move out straightaway, but you *will* be evicted and then I won't be able to help you.'

Kelly's shoulders drooped even further. 'I don't have a choice?'

'Yes,' nodded Josie. 'You could always try and find yourself another property to rent. But you need to decide soon what is right for you – and Emily. I can't hold the flats for too long. There are other people on the waiting list.'

'Mummy, can we go now?' Emily asked. 'I want to see Nanny.'

Kelly smiled at her. 'Sure we can, poppet. You get your coat on, I won't be a minute.'

Josie sighed. Underneath the hard exterior, she could see a frightened young woman. Yes, she lived on a rough estate and mixed with a few rough characters, but this wasn't the east end of London.

Already she could feel herself warming to Kelly's plight as she watched her fasten up Emily's coat. Josie knew she could help her. It would be hard work trying to pierce Kelly's durable shell, but persistence was her middle name. How many hostile people had she befriended over the years? They hadn't all been success stories but she had a feeling that Kelly could be one of them.

'I can help you through this,' she offered.

'I don't need your help,' Kelly replied curtly. 'I don't need anyone's help. I can manage on my own.'

Hmm, thought Josie, maybe not! Even so, she wasn't perturbed by the tone of her voice.

'I'm sure you can,' she agreed. 'Now, you need to sign here and we're done. Then there are the flats to view.'

CHAPTER TWO

'So who else do you know on the Mitchell Estate?' Josie asked Kelly later that afternoon, as she walked down the path towards a block of four flats.

Kelly shrugged her shoulders as she followed behind her. 'I know loads of people but no one I'm close to. I see Lynsey Kirkwell every now and again.'

Lynsey was another of Josie's tenants. She was twenty-two, with three children each having a different father, and her family was notorious. Josie knew her brothers, too; Michael and Stevie were the elder two of three, Jay being the youngest by ten years.

'Funny choice of friend.'

'I met her in the health centre when I took Emily for her first weigh-in. She was nice to me. Scott's not keen on me having friends, but Lynsey was okay because he knew her brothers.'

'But she's so untidy!' Josie screwed up her face. She wanted to say 'filthy', but knew where her professional boundary lay. Lynsey had been one of her failures. She thought back to the last visit she'd made to her flat; wallpaper on most of the walls had been torn, crayon drawings and swear words prominent over the bottom half. The furniture and appliances were up-to-date and brand new but there wasn't really a need for the top-notch carpeting as there had been nowhere to stand without treading on someone's clothes. The smell of body odour and chip fat stayed with Josie for hours afterwards, clinging to her coat, no matter how much body spray she squirted on it.

'Is Emily with your parents?' she asked next.

'None of your business.'

Josie chose to ignore the hostility in Kelly's voice. 'Let's look at this flat first and the other one is further down.'

Kelly watched as Josie struggled to undo the frozen padlock on the steel door that covered the front entrance. 'Why are there so many boarded-up properties around here?' she asked.

'It's called vandaglaze.' The door gave out an almighty groan. 'It means the buggers can't damage it. It saves us thousands. You should see what they do to these places if they get in. Mind the step, now.'

Kelly waited for Josie to kick away the colossal mountain of junk mail and final demands. Then she followed her down a narrow, dark passageway. She wrinkled up her nose at the smell that assaulted her nostrils.

'New plaster,' Josie explained when she noticed. 'It smells like pee, doesn't it? But it'll go when the property has been ventilated.' She ushered her into a fair sized room. 'Bedroom one. Needs a lick of paint and swift removal of the ghastly seventies swirls.'

One step to the right.

'Bedroom two... Emily's, maybe?'

Kelly dragged heavy feet behind her as she walked across to inspect the cupboard in the corner of the room. She tugged at a piece of stray wallpaper around the doorway. It fell onto the manky cord carpeting that had been left behind. She shook her head in dismay. How could this woman standing beside her think that *this* room was good enough for her daughter?

Josie sighed in irritation as they moved through into the living room. She could clearly see the damage caused by Mrs Corden's five dogs – which had been removed by the RSPCA – claw marks on both doors, teeth marks on the doorframe. The room hadn't been decorated in a good many years, the paintwork yellow and peeling. Even the UPVC windows had stains of nicotine imprinted in them.

Kelly went through the door leading into the small kitchen. Another overpowering odour emerged when she opened a cupboard door.

'It's due to have a re-fit next year,' Josie explained when she saw Kelly pull back her head. 'You'll be able to choose from three styles and colours.'

'Do people really live like this?' Kelly eventually found her voice. She kept her back towards Josie while her eyes flitted around in revulsion. 'I don't know how you do this job. It's gross in here.'

'This is nothing compared to some of the places I visit. This estate has a large number of social housing properties but, fortunately for me, the city council owns most of them. Mitchell Housing Association is a drop in the ocean. Besides, showing people around empty properties is the better part of my work. I much prefer it to when people have been there for a while and made their mark, if you know what I mean.'

People were often confused with Josie's role of housing officer, especially the tenants, who thought she pushed her nose in where it didn't belong. For work purposes, the estate had been split into patches and she and Ray had 600 properties each to look after, no matter what the complaint. One appointment could find Josie holding someone's hand as they cried for the loss of a loved one while she sorted out their benefits, the next she could be laying down the law with a noisy family hell bent on causing chaos for the rest of their street. She could be sorting out an alleged dog barking complaint just as easily as reporting a dead cat run over on the main road, a mound of rubbish being dumped on the odd patch of grass or having a cup of tea with a new tenant. On the odd occasion, Josie had to evict someone for anti-social behaviour, it was usually followed by showing a desperate family around a scratty property they'd have to make their home from now on, due to theirs being repossessed.

'Most of my tenants live respectfully,' she added, after Kelly had gone quiet again. 'We do have the odd ones who won't help themselves. That's why the property is in such a mess. There's only the bathroom left, do you want to see it?'

Kelly shuddered as she turned back to face her. 'I'm not looking in there after seeing the state of everywhere else.'

Josie smiled. 'That's my USP,' she said, leading the way to the newly refurbished room.

'Your what?'

Josie grinned, feeling awkward. 'My unique selling point. It's just had a makeover. You'll be the first one to pee in the toilet – unless the workmen beat you to it.'

*

As Josie made her short trip home at the end of the day, she couldn't get Kelly Winterton out of her head. It seemed a peculiar set-up, Kelly and Scott. Most couples on the Mitchell Estate who committed benefit fraud claimed they were living at separate addresses so that they could each get their hands on a single parent allowance. 41 Patrick Street had been set up as if Kelly didn't exist and it seemed intentional. But Kelly did exist. And she said Scott loved her. It didn't ring true to Josie.

She sat in the small queue of cars waiting for the traffic lights to turn green, all the time thinking that Kelly didn't seem right for the girlfriend of a thief. It was as if she'd given in to life at an early age. Yet she certainly seemed to love Scott, so did he owe her in some way? Josie made a mental note to find out more background information about the couple.

The outside light shone brightly when she pulled into the driveway. Home for Mr and Mrs Mellor was a semi-detached house in a quiet, leafy cul-de-sac that Josie had been left in her mother's will. Inside, the pampas bathroom suite and drab, wooden kitchen units had been swapped for white enamels, chrome fittings and natural woods. Oppressive, worn carpets had been replaced with wooden flooring and rugs. Curtains that had hung at the single-glazed windows for years had been ripped down and, in their place, coloured-blinds and tag-topped linen had been put up, now in front of double-glazed units.

It still hadn't made the house into a home though.

'Finally, you're back.' Stewart's voice came booming from the kitchen as she walked through the front door.

Josie's heart sank at his tone. She pulled off her coat and decided to ignore it.

'Have you had anything to eat yet?' she asked him.

Stewart came from out of the shadows, his eyes as dark as his mood. 'Thought I'd wait for you. I wasn't sure what time you'd be back.'

Josie moved past him and into the kitchen, sighing loudly as she looked around the worktops. A knife stood erect in the butter tub, a dirty plate next to it and the bread by its side, fallen slices left out in the air. On the kitchen table, three mugs congregated around an empty crisp packet.

'You must realise how time flies when you're in all afternoon,' she replied as she set about tidying the room. 'Couldn't you at least clean up after yourself?'

Stewart gathered together the dishes and dumped them into the kitchen sink. 'It's not worth washing three mugs and a plate. You can do them after tea. What are we having, by the way?'

'It'll have to be something from the freezer, I suppose. I didn't have time to do any shopping today.'

Josie had planned to go to the supermarket to stock up during her lunch break, but an alleged complaint about a dangerous dog had come in that had taken an age to sort out. The tenant had insisted she call the police, which she wouldn't do before investigating further. Josie had to take both sides into consideration before she made a decision as to who was in the wrong. She'd arranged to see the dog's owner tomorrow to get their account. It was something she wasn't looking forward to: the owner's bark was far worse than the dog's.

'Not again.' Stewart sounded in pain. 'Why can't you come home earlier and cook something interesting? Like shepherd's pie or roast chicken and all the trimmings. You used to cook all the time.'

'All the time was when you would have been appreciative of it. Don't you realise that I work long hours, too?' Josie ferociously squeezed washing up liquid into the bowl and ran the hot water. 'Oh yeah, of course you do. You're always quick to rub that in my face.'

Almost sullenly, Stewart pushed past her. 'I'm going to have a shower and then I'll be on my computer. Shout me when it's ready.'

'Stewart! Wait!' Josie called out, the compassionate side of her refusing to give up. 'What's wrong?'

'What's *wrong*?' he repeated her question with a sneer. 'As soon as you get home, you start moaning at me. The minute you walk through the door, it's 'why haven't you done this, Stewart' or 'did you remember to do that, Stewart'. I can't understand why though because you never do anything for me. You can't even cook something for me! Instead I have to make do with supermarket ready-meal garbage.'

'That's not fair,' Josie retaliated. 'You finished work at half past two; you could have gone to the shops this afternoon. You could have prepared some vegetables. You could have put a chicken in to roast so that I could finish off when I got in.' She pointed to the worktop. 'And you could have tidied this mess up, so that I don't have to. There are two of us in this marriage.'

'You're always coming home later than you say,' Stewart added, ignoring her jibes. 'You seem to think that job of yours is far more important than me.'

'Of course it isn't,' Josie snapped. 'You know I like to come home as soon as I can.'

'To your house, not to me.'

'No, I –'

With him scuttling out of the room after slamming the door, things suddenly became brighter again. Josie rummaged in the cupboards for something to lessen his bad mood. At the same time, she couldn't help thinking that surely some women must be welcomed home with a meal on the table, a bottle of wine chilling and good conversation every night. Why did she always feel as though she'd be coming home and treading on eggshells? It seemed worse than being at work at times.

Half an hour later, Stewart emerged in the doorway again, smelling clean and fresh. At five-foot ten, he stood eight inches taller than Josie, but she often felt like it was eighteen as he towered over her. Thin build, with the beginnings of a paunch on his stomach, his fair hair hung down in waves and always looked as if it could do with a good styling. But then who was she to criticize? Josie's brown hair was two different colours due to the blonde dye that she had fatefully tried out last year. It may tumble down below her shoulders but she hadn't the heart to get it dyed again. Neither was it worth hearing Stewart moaning about her wasting yet more money stripping it back to its natural colour professionally. Still, she supposed it didn't look too bad when it was tied up.

'I'm going out,' he informed her, grabbing his jacket from off the chair.

'But I've put some pasta on to cook! I remembered I bought some mince the other day. I'm making spaghetti bolognaise.'

'Can't be bothered to wait.'

'But... where are you going?'

'I told you – out.'

'Don't go, Stewart!' Josie cried. 'Please wait.'

The door slammed shut behind him.

'Piss off, then!' she shouted in frustration. 'See if I care.'

CHAPTER THREE

The following morning, Josie picked up her folder, fastened the zip on her work coat and stepped out of her car into Clarence Avenue. The January weather was continuing its cold snap and she pulled the collar in close to her neck, praying that Amy Cartwright would be in this time. Even though the appointment was pre-arranged, Amy often forgot she was coming.

The young girl that came to the door didn't look any older than thirteen, but in reality she was nineteen. Unfortunately, her mental age was still that of a thirteen-year-old when she'd been taken advantage of.

By the state of her appearance, it didn't look like she was coping very well this week. The heavily-built teenager's face was fraught, her dark hair was unkempt, her eyes downcast. Most of her six-month-old son's breakfast had found its way down the front of her pyjamas.

'Hi, Amy.' Josie changed her worried face to a cheery one. 'Had a late start this morning?'

'Reece kept me awake all night,' Amy explained tearfully. 'He won't stop crying.'

'Let me take a look, see if I can figure out what's bothering him.'

Josie followed her through into the lounge. Her shoulders sagged at the state of it. Amy and the baby didn't have much in the way of clothing, but every piece of it seemed to be littering the floor. A disgruntled Reece was propped up on the settee, with a cushion under his arm to stop him falling.

'You need to put some of your clothes away,' Josie said matter-of-factly. 'Can you fold them up into a neat pile on the armchair for me first, please?' Amy obliged and Josie picked up the baby. 'Hey, little man,' she soothed. 'What's wrong with you?'

'I've fed him this morning,' Amy spoke out, defensively. 'And

I've changed him twice because he had a really stinky nappy.'

'He's probably cutting a tooth. I'm sure there's nothing else wrong with him.'

'But why doesn't he stop crying?'

Josie played teacher again. 'Have you ever had a bad tooth, Amy?'

'Yeah, loads. My dad said I ate too many toffees when I was a baby.'

Josie nodded. Baby Reece seemed fine to her. Although she didn't profess to be a midwife, she suspected he was just being a bit grouchy because he'd missed his sleep. His cheeks were tinged with red, he didn't feel exceedingly warm to the touch, he was dry and he'd been fed. She laid him back down on the settee and reached for his rattle.

'He's tired because he's been kept awake by the pain of his teeth coming through. Why don't you try him with a bit of teething gel and see if he settles then?'

Amy went through to the kitchen and Josie followed her. Apart from a small pile of dishes in the sink, the room was cluttered but clean. Josie opened the larder door and checked its contents; it was full of mostly canned foods, but there were lots of them, so there was no need to make a shopping list yet.

'How are you feeling this week? What did the doctor say about your asthma?'

'He gave me another inhaler.' Amy pulled it from her pyjama pocket. 'It's purple.'

Josie smiled at her innocence. Amy was still a child, looking after her own. Because she wouldn't tell her parents who Reece's father was, let alone Josie, Amy's father had thrown her out onto the streets. Josie had tried to talk him round but to no avail, and Amy had been put into a small flat in Clarence Avenue, on the opposite side of the estate from everyone she knew. Her mum, afraid of what her husband would do to her, visited on the quiet every now and then, but other than her, Amy had no one to turn to. What a position to be in – nineteen, no family contact, no partner to help her, no future to look forward to. Still, if Josie made a difference to one young mum on the estate, it was something. Job satisfaction, she would call it.

Once Reece had been placated, Josie pulled out a blank to-do list and started to fill it in. Amy needed to pay an instalment on her electricity bill, sort her dirty washing into two piles ready to load, and take Reece to the clinic. She also wanted her to join in with the mothers' and toddlers' group on Friday over at the community house, a neighbourhood one-stop shop run by volunteers from the estate. Surprisingly, Amy was willing to give it a go this week. Shyness usually stopped her.

Confident that everything was in hand, Josie made her way to her next call. Charlotte Hatfield was twenty-three and had four children under the age of five. She also had a violent partner she'd fled from several times, and was currently hiding out on the estate. Josie had seen Charlotte twice already but was finding it hard to break down the barriers.

Charlotte came to the door, cigarette in one hand, baby held firmly in the other. Like Amy, she was wearing pyjamas. Her greasy hair hung limp, the bags under her eyes as dark as liquorice. The skin from her bottom lip was peeling off.

Charlotte didn't speak, just left the door open for Josie to follow her. The living room they went into was sparsely furnished, with a tatty settee, chair and coffee table that Josie had managed to find for her, and bare plastered walls that had yet to be decorated. Two large windows were at either end of the room, but only one set of curtains had been pulled apart. In the middle of the floor, the twins – four-year-old boys – raced cars along the bare floorboards. Two-year-old Joshua sat at his mum's feet.

'Shift out of my way, Callum,' said Charlotte. 'Jake, stop screeching at the top of your bloody voice, will you?'

'How are things?' Josie sat down on a stripy deckchair that would be better placed outside in the garden. She gathered together her paperwork and opened Charlotte's file. As she looked up, she noticed the remainder of a black eye. Charlotte's hair hid most of the bruising, but it could clearly be seen when she turned to face her more.

'Okay,' Charlotte answered. She sat down on the worn settee, resting the baby to the side of her chest.

'Has Nathan been in touch?'

'No!'

'Then how did you get that bruise?'

'I fell.'

Josie raised her eyebrows. 'Are you sure?'

Charlotte glared at her. 'I told you, didn't I? Don't you believe me?'

'Well –'

'He's not been here, okay? But he'll find me eventually. He always does.'

'Then how did you get the injury?' Josie knew she was pressing things but refused to back down. Sometimes it worked and people opened up to her, sometimes it didn't and she'd be sent packing, but it was always worth a try.

'He rang my mobile,' Charlotte spoke eventually. 'I was having a lie down. I'd had a shit night with Poppy. She'd kept me awake for most of it and then Callum got me up at the crack of dawn with tummy ache. I found out later that when the phone rang, Jake had picked it up. It was easy to get the street name out of him. Nathan asked a woman who was in her garden if anyone had moved in recently and the stupid cow pointed me out.'

Josie sighed loudly.

'He threatened to take my kids!' Charlotte raised her voice.

'I wasn't blaming you.'

'No, but you're judging me, aren't you? Your sort always does.'

'Not all of us do that, Charlotte.'

The baby squirmed. Charlotte settled her into the crook of her arm. 'He's not taking my kids,' she said defiantly. 'I won't let him do that.'

'He wouldn't be able to do anything if you'd press charges against him,' Josie urged, raising her voice over the twins crashing their cars together. 'He'd be locked up for a long time, the injuries he's caused you before.'

'No, I won't do it.' Charlotte shook her head. 'What if he gets off with it? I'll be turfed to another new town, new neighbourhood, new everything with nothing from a previous life. No furniture, no money, no one to turn to.'

'But wouldn't you like it to be over?'

As the boys' cries became noisier, Charlotte cracked. 'Will you pair shut up with that racket before I smack both of your arses!' she screamed. 'What do I have to do to get some peace around here, for fuck's sake?'

'Hey, come on now,' Josie tried to calm the situation. Both Callum and Jake hadn't taken any notice of their mother's outbreak, but little Joshua had burst into tears.

Charlotte looked at Josie with loathing. 'You have no idea what it's like,' she said. 'I've moved three times in a year to get away from him and each time he finds me again. Each time, it gets worse. I can't keep moving and I'm sick of being the one who has to do everything. And it's not good for the kids.'

'So what *do* you want to do about him?'

Charlotte shrugged her shoulders in resignation. 'I don't know, but I'm fed up of running. Even a harassment warning doesn't stop him. I miss my family. Maybe I should go back to Leeds and settle down near them. Maybe Nathan wouldn't want to follow me there.'

Maybe, maybe, maybe. Maybe next time he'll give you one slap too many and there'll be no one to look after the kids. Josie shuddered and kept her thoughts to herself.

'I'll help you,' she said, 'whatever you decide to do. In the meantime, I'll fit you the panic buzzer I've brought with me that will link you to our control room. If Nathan arrives and you don't want to see him, press it, and if we can, we'll get a police officer to attend as soon as. And if it's office hours, I'll do my utmost to attend myself.'

Charlotte looked away. Josie knew she'd probably heard it all before. Lord knows, she wished there was more she could do about it, but there were only so many hours in a day.

And anyway, who was she to dish out advice? In some ways, she was no different from Charlotte – wasn't she ruled by the mood swings of a man?

CHAPTER FOUR

'Mummy, can I watch the penguins?' Emily shouted up from the bottom of the stairs.

Kelly stretched out her legs. Through tear-swollen eyes, she stared at the clock on the bedside table. Half past seven: the day had hardly begun.

'Okay,' she shouted back, 'but be careful with the DVD.'

'I'm not a baby!'

Kelly had to agree. It didn't seem a minute since Emily had been born; now she was due to start school in September.

Moments later, Emily came running into the bedroom. 'Mummy! Where is it? I can't find it anywhere.'

'In a minute, Em.' Before she could complain, Emily tore off again.

Sighing heavily, Kelly pulled away the duvet and then promptly pulled it back again. What was there to get up for? It would have been different if Scott had been lying beside her. Usually she'd get up around eight, leaving Emily to climb into her empty space and flick on the portable television. But that had all changed since he'd been sent to prison.

'Mummy!'

'I'm coming! Have you looked under the settee?'

'I can see Jay's car.'

This time Kelly got out of bed quickly. She pulled on a pair of jeans and a jumper, wondering what he wanted this time. She'd refused to speak to him when he'd called around last week after the court hearing.

Kelly opened the front door. 'What do you want?' she snapped.

Jay hovered on the path for a moment, his hands thrust deep into his coat pockets. 'Can I come in?' he asked eventually.

'No, I don't want you calling when Scott isn't here.'

'I've got something for you,' his foot tapped on the door step, 'and I'd rather not give it to you here.'

Kelly sighed but held open the door.

'Hiya, Jay,' Emily greeted him as they went through into the living room. 'Daddy's not here. He's gone to work away, for a very long time.'

Scott had told Emily that she'd need to be a good girl if he had to go away for a while. He didn't want to see her if he was sent down and Kelly wouldn't take her anyway. She felt Emily was too young to go into a prison environment, even though it would be an open prison. In fact, she wasn't sure that she wanted to go there herself yet. Regardless, with any luck, he'd be out in three months – if he kept his nose clean.

'You'll just have to put up with me, little monster, won't you?' Jay told the little girl. He nudged her gently, almost knocking her over. Emily giggled loudly.

Jay Kirkwell was twenty-eight with stylish, dark spiked hair, olive skin and a tall, thin physique. Of the three brothers, Kelly liked him the most; she tolerated all of them, for Scott's sake, but Stevie and Michael were rough, more aggressive. Jay had a softer side to him. He would always use his mischievous grin to try and make her smile.

But he would get nowhere trying that technique today.

Work shy hands pushed a white envelope into hers. 'There's five hundred quid. It's to help out, while you're on your own.'

Kelly reached inside and pulled out a handful of twenty pound notes. All at once she realised that Scott even had a contingency plan. Just how big had that last job been?

She slumped down on the settee. 'Why weren't you caught?' she questioned Jay sharply.

'Because I wasn't there.'

'Come off it. Wherever Scott was, you were never far behind. And your brothers had been on the job, too. You'll be telling me it was your night off next.'

'No. I –'

'Don't tell me that you weren't involved – you went slinking off to the kitchen beforehand, to talk to him about *the job*.'

'That's not how it –'

Kelly held up her hand to quieten him but Jay continued anyway. 'I know you're angry with me. You're right, I couldn't stop them. But –'

'I lost count of how many times I begged Scott to go straight but once a thief there's always another better opportunity that's a dead cert. At least we managed to spend Christmas together as a family.'

'Three months is nothing, it'll go by in a flash. Scott will be –'

Jay knew he wouldn't get through to her so he left the sentence hanging. She had every right to be angry with him. He hadn't been able to stop them.

Jay wasn't looking at her now, but Kelly still glared at him anyway. She was too angry to speak. It didn't seem fair; two of his brothers and her partner were in jail and he was free to do as he pleased.

'Is that all?' she asked, when they'd been sitting without conversation for a while.

Reluctantly, Jay got to his feet. 'Suppose so.' He turned back before reaching the door. 'You can ring me anytime you need help. Don't push me away.'

Jay had penetrating eyes, the deepest of blue irises that would make the harshest of women fall under his spell in seconds. But they were wasted on Kelly. She stared back until he lowered his gaze.

'I don't want to ring you, I don't want your help, and,' she thrust the envelope roughly back into his hands, 'I don't want the money.'

'Kelly, it's dog eat dog out there. You're going to need help, whether you like it or not.' Jay held out the envelope until Kelly reluctantly took it from him again.

'Give me a bell if you need me,' he reiterated.

Sinking down on the settee once he'd gone, Emily jumped up beside her mum and snuggled into her chest. She began to play with her hair.

'I like Jay, Mummy,' she stated. 'Will he come again?'

Kelly sighed. 'I don't know, Em, but we'll cope on our own.'

Content with this, Emily turned her attention back to the penguins.

Kelly's eyes glistened with tears as she realised how uncertain her future had become in the space of a few days. She knew the coming weeks would be tough but, despite what Jay thought, she could cope on her own until Scott was released. Well, she could as soon as she had the appointment with Josie Mellor out of the way.

Josie had to admit to being pleasantly surprised at the immaculate condition of 41 Patrick Street as she looked around the upstairs rooms. It never failed to amaze her how some families on benefits did better for material things than she herself did with two full time wages coming in. Everything looked brand new: brown leather settees, a large widescreen television with built-in DVD recorder, modern wallpaper and curtains, the latest collection of vases, candles and picture frames. It would be tough for *her* to move out, never mind Kelly.

'This looks lovely,' she tried to jolly her up as they went from bedroom to bedroom. 'And downstairs is equally as nice.'

'I still can't believe you have to check it at all.' Kelly reached for Emily's hand. 'How can you live with yourself? I've been here for five years and I've never caused you any trouble.'

'You'd be surprised at the things I've seen when tenants have abandoned properties.'

Kelly rolled her eyes. 'Like what exactly?'

'Walls knocked down, doors blocked in, fires and kitchens ripped out,' said Josie. 'That's why we introduced the tenancy conditions. Anything done without permission needs to be brought back to standard or we'll re-do the work and issue a charge.'

'I hope you're not referring to me. Me and Scott wouldn't do –'

'No, I'm not referring to you at –'

'But you are going to make me move into that heap of junk you call a flat in Clarence Avenue?'

'I know it's not ideal,' Josie tried to sympathise without sounding patronising, 'but you can make it homely. Then, when you've lived there for a while as a registered tenant, you can go on the transfer list and move somewhere else.'

'And the chances of ever getting to the top of that list are...?'

'That will be up to you, and how Scott behaves when he comes out of prison.'

'Is Daddy in prison, Mummy?' Emily tugged on Kelly's hand.

'No, he's not, Em,' Kelly reassured her. She stared coldly at Josie. 'Can you at least try and be careful what you say?'

Josie didn't falter. 'This isn't my doing. Things have to change. I know you don't like it but that's the way it is. Scott must have known the risk with every job he did and you didn't say no to a life surrounded by material wealth because of it, did you? So you'll have to make the best of your time there.'

'But why Clarence Avenue? Can't we move to somewhere else?'

'No. When Mr Johnstone signed the tenancy agreement on Patrick Street, the only probable reason he managed to get a three-bedroomed house was due to low demand. We had a huge problem letting properties a few years ago but rising house prices have forced more people onto the renting ladder. Clarence Avenue is all we have for you at the moment.'

'They're both doss holes, if you ask me,' Kelly argued. 'I can't believe that you think I'd want to live in *any* of them.'

'Like I told you yesterday, you have no choice. It's either Clarence Avenue or you can find yourself somewhere to live. I think it's better if you go with the first choice, don't you?'

Later that afternoon, Kelly walked briskly up Clarence Avenue, pushing against the freezing wind. She held on tightly to Emily's hand as she skipped along, singing a nursery rhyme. They drew level with the first flat she'd seen yesterday and Kelly shuddered, remembering the inside of the property. The walls had been nicotine yellow, a shade she'd never seen on a colour sample chart from any DIY store and it had smelt like someone had used the place as a toilet.

Kelly chanced a quick look at the garden as she marched past. The weeds that had survived the winter had overtaken what looked like a rockery embedded in the middle of the postage-stamp sized garden. The obligatory mound of black waste bags formed another corner display, their contents shred across the path. Dried up baked beans, remains of a roast dinner and... urgh, she didn't want to think about the rest. At least the inside of the flat she'd decided to take had seemed a little more habitable.

She pushed her way through the overgrown hedges again.

'Mummy, I'm wet,' Emily wailed.

Kelly kept a hold of her hand as she guided her down the steps. 'Nearly there,' she gave her voice a sing-song tone. 'Then we can see our new home, Emily. Isn't it exciting?'

Kelly opened the door and bent down to have a nosy at the mail that had been pushed to one side when she'd been shown around. Dozens of leaflets advertised two for the price of one pizzas and double glazing. Red bill reminders for the previous tenant, the odd letter addressed to the new occupier and free newspapers aplenty.

'Pooh, it stinks.' Emily covered her nose with her hand.

Kelly encouraged her to climb the concrete stairs with a gentle nudge on her shoulder. A ninety degree turn to the left led them into a long hallway, made brighter by the vast but narrow landing window behind them. Four doors led off it. The first one on the right revealed the larger of the two bedrooms. Next to that was the bathroom. It was half the size of the one Kelly was leaving, with damp patches that needed to be papered over or, at the very least, painted. The door on the left led into the other bedroom.

Kelly walked the few steps towards the last door and pushed it open. It led into the living room.

'And it's cold,' Emily added, when Kelly hadn't answered her.

'It won't be, once we move our stuff here and put the fire on.'

'But it will be dark soon and I don't like the dark. I'm scared, Mummy. I want to go to Nanny's.'

'It won't be dark for ages yet, and I promise we'll be gone long before then.' Kelly squatted down to Emily's level and pulled her daughter into her arms. 'It's going to be fun living here, Em, wait and see. You can have your room decorated however you like. Do you want Barbie again? Or do you want something else now that you're growing into a young lady?'

'Can I choose my room first?'

While Emily raced around, determined on making as much

noise as possible on the bare floorboards, Kelly checked the windows. Child locks had been fitted, but nothing to deter the thieves: at least they were on the first floor in this block. She ran a hand over the freshly plastered chimney breast. If only the other three walls were in the same state, she could get away with a lick of paint. But they weren't. The fresh plaster had been where the previous tenant must have ripped out the fireplace and hadn't put the damage right. The housing association had re-fitted another one, ripping off some of the wallpaper and plastering over a good deal of what was left.

Kelly looked out of the large window and surveyed the neighbouring properties. She was in a block of four flats: other than the two blocks above hers in Clarence Avenue, the rest consisted of semi-detached properties, similar to the one she was being forced to leave, but they were nowhere near as tidy. The garden in the house opposite had more rubbish bags there than in her new garden and a soggy, single mattress had been dumped on the path. On the patch of grass in front of a bay window, the shell of an old hatchback balanced precariously on piles of house bricks, the wheels having long ago vacated the body. The windscreen was missing and the number plates had been removed to claim anonymity.

Kelly tried to calm the fear mounting inside her. She'd spent six nights on her own since Scott had gone. Only now was it beginning to sink in that he wasn't coming home for a long time – wasn't coming home to Patrick Street at all, in fact. He'd made sure of that.

'I've picked me room, Mummy,' Emily shouted through, bringing Kelly back to the present with a jolt. 'Come and find me!'

'My room, Emily. I've picked *my* room.' Kelly raised a smile as she walked through to the bedroom. 'I can't see you,' she played along with her. 'Are you hiding from me?'

Emily giggled as Kelly flung open the cupboard door. In a fit of fun, she grabbed her daughter and began to tickle her.

As they collapsed into a heap of laughter, Kelly's nerves began to centre. Maybe it was inevitable that she'd be anxious about moving here, but what choice did she have? She had to live somewhere and here was as good as any place. It had a roof and four walls, much more than some people had, and she already had furniture – well, most of it would fit in.

It would keep her warm and dry, though, and that's all that mattered, really. And she would be safe, even on her own – if not entirely happy. Eventually she'd get used to every creak of the floorboards, every bang of the hot water system, without jumping out of bed to investigate the locked door.

'I think we'll go up into town tomorrow morning, Em, and buy some roll ends of wallpaper. Then in the afternoon we'll start to pack up your things.'

'I have lots of things, don't I, Mummy?'

'Yes, you do.' Despite her reluctance, Kelly would have to ask Jay to lend a hand with some of the bigger items, but she promised herself it would only be this once. She looked around the room again. Number 33 Clarence Avenue, their new home. Well, it would be when she'd finished with it, Kelly resolved.

'Yoo-hoo! Anyone home?' There was a light rap on the door. 'Thought I'd come and see for myself as you said you'd be measuring up for curtains.'

'Nanny!' Emily rushed towards her.

'You call this home?' Kelly griped as her mum, Jill, came into the room. Their stature and height were the same and, apart from a few grey hairs instead of an allover brown, their resemblance was uncanny. Emily had the Winterton button nose too.

'Clarence Avenue isn't as bad as everyone makes out,' Jill tried to reassure her daughter.

'It'll do, I suppose. Looks pretty rough to me, though.'

Jill glanced around the bare living room. 'You can make it nice, love. You seem to have a flair for this kind of thing.'

'It's going to cost me a fortune to get it half decent,' Kelly continued, knowing that her mum really meant the inside and not the outside of the property. 'There's a stack of decorating to do, and cleaning. Everything needs to be scrubbed again before I'm moving one piece of furniture in. I can't believe the association let it in this state.'

'Have you thought about what to do for money until Scott gets back from you know where?'

Kelly was confused. 'I don't follow,' she said.

'Your dad says they're advertising on the twilight shift at Miles' factory. Four 'til eight. It's a little unsociable but it could work out well for you. I could look after Emily.'

'Yeah, can we, mummy?' Emily chirped in at the mention of her name. 'I can stay with Nanny.'

'And you know lots of people there. There's Pam, for a start.' Pam was Kelly's auntie. Her cousin, Estelle, worked at the factory too.

'I'm hardly going to have time to do anything else with all the decorating they're expecting me to do in this dump.'

Jill shrugged and walked over to the window. 'I just think there's more to you than a stay at home mum.'

'Actually, I was thinking of doing a college course.'

Jill turned back to her daughter and smiled. 'I think that's a great idea. What do you fancy doing?'

'I'm not sure, thought I'd suss it out.' Kelly back-pedalled slightly. 'I know that being a mum is the best job in the world but Em will be starting school in September. I don't know what I'll do with myself then. Maybe if I start a course while Scott is – erm,' she looked at her mum again, 'working away, I could always say I felt the need to fend for myself in case he went to work away again.'

'Maybe if you went to college during the day, you could manage the twilight shift?' Jill pulled a bag of sweets from her handbag and gave them to Emily. 'It's not rocket science and it's repetitive but you know the money will be good. And it beats scrounging off the social. I've always thought better of you than that.'

Kelly huffed. 'Knowing my luck, I'd probably be hopeless at it.'

'You won't know if you don't try.'

'But what if I'm not good enough?'

'Then you'll get better with practice. You're a smart woman, love, and not everyone on this estate needs to play the part of an extra in *Shameless*. Don't get dragged down with the rest of them,' she advised. 'You can get yourself out of this situation if you really want to.'

Kelly said nothing. She knew she needed to secure her future but she wouldn't make her mind up yet. There was so much changing in her life right now. She had all her furniture to pack up, her change of addresses to sort out, and she still had to go and see Scott, which was another thing she kept pushing to the back of her mind.

CHAPTER FIVE

'Please tell me that's all of it.' Jay crammed two more boxes into the back of the van he'd borrowed. 'I don't know about you, but I'm knackered. I think you owe me a beer when we've shifted this load.'

'I think I can run to that,' Kelly answered. For all her misgivings, she wouldn't have managed today if it wasn't for Jay and his offer of a van. Her mum and dad had helped her to box up the remainder of their belongings yesterday, keeping Emily with them overnight so Kelly could shift the heavier items without her getting in the way this morning.

Jay pulled down the roller shutter and secured the padlock. 'I reckon we'll have this unpacked at the other end in a couple of hours. Do you want to see if we've forgotten anything?'

Kelly went back into the house and wandered around each room, checking cupboards, pulling out kitchen drawers, but she hadn't missed anything. Finally, she made one last trip to the living room. She held back tears. Never again would she open her curtains and feast her eyes on old Mrs Shelby across the road at number forty, who'd wave whenever she saw her; be woken up by the boys from number thirty-two coming home from the pub at the weekends; be able to nip in to see Sue, her mum's friend, at number seventeen to check on how her grandson was doing.

She had so many memories, good and bad: bringing Emily home from hospital, her first Christmas, her first birthday. Painting the living room walls buttercup yellow for two days until she and Scott couldn't live with it any longer and had to do it all again in pale lemon; the police knocking on the door every time there had been a robbery or break-in to check for stolen goods. Kelly had lost count of how many times that had happened during their relationship.

'Ready?' said Jay as he came back inside.

Kelly turned towards him. 'It's not fair,' she choked back tears. 'Why should I have to move out because of that thoughtless git? This is my home, too.'

'Don't worry. I'll help you in Clarence Avenue. It'll be like this place in no time – only don't try and badger me into any wallpapering. I'm crap at it. It always rolls down the wall again, no matter how much paste I put on.'

Kelly's lips twitched, thankful that he was trying to make her smile.

'Has Scott called again?' Jay asked.

'Yeah, last night.'

'And am I taking you to see him?'

'I'm not sure.'

Jay nodded. 'I thought you'd say that. But he needs you, Kel. I can't imagine what it's like in there but I know he'll be missing you.'

The lone tear that had trickled down Kelly's cheek now headed towards her neck. She wiped it away abruptly. 'He should've thought about that before he did that last job. I told him not to do it.'

'Don't you think he regrets that now?'

Kelly had asked herself that more than once over the past fortnight and it was eating her up inside. *Had* it all been a mistake? Had he been unaware of his actions? She needed to see Scott, ask him why he'd done it – to hear him say he hadn't realised that he'd put their lives into jeopardy. But it was too raw.

'I'm not ready to forgive him yet. Look what's happened because of his stupidity.'

'I know. You've every right to be upset.'

Yes, she did have every right to be upset. But Kelly didn't want Jay to see her like that. Despite her anguish, she held her head up.

'Upset is one thing, but feeling sorry for myself? I'm better than that.'

Jay flashed a smile. 'Of course you are, but everyone's entitled to throw a wobbler every now and then. It's only natural.'

Kelly sniffed, knowing that if she stood there much longer,

she'd start crying properly. 'Let's get out of here,' she said, trying not to think that, as she walked down the path, it was for the very last time.

The following week, Josie was in the office, about to start on the massive task of clearing some of her paperwork. There were six people in that morning as she pulled out a bundle of files from her in-tray. Moments earlier, Debbie had finished her stint on the reception counter and was eating an apple while flicking through a pile of messages. A telephone went unanswered as Irene and Sonia argued over who was going to take over from her.

Where was the office manager when they needed her, Josie thought? Kay Whitehead had been their manager for the last seven years but most of that time had been spent working at their head office in Warbury on special projects – so special that none of her staff ever knew what she was doing. Sometimes the office ran okay without her being there: she was, she insisted, only a phone call away. Sometimes, however, things became a little lax and the staff started to rule the roost.

'Reception okay this morning?' Josie asked Debbie as she searched out a tenant's file from the large cabinet by her side.

Debbie nodded. 'Gets a bit boring, though, listening to everyone moaning.'

'Do you fancy coming out on the patch with me for a few visits? People will still moan but it's better than being inside – well, most of the time.'

Debbie nodded a little more eagerly this time. 'I'd love to.'

'Great. I'll sort it out. All you need to wear is trousers and flat boots or shoes. I'll find you some armour to change...' Josie grinned at the in-joke regarding their work wear. 'I'll find you a coat to wear.'

'Cluck, cluck, cluck, you're doing it again,' Ray teased, smirking at Josie as he sat down at his desk.

Josie stuck out her tongue.

'Whatever you do,' he shouted down the office to their new recruit, 'don't let her tell you the rules of a housing officer. They'll put you off our job for life.'

'Rules?' queried Debbie.

'Ignore him,' Josie soothed her as she frowned at a grinning Ray. 'I'll introduce you to them one at a time.'

When Josie next went out on her own, she spent a pleasant half an hour with Amy and Reece Cartwright. As she left the property she looked up the road. As she'd expected, Kelly Winterton had been hard at work. There was a pile of empty boxes crunched up neatly by the side of the wheelie bin and curtains were hanging in arcs at each of the windows.

As she drove past, Josie spotted Kelly on the pathway. She was quite a way through cutting back the hedge that separated the path from the small garden. Pleased to see her making an effort already, Josie decided to stop.

'Now that's what I like to see,' she said as she walked down the steps towards Kelly.

Kelly stood up straight and put a hand on the small of her back. 'It's bloody killed me to get this far, but I was sick of getting soaked when we moved in.'

'It looks great. And it's nice to see someone *doing* something rather than me having to enforce it with a dozen warning letters.' She was about to ask where Emily was when she appeared behind her mum.

'Hiya, lady,' Emily smiled a row of milky-white teeth. 'I'm helping Mummy clear the garden. I'm on litter duty.'

Kelly and Josie shared a smirk. Emily had numerous cuttings stuck to her red pom-pom hat, and a child's pink rucksack stuffed with crisp packets, toffee wrappers and the odd shrivelled leaf.

'What a good girl.' Josie bent down to her level. 'I think you can come and do my garden when you've finished here. You're doing a wonderful job.'

'Mummy says I have to leave the grown up stuff for her to tidy up,' Emily pronounced, picking up the rucksack ready to return to her duties.

'Is she always that sweet?' Josie spoke to Kelly.

Kelly stopped mid-shear. 'You should've been here last night when she was crying for most of it.'

'Hello, ladies,' said someone behind them. They both turned to see a small woman. She looked to be in her sixties, with shots of grey running through her dark hair.

'Hello, Dot,' Josie smiled warmly. Dorothy Simpson had lived in the flat below Kelly since she'd lost her husband to lung cancer. She was the first tenant that Josie had taken on a viewing when she had started working for the association. 'This is Kelly. She and her daughter have moved in downstairs.'

'Yes, we met briefly earlier, and I like her already.' Dot smiled at Kelly. 'Especially if she's tackling the garden. I'd do it myself, but my arthritis is playing up at the moment.'

'There's no need,' Kelly told her. 'I'll keep it in order all the time from now on. I can't stand any kind of mess.'

Dot beamed even more when she spotted Emily. 'Hello. Would you like to see if I have any chocolate biscuits left in my tin?'

Emily shrugged shyly but took hold of Dot's hand anyway.

'If you ever need a baby-sitter for an odd hour here and there,' Dot said as she opened her front door, 'give me a nod. I'd love some company.'

'She seems nice,' Kelly said, as she continued to shear.

'Yes, Dot's one of my prize tenants. She's the chairman of Clarence Avenue Neighbourhood Watch, helps out at the church on Samuel Street. She's always running errands for people less fortunate than herself, too. I've never...' Josie stopped in mid flow as a black and white collie ran past on the pavement. She put her folder down on top of the low wall. 'I won't be a minute.'

Kelly couldn't resist going to investigate as Josie shouted Tess at the top of her voice and raced up the path.

Josie tore after the dog, grabbed for her collar and walked her back the way she had come. She marched Tess down the path and finally managed to tie her up in the garden again. As usual, Mr and Mrs Thomas weren't in to reprimand. Josie made a mental note to pop in next week when she called to see Amy.

Kelly had finished the hedge and was bagging up the last of the cuttings when Josie came into view again.

'You certainly have a varied role as a housing officer,' she grinned as she clocked the red glow of her cheeks.

'She's a good dog really, but she's always escaping. Between you and me, I've given up with her owners. I've had to tie her up in the back garden. It's not something I like doing but what else can I do? It'd be a trip with the dog warden if she's caught wandering the streets again.' Josie held up muddy palms. 'Don't suppose you'd take pity, offer me a cuppa and let me wash my hands?'

Kelly could hear Scott's scornful tone as he said 'absolutely no fucking way' quite clearly in her mind. But Scott wasn't here to say it aloud. Loneliness made her nod her head.

Once Kelly had checked that Emily wasn't badgering Dot too much, they went upstairs to the flat and into the living room. Josie glanced around. Although the floorboards had still to be covered, it was almost a replica of the room Kelly had left behind in Patrick Street: the large coffee and cream swirl rug, heavy ivory curtains hanging from a thick chrome pole. The settees had been placed in an L-shape on the back walls. Three wooden-framed photographs of Emily hung strategically above the tiled fireplace.

'It looks fantastic,' Josie enthused, before sitting down on the settee nearest to the window. 'It must have taken you ages to get rid of the yellow stains.'

Kelly ran her hand over the door frame nearest to her. 'Three coats of white gloss. To be exact, it was three coats of one-coat gloss. And if you think this is bright, you should see Emily's room – Princess Pink.'

Josie unzipped her folder and pulled out Kelly's paperwork. 'Do you mind if I run through this while I'm here?' she asked when handed a mug. When Kelly didn't reply, she continued. 'Did you go and sort out your benefits last week?'

'Yeah.'

'What about your bills? Have you registered the suppliers in your name?'

Kelly nodded this time. Josie could feel her resistance to the questions.

'That's good,' she continued, 'because if you ever want to get out of here, you'll need to prove you've been a tenant long enough to qualify.'

'I told you I'm capable of surviving on my own,' Kelly muttered.

She turned to stare out of the window.

Josie put her drink down on top of a coaster. 'I haven't called to spy on you. These are routine questions I ask all of my new tenants. I'm simply interested to see how the place is coming on. You have a real flair for making a home.' Her eyes raced around the room again. 'I'm genuinely amazed to see how much you've done in such a short space of time. Some of the tenants I signed up during the same week as you won't have moved in yet, let alone started any decorating. Now that you've done that, though, have you thought any more about getting a part time job to tide you over?'

Kelly sat down on the other settee. 'Yeah, I need to do something. I don't know how people manage on benefits.' She grimaced, knowing how it would sound to Josie but when she'd lived with Scott, everything had been acquired without question; now she was fending for herself, she had to watch every penny.

'Why don't you come with me to look around Mitchell Academy?' Josie suggested. Mitchell Academy was a high school on the estate that had been used as a community college on its closure. Originally the building had housed six hundred pupils, but government cuts had insisted that it amalgamated with another school three miles away. 'What do you fancy doing?'

Kelly sighed. 'I don't know what I *can* do. It seems so long since I left school. My mum reckons I could get some work at Miles' factory because my auntie works there. I might give it a go.'

Josie nodded. 'Great. It will alter your benefits if you do over eight hours a week but I think you could easily combine the two. My husband works at Miles' Factory; he does the day and noon shift.' She checked her watch and shot to her feet. 'I'd better get going. I need to call another couple of times yet though, just to see that you're settled. Is next Thursday morning okay for my next call?'

'Yeah, I suppose so. And I'd better rescue Dot from Emily.'

'Don't you mean rescue Emily from Dot?'

Kelly shook her head. 'I know exactly what I mean. That child can talk the hind legs off a donkey, given half the chance.'

Josie smiled to disguise her feelings. Her biological clock had been ticking for quite some time now but Stewart wanted to wait until the timing was right for him too. Then again, with the relationship how it was, there didn't seem much point in trying for a baby if they weren't more of a unit first.

'I'll show myself out and thanks for the drink,' she said. 'I don't accept such offers from everyone I visit, you know.'

Later, as she went back outside to finish clearing up, Kelly recalled Josie's visit. She found herself warming to the woman behind the coat of authority. Josie had no airs and graces, no false chit-chat. She was straight, to the point, yet never rude with it, and she didn't judge people. But it was her ability to care without being patronising that she really found admirable.

It also made Kelly realise how much she'd given up for Scott. She was twenty-four-years old and not a friend to her name. Everyone she'd been close to had eventually been driven away in case they became too familiar and saw or heard too much. If she *had* had someone like Josie around all the time, to share her concerns and talk over her worries, maybe she might not have got into this mess.

Still, Kelly sighed, Josie was a housing officer. To her, a visit was part of the job. Kelly knew she must visit lots of tenants and make them feel that she was someone in authority to be trusted. But it did seem a pity that the arm of friendship she was offering came with strings attached.

CHAPTER SIX

It was nearing six thirty when Josie got home from work that evening. She knew she didn't have to rush because Stewart was on the noon shift, two-til-ten. It made her feel sad to realise how much she relished coming home to an empty house. Every other weekend she'd be thinking that the next week, when Stewart was on days – six-til-two – it would be different. But by each Friday night, she couldn't wait for his noon shift to start again.

She hung up her coat and checked the mail: a gas bill, two circulars, a bank statement for her and a bank statement for a Mrs S Mellor. She sighed. She'd rung the bank on several occasions to complain about the computer-generated error but still they kept coming. She left it on the kitchen table for Stewart, along with his monthly car magazine.

After running the hoover around the living room, she ate a quick meal and then decided to savour the peace and quiet by finishing off the last three chapters of the romantic comedy she was reading, but she was also keeping one eye on the time, as there was a film she wanted to watch at eight.

At quarter to ten, she woke up with a jolt to see the film credits rolling. Damn and blast, she'd missed the ending again. She walked through to the kitchen, made a cheese and tomato sandwich for Stewart and two slices of cheese on toast for herself.

She was halfway through it as she heard his car pull up in the driveway. Automatically, she switched on the kettle and slid the sandwich across the table, reaching across to bring the salt and pepper nearer.

'Hiya, love,' she greeted him cheerily. 'It's a bit nippy. Have you had to scrape the ice off your car?'

'Yeah, it's not fit for a dog out there.' Stewart shrugged his coat off and threw it over the back of the nearest chair. He lifted up a corner of bread from the sandwich and frowned. 'Couldn't you have toasted it for me?'

Josie sighed. No rush to kiss her on the cheek, then. 'You had that last night. I thought you might like a change.'

'I'd rather have a curry.'

'Well, order a takeaway if you want to suffer with indigestion all night.' She pushed past him into the living room, taking her toast with her before he pinched it off the plate.

Fifteen minutes later, Stewart was still in the kitchen. Josie cocked an ear and yes, he'd turned on the portable television rather than come through and sit with her. Fuming to herself, she switched off the set she was idly watching, plumped up the cushions and took her dishes through.

'I'm going to bed,' she told him. 'You can slob out on the settee in the living room now that I've gone.'

Without waiting for his response, Josie slammed the dishes into the sink, noticing the chaos all around her. Honestly, how much mess could you make eating a cheese sandwich? But then her eyes flicked to the table to see the sandwich still there. Next to it was a bottle of tomato ketchup, Stewart's favourite – with cheese on toast.

'Bloody hell, Stewart,' she cried. 'Isn't anything I do good enough for you? What a waste.'

'Stop whining,' Stewart muttered, not taking his eyes from the TV screen. 'I'll have the sandwich for my dinner tomorrow.'

'That's hardly the point.' Josie reached for the washing liquid, then immediately put it down again. Stuff it: she wasn't going to wash them now. They could wait until the morning. After all, Stewart would never think to do them; it certainly didn't bother him when the bowl overflowed.

With every step she took up the stairs away from him, Josie's shoulders drooped a little more. She thought back to the nights when she used to rush upstairs half an hour before he was due home to change out of her sloppy joes and into fresh clothes to look nice for him, applying a little mascara and a smidgeon of lipstick and running a comb through her mass of hair. Come to think of it, Stewart had hardly noticed her then. That's why she'd stopped making an effort.

Her mind still whirred over an hour later as she tossed and turned in her bed. She knew Stewart had taken her advice and moved through to the living room because she could hear the television blaring out. He was watching some action film: she could clearly hear gun shots and every scream for mercy.

Josie lifted her head and pummelled her pillow before resting it again, wondering why things had become so difficult between them. You'd think they'd have so much in common, both of them losing their mums in their late twenties. Stewart had never known his father either. He'd died before he'd been born. His mother had taken care of his every whim until she'd died too, so when he'd moved in with Josie, she'd found herself back in her previous role of carer. Over time, it had become easier to give in to his demands, keep the peace – live the lie.

It had been the same with her mother. Was that all she'd ever be, she wondered, a skivvy to domestic chores? Ever since their wedding day, Josie had taken care of Stewart in the same way she'd taken care of her mother: cooking, cleaning, shopping, washing, and ironing. Maybe that's where she had gone wrong. But looking after people was the only thing she knew how to do. Josie's dad, Jack, had died suddenly of a heart attack when he was forty-two. Josie had only been two at the time so she had no memories of him at all. Her mum, Brenda, had been distraught. Widowed at forty, she'd complained bitterly about her life being over. She had never remarried: there had been a few 'uncles' along the way that Josie could remember, but no one had moved in. They'd stayed in the same house – at least Brenda had been lucky enough not to have a mortgage weighing heavily on her shoulders.

A few months after Josie's fifteenth birthday, Brenda was injured in a car crash and was never able to walk unaided again. She wasn't confined to a wheelchair as such but, due to not using her legs as much as she was capable of doing, the muscles wasted away and she became housebound. Depressed with her situation, Brenda became spiteful and jealous of her daughter's position. She constantly reminded Josie that she could go out whenever she wanted and that she didn't have to sit alone all day and all night too. Trapped somewhere between pity and hate, Josie would stay in to keep the peace. Missing out on her carefree teenage years, she'd borrow books from the local library and read while her mother fell asleep on the settee. It was easier to give in and, after all the housework that she'd had, as well as finding time for homework, there hadn't been much time for anything else.

Josie hadn't been quick to make friends at college, and was glad of the receptionist job that came up at Mitchell Housing Association. The head office had only been minutes away in her car, giving her time to call home every lunch to see to her mother. Things had become more difficult when she'd moved onto the Mitchell Estate as an administrative assistant, but she'd still managed the trip, most of the time eating a sandwich en route.

When she was promoted to housing officer two years later, Brenda tried to talk her out of it. Although she still had office hours of nine to five, there had been lots of evening meetings to attend and Brenda didn't like anything that ate into the time her daughter should have been there to wait on her hand and foot. But Josie, for once, stood her ground and at last gained some control in her life. She enjoyed her job. It had been tough at first, but once she got used to it, she found job satisfaction. She could see the results of her labour, she helped to improve people's lives and quite often was thanked for her efforts. Not all of the tenants were bad news. There was a terrific display of community spirit. Ninety per cent of them were workers, law-abiding people who made up for the other ten per cent of rubbish.

Josie looked after her mum until Brenda had two strokes in quick succession and it became impossible for her to cope. It was then that she had to make the distressing decision to put her into a nursing home. Brenda needed constant care and attention, way beyond what she could give. It broke her heart to let her go, but as soon as she settled her into Grove House, she knew she'd done the right thing. Josie had visited every other day until another, more severe stroke took her life eight months later.

As well as sorrow, Josie could remember feeling immense relief she'd been free at last to do what she wanted. She tackled some decorating and took a short break to York, her first ever time away from home, where she stayed in first-class indulgence. As the weeks rolled into months, she started to go on the odd night out with some of the girls from work or they came to hers for a takeaway and a bottle of wine. She started to meet new people and her confidence was given a boost. Six months later, she met Stewart. Now, memories of better times became overshadowed by a lack of passion. Perhaps this is how all marriages go, Josie considered.

She stopped in her tracks, her eyes opening wide in the dark of the room. Had she been aware of what was happening, just like Kelly Winterton? Had she turned a blind eye, even though she had done it unintentionally?

With that ugly thought, Josie switched off the bedside lamp and buried her head underneath the covers.

'Not again,' Kelly sighed, later that same night. Slowly she dragged herself to her feet, her daughter's wail for attention getting louder by the second.

'Hey.' Kelly pulled her into her arms. 'What's up with my little monster?'

'I want to go home. I don't like it here, Mummy.'

'Would it help if I sat here for a while?' she whispered, knowing full well that Emily would be asleep again soon. Her eyes had already started to close.

Kelly tucked the duvet closer around her small body and looked at her watch. Eleven thirty: she'd only been in bed for an hour. She chewed lightly on her bottom lip. Even though Emily was safely tucked up in her own bed, the room was new, the place was new and the street was new. Through no fault of her own, her child had been dragged away from everything that she knew as her security. Kelly could understand her disorientation.

Her eyes scanned the room that she had struggled to decorate before she moved in. Emily had decided that she wanted everything as pink as possible: duvet, walls, curtains, lampshades. Kelly had drawn a line at a fluffy pink carpet when the men from Kenny's Carpets had fitted flooring throughout. Jay had told her Kenny owed him a favour and she could choose whatever she wanted for free. Kelly had resisted at first, but after a few days she couldn't bear to see those shabby floorboards any longer and gave in. Most of Emily's toys had been hidden away in the cupboard above the stairs, making the bedroom look far tidier than it would have been at Patrick Street.

Peering down at her restless child, a perfect miniature of herself, Kelly couldn't help but feel a huge surge of love. Emily had certainly arrived at the wrong time in her life, but she was so glad that she had her now. She was her hope for the future, a ray of sunshine in an otherwise dull world – just like, Kelly supposed, she had been for her mum at one time.

Minutes later, sure that Emily was safely back in the land of nod, she left her room, made a coffee and dropped into the nearest settee. The living room was quiet except for the noise of the dripping tap from the bathroom. Even with the door shut tight, she could still hear it. Drip, drip, drip. She felt tears welling up in her eyes. Before long, she was sobbing like Emily.

The walls seemed to close in around her, suffocating her with their loneliness, dragging her down to despair. She hated it here in this flat and thought about her pending visit to see Scott. Jay was taking her in the morning. Even without the two hour car journey, she wondered if she really wanted to go into that environment. She'd heard too many stories to think that any prison cell could be void of a mass murderer or some evil bastard ready to slit your throat at the mention of slopping out.

Kelly wanted to hate Scott for what he'd done, but she couldn't. What if Jay was telling the truth? What if Scott did need her more than she thought? Could she abandon him after five years together?

Questions, questions, questions.

Kelly's eyes had closed for all of ten minutes before she was jolted awake again by the sound of the techno beat bursting out from the flat next door. Before her tears had started to fall for the second time, Kelly heard Emily beat her to it.

She sighed loudly. Would either of them settle in Clarence Avenue?

*

Over at Josie's house, it was an hour later that Stewart finally came to bed.

'I'm going in at six tomorrow,' he said, not bothering to kiss her goodnight. 'We've got lots of work on so I might as well do a few hours overtime while I can.'

'Okay,' Josie answered, before he dragged over the duvet and slept with his back towards her – the same thing he'd done for as long as she could remember now. She wondered why she thought it would be any different tonight.

The following morning, Stewart was up and out of the house before Josie got out of bed. Making all the difference to the start of the day, she set off to work with a spring in her step. Driving through the rush hour traffic, the radio belting out its tunes, she sang along to the lyrics at the top of her voice and wondered how long the feeling would last.

It was all of thirty minutes – enough for her to grab a quick cup of coffee – before the first phone call came in. There had been another burglary over at Wilma Place, a row of bungalows for the elderly. Someone had made another complaint about Gina Bradley's twins. That was the third one she'd had that week. Josie clicked onto the computer system and opened up the case. That was the beauty of hard drives, she surmised. If they were still using paper files, Clare and Rachel's files would be at least two inches thick. And that was one case of the Bradleys – for once, it wasn't their older brother, Danny. Nineteen-years-old and he'd already been into juvie twice for burglary and car theft.

Josie grabbed her car keys and coat. If she left now, she could see if Gina was in before she started her other appointments. She might as well get it over with first – it wasn't going to be pretty.

CHAPTER SEVEN

With all the courage she could muster, Josie unlatched the broken gate and walked slowly up the path towards Gina Bradley's front door. Every heavy step made her feel like turning around and running away. Although she knew Gina Bradley hated her with a passion, Josie tried hard not to show that the feeling was mutual.

She was about to knock on the door when it was yanked open. Gina stood there in all her splendour. She was a little woman but 'fat' and 'round' were too kind for her description. Looking like she hadn't seen a shower in weeks, she was wearing black leggings that threatened to walk off on their own, filthy white socks and a grey sweatshirt three sizes too small. Her hair had been dyed bright red this month, and with no makeup on her pale face, she reminded Josie of a matchstick – a jumbo matchstick.

'I suppose you're about due a visit,' Gina drawled, looking pointedly down at Josie from her advantage of being three steps up. 'What the fuck do you want this time?'

'Morning to you too, Gina,' Josie replied, trying to sound confident. 'Can I come in?'

Gina turned away from her but left the door open. Josie squeezed her way through lager boxes stacked high in the hallway and followed her into the living room. From where she was standing, she surveyed the mess. At least a dozen dirty cups on the coffee table, piled next to them, plates containing the remnants of two different meals. Gossip and fashion magazines were scattered over the floor, beside nail varnish and bags of cotton wool pads. Clothes seemed to be strewn over every seat.

Gina flopped down onto the settee, not bothering to move anything.

Josie pulled her coat down as far as it would go to cover her bottom and perched on the edge of the chair. She didn't want to sit in anything suspect.

'I've had more complaints about the twins,' she began.

'Oh?' Gina lit up a cigarette and took two long drags before she spoke again. 'And which nosy bastard has reported them this time?'

'You know I can't tell you that.'

Gina glared at her. 'I can't see why not. I always guess who it is by the complaint. Anyway, what are they supposed to have done this time?'

'They've been causing a nuisance up at the shops. They've –'

'Doing what?'

'Hanging around the outside, swearing at customers, begging for cigarettes, following people around in a threatening manner. On one occasion, a purse has gone missing.'

'I hope you're not saying that one of my girls nicked it.' Gina looked outraged.

'No, I don't have any proof but –'

'Then I'd shut your mouth if I were you or I'll have you for slander.'

Josie swallowed. Things were going no better than she'd envisioned, but she tried to stay calm.

'They've also been seen throwing eggs at Mrs Robson's bungalow,' she added.

Gina nodded and took another drag. 'So she's complained has she, the moaning old bag? I'll –'

'It wasn't her,' Josie told her truthfully. 'You know she keeps herself to herself.'

'She's a nutter.'

Josie ignored her, not wanting to be drawn into discussing anyone else. Just then, she heard the front door open and slam shut. She held her breath for a second, unsure what to expect, which member of this nasty family she would encounter next.

'What the fuck is she doing here?'

'Hello,' Josie greeted the scowling girl. She was followed by her identical twin sister, who ignored Josie and went into the kitchen.

'She's come about you two.' Gina stubbed out the remains of her cigarette and lit another one straight after. 'Do either of you know anything about a purse being nicked at Shop&Save. Clare?'

'No, we bloody don't.' Clare folded her arms across a blossoming chest. 'So don't start blaming me and Rach for it. We were home all night, weren't we, Mum?'

Gina snorted. 'That's right, love, you were.'

Josie sighed and stood up. It was like talking to a brick wall.

'I don't have any proof this time, Gina,' she said, 'but you can't keep on letting your girls rule the roost. Sooner or later, they're going to go too far.'

Gina pushed the pile of plates to one side and put up her feet. 'They're kids,' she yawned, stretching her arms above her head. 'They'll grow out of it.'

'Danny didn't.'

'Keep Danny out of this!'

'I was just saying.'

'Well, don't,' Gina warned. Her top lip curled up scathingly. 'If you've said what you've come to say, then sling your hook. Danny's still in bed, and if I start raising my voice, he'll wake up – and you don't want that, do you?'

Josie certainly didn't. Danny Bradley scared her more than Gina. An evil specimen of a young man, it gave her the creeps even looking at him.

'Yeah,' said Rachel. She sat down next to her mother. 'Fuck off out of our house with your airs and graces.'

Josie stood her ground. 'Think about what I said, Gina. This can't keep happening.'

Gina did nothing but stare at her.

Feeling dismissed, Josie couldn't leave the house quick enough. Getting into her car, she drove to the next street, parked up again and took a breather. She held on to the steering wheel to stop her hands from shaking.

That bloody family. Who the hell did they think they were? She felt frustration rip through her. She was no match for them. They knew every benefit scam, every way to beat the system. Their father was no better; Pete Bradley was a complete layabout. Josie wondered if he'd ever done a day's legal work in his life.

And that was just the one house. Gina's mum and dad lived two doors further down. Three doors after that was Leah Simpson, Gina's younger sister. Stanley Avenue was overrun with that family because no one else wanted to live near any of the Bradleys.

Josie's nerves began to settle again. Although there were lots of decent people on the Mitchell Estate, there were plenty of badly behaved families, too – yet none of them got under her skin as much as the Bradley's. The lot of them thought they were above the law. But one day, one month, one year, one of them would do something, and she'd have the power to get them out. Until then, Josie would have to build up the evidence against them and bide her time.

The two-hour car journey to visit Scott had been a nightmare due to heavy rain and an overturned lorry on the motorway. Then there had been the humiliation of the search procedure and the intimidating atmosphere of the prison environment. But just seeing his face break out into a smile when he spotted her walking towards him in the visitors room made it all worthwhile for Kelly.

For a minute or two, anyway.

'It's good to see you, babe,' Scott whispered, as he hugged her.

Kelly glanced over his shoulder cautiously, not daring to meet anyone's eye, fearing she wasn't allowed to touch him. But it seemed okay – lots of men were doing the same before they sat down.

There were approximately twenty tables arranged in rows up and down the room. All the prisoners had red bands around their torsos. The woman on the next table had two young children with her as she chatted excitedly to the man she'd come to visit. Luckily for Kelly, the 'working away' lie seemed to be doing its job. There was no need to confuse Emily.

People were talking, laughing, moaning, smiling – but Kelly couldn't find anything to smile about. Somehow a prison visiting room hadn't featured in her life plan.

Scott motioned to a chair. 'How's Em doing?' he asked.

'She's okay, I suppose,' Kelly replied. 'One minute she's fine about you not being there. Other times, she's upset. But I'm glad I've got her – I hate being on my own.'

'Is Jay keeping an eye on you?'

'Yeah, he brought me here today.'

'Good. I told him to look after the pair of you.'

'He shouldn't have to look out for us! That's supposed to be your job.'

Scott groaned. 'Don't let's go there, Kel. It's not like I can do anything about it now. Think of me, stuck in here, it's enough to drive any bloke loopy.'

Kelly ignored his self-pity and went straight to the main point. 'Did you get the letter from the housing association?'

Scott's top lip curled derisively. 'Yeah, but I'm not worried about it. You shouldn't be either.'

'But you'll have a bill for about two grand!'

'Which I can pay off at a couple of quid a week because I'm on the dole.'

Kelly frowned. 'You're not grasping the seriousness of the situation!'

'Rules are made to be broken.'

She folded her arms. 'But I don't want to live like that anymore. Besides, the house is still your responsibility while you're in here. Josie says empty properties are like a magnet on the estate. You'll have to pay for any damage.'

'Who the fuck is Josie?' Scott questioned. 'Not that interfering bitch from Mitchell Housing? And what do you mean by empty property? Don't tell me you've moved out!'

Kelly seemed surprised he hadn't realised sooner. 'Yeah, of course I have,' she said. 'I had to go and see Josie. She told me what would happen if I stayed at Patrick Street – they would have evicted us!'

Scott shook his head to protest. 'No, they wouldn't. She's trying to scare you. They can't evict me. They have to take me to court and I would've been out of here before that happened.'

'Maybe, but –'

'You should've stayed where you were. Now the house is empty, they've got more of a case – I could lose my tenancy rights! You've ruined everything, you silly cow.'

The icy look Scott threw Kelly chilled her bones. 'And how

exactly have *I* done that?' she snapped. 'You being in here means that I *can't* stay at Patrick Street. They turfed me and Em out and it's *your* fault. How could you do that?'

Scott looked around the room as a couple of heads turned in their direction. One of the wardens started to walk towards them.

'Keep your voice down, Kel.' Scott cocked his head a little. 'Let me get this clear. The letter wasn't an empty threat?'

Kelly shook her head.

'They can't fucking do that! That's my home.'

'*Our* home,' corrected Kelly. 'At least it *was* our home until you got sent down. They've moved us to a flat – on Clarence Avenue.'

Scott's eyes bulged. 'Fucking hell, this is getting worse! If you're on Clarence Avenue, where am I supposed to go when I get out of here?'

'You haven't even asked how I am!'

Scott sniggered. 'I know you'll be coping. That's what keeps me going in here, knowing that you'll have everything under control. Well, it was until you told me about Patrick Street. Why didn't you stand your ground? They wouldn't have evicted you if you'd refused to go.'

'They would because I'm not mentioned on the tenancy agreement. My name isn't on any of the utility bills either. I'm registered for benefits from Christopher Avenue, my mum's address. Why did you do that?'

The warden had stopped a few feet away from them, content to linger for now. Scott settled back in his chair again.

'I didn't do it on purpose, if that's what you're thinking. I knew we could claim more money that way but I didn't know this would happen.'

Kelly huffed. '*You* said you'd never get caught. *You* said you'd never get sent down.'

'I say a lot of things. It doesn't mean everything always goes to plan.'

Kelly pushed her chair back with her feet but it didn't create enough space. Right now, she didn't want to be near him. All he seemed to be concerned about was his own welfare.

'What about me?' she asked. 'And Emily – what about her?'

Suddenly Scott's tone changed. 'Come on, Kel, this was never going to be easy, you coming to see me in here. I'm sorry, but when you're locked up, you do nothing but think of yourself.' He looked straight into her eyes, throwing her heart into turmoil. 'It's the thought of getting out and being with you that gets me through each day. Don't give up on me.'

'Then give up Patrick Street,' said Kelly. 'The longer you have it, the more rent you'll owe when you do get out. And you'll be moving back with me, anyway, won't you?'

'Yeah, course. Listen, I need you to do something – I need you to go and see Philip Matson, over in Bernard Place. He has some of my gear and I want you to get it back. I've been thinking and I don't trust him with it until I get out.'

Kelly narrowed her eyes. 'What kind of gear?'

'A bit of insurance.' Scott raised his hands in the air. 'Nothing to do with drugs, you know me.'

'Yes, I do know you. What have you been up to?'

'Something and nothing, babe. Nowt you need to worry about anyway, but I need you to keep it for me at Patrick – Clarence Avenue.'

'No way!' Kelly shook her head furtively. 'I am not doing your dirty work for you. What do you think I am, your lackey lad? Get Jay to do it.'

'I don't want anyone to know about it. It's a job I did on my own, so I don't want Stevie and Michael finding out. They'll only want a cut. And, I told you, it's not safe in Matson's hands.'

'A cut of what?' Kelly questioned further.

'Never you mind.'

'No, I won't fetch it unless you tell me what –'

'Just do it, Kel.' Scott's tone held a hint of menace. 'I don't –'

Kelly stood up. 'That's why you wanted me to come and see you,' she hissed. 'You're not bothered about me or Em.'

Scott stood up too. ''Course I am, babe. This money's for all of us, when I get out.'

'Money?'

'Yeah, I –'

'How come I didn't know about it?'

'I'm telling you now!'

The warden was on his way over again. Kelly turned to walk away. Scott reached up and lightly touched her arm.

'Please, Kel, do this one thing. Remember the good times ... didn't I always look out for you ... and Em?'

CHAPTER EIGHT

Jay was waiting for Kelly in the prison car park. He noted her red eyes as soon as she opened the door.

'I take it the visit didn't go to plan?' he remarked.

Kelly buckled up her seatbelt and shook her head. She didn't want to talk about it – least of all to a Kirkwell. Thankfully, Jay started the car and moved away from the building.

How had she let this happen? She asked herself the same thing over and over as Jay drove back onto the motorway. Her partner – the man she loved – had shown his true colours today. He didn't care about her. All he was bothered about was himself.

She turned to Jay at last. 'God, what a pushover I've been. Good old Kelly. Never one to make a fuss, always keeping the bloody peace. Fat lot of good that did me.'

'This isn't your fault,' Jay replied.

'Yeah, right. I should have been stronger, told him not to do that last job. I should have been more forceful, demand that he keep away from you and your bloody brothers. I should have told him –'

Kelly stopped sharply before she let slip about the parcel. She turned away to look out of the window again.

The landscape passed by in a blur. Kelly sensed that Jay wanted to carry on talking, but she wouldn't let him. She couldn't trust him – couldn't trust any of Scott's friends. And if she couldn't trust Jay, why should she try to make him feel better?

As they left Scott further and further behind, Kelly knew now that she would have to dig deeper to find the strength to rely on herself and herself only – regardless of whether she wanted to or not.

*

Before she made her next visit to Kelly, Josie dropped into Mitchell Academy to fetch two prospectuses. She'd been pondering whether to get a qualification in counselling for some time now. It could possibly help her with her work but, more importantly, it might make her find out more about herself. However, there was one thing stopping her – or rather, one person. Stewart – Josie knew he'd hardly be pleased with the prospect of his wife being away from home for another night a week, even if it was only for two hours at a time. When he was working on the late shift, most nights he would ring to see if she was at home. It made her feel like a prisoner on a tag clocking on with her probationer.

No, Josie decided there and then that she was going to do this. She'd just have to think of something to throw Stewart off the scent.

Ten minutes later, she knocked on Kelly's front door. When she answered, Josie realised in dismay that Kelly had made more of an effort than she had. Fully made up, she wore dark jeans and a fashionable red sweatshirt. Consciously, Josie closed her coat to hide the fact that, to Kelly, with her extensive and stylish wardrobe, she would look like she only had a few outfits to her name.

'You must be psychic,' said Kelly, strangely glad to see Josie. 'I was about to flick the kettle on.'

Once upstairs, Josie's eyes swept over the living room, noticing that it was as tidy as it had been on her last visit. Emily lay on the settee, her feet waving in the air, her chin resting in her hands.

'Hello, Emily, what's Dora the Explorer up to today?'

Emily turned her head, her eyes opening widely. 'You know who Dora the Explorer is?'

'Of course I do! She's a very clever girl.'

'I like the penguins best.'

Josie was stumped at the mention of penguins. She turned as she heard Kelly behind her.

'I've brought you a prospectus from Mitchell Academy. I thought you might like to see what's available for you to try out.'

Kelly pushed Emily's legs to one side and sat down. Emily put her feet into her mum's lap as Kelly flicked through the booklet.

'I'm thinking of enrolling on a counselling course,' said Josie, trying to start the conversation up again.

Kelly looked up. 'I thought counselling was part of your job?'

'I suppose it is,' said Josie. 'But I'd also like to be qualified to do it properly. And, although no two cases are the same, who's to say there isn't a better way to deal with a situation?'

'I think you're good at your job. You have a way about you. Scott warned me off people like you – people in authority.'

Josie smiled: praise indeed.

'Josie, will you read me a story before you go?' Emily came towards her with a book.

'Manners, young lady.' Kelly tapped her daughter's thigh lightly. 'It's rude to interrupt. Wait until we've finished talking, please.'

A knock at the front door interrupted their conversation for a second time. Emily rushed to her feet but Kelly pulled her back.

'What did I tell you about answering the door?' she scolded. 'That's always Mummy's job.'

An awkward silence descended as Jay followed Kelly into the living room.

'Jay!' shouted Emily.

'Hey there, maggot.' Jay picked her up and slung her over his shoulder. Emily started to squeal and giggle.

Ill at ease, Josie quickly got to her feet. She wondered why he was calling, although she wouldn't ask. Tenants were allowed visitors. It wasn't as if she had – or would even want – control over who came and went.

'Hello, Jay,' she said. 'How's your mother?'

Jay nodded. 'She's okay, ta.'

Josie spotted the flowers Kelly was holding.

'These are from Scott,' Kelly said. 'There's nothing sinister going on. It's my birthday tomorrow.'

'Happy birthday,' Josie offered, with a faint smile. 'Right, I'll be on my way. I was nearly finished anyway. One more visit in another four weeks and that'll be me done officially. It's obvious you're doing okay.'

Kelly sighed. What the hell would Josie think of her now? She must wonder if she associated with every villain on the estate. And it had been fun, she realised, talking to someone different for a change, even if she was a housing officer and therefore known as the anti-Christ.

Josie couldn't contain herself when they were alone, though. 'Does he come round often?' she said, as Kelly opened the front door to let her out.

Kelly shrugged a shoulder slightly. 'He's been a few times since Scott was sent down. Why?'

'Be careful, hmm? I really like Jay, but maybe you or I don't know what he's really capable of.'

'Like Scott, you mean.'

'No,' Josie faltered. 'I –'

'Keep your nose out of my business.' Kelly's eyes held a look of fury. 'You can't run my life for me – and don't bother calling again if you think you can.'

She closed the door. By the time she'd climbed the stairs again, her earlier thoughts about a friendship forming had been dismissed. It was Josie's job to see that she was settled. Maybe that was all she'd ever intended. Kelly now felt foolish thinking anything else.

Jay took one look at her face and thought better about mentioning his bad timing. Kelly marched past him into the kitchen, filled both rooms with the sound of water gushing out of the tap at full force, then switched on the kettle.

'It's not you that I'm mad with,' she shouted through to him. 'It's the situation I'm in.'

'Josie's all right,' said Jay.

Kelly sighed as she emerged in the doorway with a turquoise patterned vase for the flowers. 'I know. That's what I can't get my head around. She's a housing officer – the spawn of the devil, according to Scott.'

'Most people are the spawn of the devil according to Scott.'

'She seems different, though. Well, at least I thought she was.'

'I think she's really fair.' Jay casually flicked open the cover of the pink book on the table. Emily's eyes left the television long enough to register the information and he put it down quickly.

'I've never had a problem with her and I've known her for years,' he added. 'And she's someone you can trust not to spread your business. Mitchell's a great estate for rumour spreading. I should know, being a Kirkwell.'

Yes, thought Kelly, you being a Kirkwell is the reason why Josie wants to know my business in the first place!

Josie couldn't get Kelly's outburst out of her mind as she walked down the pavement towards Amy's flat. Sometimes she wished she didn't care so much, then she wouldn't get it in the neck when she interfered. Kelly was right: it was none of her business if Jay called round to see her every day – but that didn't stop her from feeling cynical about it.

She knocked on Amy's door but there was no answer. Josie checked her watch: she was ten minutes early. She bent down to check the lock. The key was still there on the other side of the door, meaning that Amy had to be in. Josie knocked again twice, waited for a couple of minutes.

When she still didn't come to the door, she pulled out her mobile phone, checked her file for a phone number and rang Amy. From inside the flat, she could hear the phone ringing. Concerned, she knocked again.

'Amy? It's Josie. I know you're in there. What's the matter?'

Still there was no answer. Josie quickly wrote a message on a calling card and popped it through the letterbox.

Unable to do any more, she went back to her car. Bloody typical, she thought. Now she had Amy *and* Kelly to worry about.

For Josie, the day hadn't ended at five o'clock as the office closed its doors to the public. By rights, it wasn't her night to stay late for the monthly residents meeting, but Ray had conveniently had a memory lapse and left early straight from his last appointment. He'd rung in to speak to one of the admin staff rather than directly to her. Josie wasn't the type of person to shoot the messenger, so she'd had no choice but to step in.

'It's bloody ridiculous what we have to put up with around here,' Saul Tamworth said, as he slammed his fist down onto the table. 'I'm not paying a penny more in rent unless you get something done about it.'

'Yeah, too right,' nodded Muriel Tamworth. 'It's so flipping noisy, every night.'

Mr and Mrs Tamworth lived in Warren Street, on the outskirts of the estate. Over the past few months, they'd been plagued by a gang of teenagers tearing around on scrambler bikes across the open fields behind their property – a property they'd moved into *because* of the open fields they overlooked.

'Like I told you at the last meeting,' Josie reiterated patiently, 'this is a matter for the police to deal with. It's an anti-social behaviour issue and you need to contact them every time the boys come –'

'That's no bloody use. They can't do anything either! They're always far too busy to respond to the likes of us. Seven times I rang the switchboard last night.'

Mr Tamworth was a heavily-built man in his late fifties, with grey hair and cheeks that matched the shade of his grubby red sweatshirt precisely. His wife was a fair bit younger, probably early thirties, built like a barrel with greasy hair and a face covered in acne. To Josie they seemed an odd couple, more like uncle and niece. They were two of nine tenants who had turned up for the monthly tenants' meeting – 'the gripe night', they called it back at the office. They sat on orange plastic chairs, squashed around a snooker table, in a room at the back of the community centre.

Josie tuned out of Mr Tamworth's rants and checked her watch as another tenant, Mrs Roper, joined in. 'I think it's preposterous that you can't do anything about it,' she shouted across the room. 'The noise is atrocious, it's like having a hair dryer on high speed and I can't hear my television half the time.'

Josie wondered how she could hear anything above the full volume of her television. Mrs Roper had worn a hearing aid for the best part of thirty years now. Whenever Josie visited, it was sometimes minutes before she could get her attention, even banging on the front window after trying the door.

'Yeah, and it's always late when they –'

Josie held up a hand, trying to bring things back to the agenda.

'I'll have another word with PC Baxter and see what he can do. If he's on shift, maybe if he walks around the area every night for a couple of weeks, things might calm down.'

'That isn't the point.' Mrs Tamworth folded her arms across a huge chest that sat on an even larger stomach. 'They'll only move onto somewhere else.'

Josie withheld her exasperation.

'Before *we* move on,' Mr Ashworth from number 92 William Precinct began to speak, 'I'd like to congratulate Josie on getting rid of most of the dog poo from in front of my house. It's been far more pleasant taking my daily walk.'

'Must be because you haven't let your own dog out to crap everywhere else,' muttered Mrs Pike from number 74.

Mr Ashworth sat forward in his chair and turned his head to the right. 'You always have to say something detrimental, don't you, Mrs Pike? You can't say a nice word about anyone.'

Mrs Pike huffed. 'That's because I'm always right. You let that ratty thing of yours crap all over my pathway last month.'

'I cleaned it up, didn't I? Charlie has been poorly lately.'

'I bet it won't be long before it happens again.'

'It'll be a very long time, my dear. He passed away last week.'

'Moving swiftly on,' Josie interrupted. She checked the agenda for the next item on the list: number four of sixteen. Great, she sighed – the recent spate of burglaries. And considering there had been another two during the past fortnight, plus another attack on an elderly woman that had left her severely battered and bruised, Josie knew she'd be in for a roasting – even though it was nothing to do with her job.

CHAPTER NINE

By the time everyone had made sure they'd put their point forward, some more forcefully than others, Josie finally brought the meeting to a halt at five to seven. After stacking all the chairs and washing the coffee cups, she left for home ten minutes later. With hardly any traffic on the road, she'd just get back in time for *Coronation Street*. Quickly, she sent a text message to Stewart to let him know she was on her way.

She drove the short journey through the dark streets, wondering why her tenants always worried over the most trivial of matters. Didn't they have anything better in their lives to occupy their minds, apart from moaning about the little things or going on about other people's behaviour? It was bound to be a case of the pot calling the kettle – Josie would love to get inside their homes at night to see what they really got up to behind closed doors. Then she thought of the huge age gap between Mr and Mrs Tamworth – hmm, maybe not.

Stewart was sprawled the length of the settee in the living room when she arrived home, but immediately jumped up to join her in the kitchen.

'Where the bloody hell have you been until now?' he demanded.

'Let me at least take my coat off before you start ranting,' Josie said. 'I had to cover a tenants' meeting. Didn't you get my first text message? I sent it about half past four.'

'You never told me about it last night.'

'That's because I didn't know about it then. Good old Ray decided to bunk off and I was the only one left to cover it. Have you eaten yet?' Josie unzipped her fleece and moved through to the kitchen. 'If you haven't, I can cook you something while I catch *Corrie* on the portable.'

She'd only made it to the fridge when Stewart came up behind her. He slammed his palm on the wall by the side of her head.

'You're seeing someone else, aren't you?'

'What? Don't be –'

Stewart grabbed her arm, pulled her closer and sniffed. 'I can smell him on you. You've been with him tonight.'

Josie flinched as his fingers dug into her skin. 'I haven't been near anyone else. You know I wouldn't –'

'*How* would I know? You could use that frigging job of yours as an excuse any time you want to. I wouldn't be any wiser. You could even meet him at one of your empty properties. You've got loads of opportunities, so don't deny it.'

'Stop it!' she cried. 'You're hurting me.'

'You don't see a problem with hurting ME!'

'Let me go! I haven't been seeing anyone else!'

Stewart loosened his grip and bent forward, his face an inch away from hers. 'No, you're right.' He sniggered. 'No one in their right mind would have you, would they?'

Josie let out her breath as she watched him shrug on his coat. There was so much that she wanted to say, but words wouldn't form. Instead, she watched him swipe up his car keys and leave the room.

As soon as the front door slammed behind him, she burst into tears. She sat down at the kitchen table, tentatively rolling her shoulder as she tried to ease the pain in her arm. What had got into him now? If it wasn't the house, he'd be moaning about something else. Something trivial, just like most of her tenants. It was like being at work at times. Throughout their marriage, all she'd ever done for Stewart was her best, and now even that didn't seem good enough. But then again, no wonder he thought she was a good catch. He could see 'easy life' written all the way through her like the lettering inside a stick of seaside rock.

Josie had met Stewart after a night out in the town. One of the office girls was leaving and most of the housing staff had gone for a meal to send her on her way. It was only after Josie had dropped the last of her passengers off that her car decided to splutter to a halt half a mile from home. Reluctant to walk alone in the dark, she'd rung Kay, the office manager, who had sent husband Richard to help. In the meantime, she'd opened the driver's door, released the handbrake and attempted to push it to the side of the road.

Stewart, with several of his friends, had rounded the corner on the way back from the pub to see a damsel in distress. They'd manoeuvred the car into a better position, locked it up and gone on their way. Moments later, Stewart had returned to keep her company and by the time Richard had arrived, they'd arranged to meet up for a drink the following lunch time. Josie could hardly believe her luck. He was the first man who'd shown an interest in her since her mum died.

Stewart had swept Josie off her feet. He called her beautiful and her confidence had grown. Josie knew she wasn't beautiful – far from it, with her pale complexion, wavy mass of hair and waif-like figure. But he took control of her, made her think that she needed him. And, after losing her mum, that was exactly what she did need. It took her a long while to realise, however, that what she'd first mistaken for loving concern was actually his possessive manner.

Their wedding day a year later had been quiet. Josie wasn't one for a huge affair and Stewart had agreed with his bride-to-be. But it had been a lot quieter than she had at first anticipated. Stewart had booked the ceremony at the local registry office for the month after he'd proposed. He said there was no point in waiting now that they both knew what they wanted. There had only been the two of them. Stewart had managed to persuade a couple in their late fifties to witness the occasion, brought a disposable camera at the local chemist and a suit from the high street. Josie wore a dress she'd found in the summer sales the week before and, late in August 2007, she became Mrs Josie Mellor. A quick meal afterwards – Stewart insisted on the witnesses tagging along too, giving them no time alone to celebrate – and that had been that.

It was when he came to live with her that things started to change. Like Josie, Stewart had never moved away from the family home, but his had been rented from the local council. Giving it up had been easy for him. There was no more rent to pay and what furniture he had he sold.

Before long, he began to question Josie's every motive: what time was she coming home, what time did the meeting finish, could anyone else go instead? Josie soon realised he was a control freak, often behaving like a spoilt child if he didn't have things his own way. It wasn't long until she realised that she was in the same position that she'd been in with her mother.

She stared at her weary reflection in the window as she sat in silence. She wondered if this was really what marriage was about, what everyone raved about, what other girls had craved since puberty. Was this the 'worse' part mentioned in the wedding vows she'd taken, or did it get any better?

She wondered again if Stewart still loved her. Had he *ever* loved her or had he only ever seen her as a safe bet? Good old Josie; in her mind's eye, even she could see how much of a catch she'd been. She didn't have to be exceptional in the looks department to provide a roof over his head. She didn't need to keep up with the latest fashions to wash, dry and iron his clothes. She didn't have to have a confident manner to cook him a decent meal.

One lone tear trickled down her cheek. She left it to travel down her chin, her neck, her chest, as she wondered what she should do about things.

She knew what she *should* do. But she also knew what she *would* do – absolutely nothing.

'Hello, you.' Cathy Mason flashed a welcoming smile as she opened her door to find Josie on her front door step. 'How's tricks?'

'Fine. I called by on the off chance you'd be in,' Josie explained, glad of a warm welcome for a change. 'I heard about the burglary. Are you okay?'

'Yeah, I'm fine, thanks.' Cathy's shoulders sagged. 'Which is more than can be said about my TV! Whoever the bastard was, he put a hammer through the screen. I hadn't had it long.'

Josie pulled a sympathetic face. 'It's a good job you're insured.'

'Yes, and Matt has fitted better locks now, but it still pisses you off, doesn't it? Have you got time for a cuppa?'

'Sometimes I don't believe a word of what they say about this estate and its tenants. Some of them are salt of the earth.' Josie grinned. 'I'd love one please.'

'There's a packet of chocolate biscuits in the cupboard,' she pointed. 'Help yourself.'

'So, how are you and Matt getting along? Still good, I hope?' Josie enquired, as Cathy bustled about making coffee. Cathy's smile told her everything she needed to know. She sighed wistfully. 'I wish I could have a little more happiness every now and again.'

'Oh dear. That doesn't sound good.'

'Never mind me, I'm rambling.' Josie waved the remark away with the flick of a wrist. 'Something and nothing. Have the police got any clues as to who it might be?'

Cathy shook her head. 'Nope, they just gave me a crime reference number. I'm yet again another statistic.'

'Do you think it might be linked to anyone you have staying here?'

'I don't think so, though I can't be certain.'

Cathy Mason had been Josie's saviour many times over the past three years. She'd been widowed at thirty-six, four years ago now. Josie had always liked Rich Mason. Although a trouble maker in his early years, he'd left his reputation behind in the prison cell he'd spent three years in for armed robbery. Once out, he'd made an honest woman of Cathy Riley.

But until a few months ago, everyone was under the assumption that Rich had stumbled coming home from the pub one night. One drink too many and he'd taken a tumble down a flight of steps on his way back. His neck had been broken and he'd died instantly. Having found out since that the push had been deliberate and a couple of kicks to his head had finished him off, Cathy had been left traumatised. But as always, only people close to her would know that.

It was a chance encounter that had started Cathy on the caring route. A child of the care system herself, she'd taken in her friend's daughter after her friend had threatened to kick her out. The result had been a learning curve for Cathy and, as she'd told Josie on numerous occasions, it had been nice to have company again. When she'd been made redundant for the second time in as many years, she'd opened up her home to more of the same.

Cathy only had room for four girls at a time, but she'd always help Josie out as much as she could, even if it meant giving up her room to spend the odd times on the settee. Sometimes the girls stayed a night, sometimes a week, sometimes – like in Jess Myatt's and Becky Ward's cases – months at a time. But since Matt had come onto the scene and Cathy had settled down with him, they'd been making enquiries into fostering children.

'I wish we could collar this dickhead who's been targeting the elderly on the estate. He's the bloody bane of my life at the moment.'

Josie sat down at the table and Cathy pushed a mug over to her.

'I bet he is,' she said. 'But at least whoever did mine didn't take anything of sentimental value. Other things I can replace, but not photos or jewellery – not that I have any jewellery that's worth nicking. It's all cheap tat from Primark.'

'And your window's been fixed, no doubt?' Josie's voice dripped with sarcasm.

Cathy noticed it. 'You're joking, aren't you? You lot have put a piece of plywood over the pane but that's it. How's that supposed to make a woman feel safe?'

Josie reached for her folder. 'I'll make a note to chase it up when I get back. You know these things take time.'

'Bloody budgets,' said Cathy.

The back door flew open and a skinny, young girl marched in, slamming it shut behind her. She peered across at them before getting a glass of water.

'Hello, Jess,' said Josie.

'Hi.'

'Did you get my shopping?' asked Cathy.

Jess held up a carrier bag. 'They hadn't got any of that cheese that you wanted so I got cheddar instead.' She slung it down on the table and made for the door.

'Haven't you forgotten something?' said Cathy.

Jess turned back with an exaggerated sigh. She pulled some coins from the pocket of her jeans.

Cathy held out her hand as she gave them to her. 'Thank you.'

Jess smiled sweetly and turned on her heel again.

'And?' said Cathy.

'And what?' Jess huffed.

Cathy pointed to the bag on the table. 'It won't put itself away now, will it?'

Tutting, Jess grabbed the bag. 'Jesus, what did your last servant die of?'

'Not doing as she was told. It's your own fault. You should have gone in to college this morning with Becky and you wouldn't have to do anything.'

'I didn't get up in time.'

'Becky did.'

'Becky's a swot. Besides, I don't like the lecturer this morning. He gives me the creeps the way he stares at me.'

'I'll give you a lift in tomorrow if you like?' Even though Jess had the odd day off here and there, Cathy had been pleased that she'd stayed in college since September, and marks from some of her essays were good, surprising them both. Still, Cathy didn't want to encourage her to skive off.

Jess muttered something indistinguishable under her breath as she opened the fridge. Cathy rolled her eyes to the ceiling.

Josie grinned at her. 'Looks like another satisfied customer!'

Cathy snorted. 'At least I have some.'

Kelly picked up the leaflet that Josie had left for her and shoved it into her coat pocket, then she bundled Emily down the stairs and out into the morning air. One turn right and two lefts would take them onto Davy Road, the main road which chopped the estate in half more or less through its middle. As February made way for March, the days were getting longer and lighter by the minute, and the weather had warmed up considerably after the past few weeks of frost and freezing winds.

'Will I meet lots of other kids?' Emily asked, as they made their way along Clarence Avenue.

'Yes, you will.' Kelly was pleased that Emily was looking forward to it. It wasn't her idea of fun to go along to a pre-school club, but now that she had so much time on her hands, it seemed a good idea. 'And it will be nice for you to have some friends ready for when you start school in September.'

At the pelican crossings, they crossed over Arnold Road and took a short-cut through the park at the back of the health centre. The gravel that covered the play area was scattered with litter and beer cans. The rubbish bin had been kicked off its holder and Kelly noticed that the street light at the entrance had been vandalised too. The park was deserted but Kelly hurried through it anyway. A month ago, she never even knew this area existed. Now it amazed her how many streets on the estate she had never walked before, living at the bottom of the estate with Scott.

As they emerged from the park, they came across a group of youths sitting on the wall of the health centre. They were all wearing hoodies, combats and jeans, dark and menacing even in the light of day. One of them was messing around on a skateboard.

'Wha-hay, lads,' another one shouted as he spotted Kelly. 'Cop a look at the tottie coming past.'

'What's tottie, Mummy?' asked Emily as she skipped along.

'Never you mind.' Kelly frowned as the lad walked towards her, his mates egging him on.

'Tottie is what I can't get enough of,' the lad said. He was quite an ugly fella up close: wide-set eyes, scabby skin and what looked like bum fluff on his chin made him appear more menacing than he was. He wore a black cap with the initials IA on the peak.

Idiot Arse, Kelly thought immediately.

He placed his hand on his crotch and thrust it forward. 'You fancy some of this?'

'In your dreams,' replied Kelly, pushing past him. 'And they must be wet ones – what are you, fourteen?'

'Old enough to make you groan,' he replied cheekily. He patted her backside but let her pass.

Kelly slapped his hand away and glared at him before turning back to Emily.

'What's a wet dream, Mummy?'

Kelly groaned, hating this part of the estate already. Around the corner was Bernard Place. Two days ago she'd fetched Scott's package from Philip Matson's house. Kelly hadn't liked him on first impressions either, and was glad that he handed it to her without any fuss. The parcel looked like an old shoe box, and was completely covered in duct tape. Annoyingly, there was no way she could look inside it without Scott knowing.

Everything was good between them now. Scott had rung shortly after she and Jay had arrived home from the visit and apologised for being short with her. He said he was looking forward to her next visit, but Kelly wasn't sure she could face going again.

'Will there be lots of books?' Emily broke into her thoughts.

'You'll have to wait and see,' Kelly told her with a smile. Emily had become obsessed with a set of pink teddy bear books that Dot had given to her.

It took them another ten minutes to walk to Mitchell Academy. Once she'd found the right way along the corridors, Kelly pushed open a door. The room was as bright as you would imagine: toys piled high, spilling out of red and green plastic boxes. Above them hung a colourful collection of alphabet letters made out of cardboard and screwed up pieces of crepe paper. Kelly spotted roughly fifteen children walking around in a circle, singing and shouting 'ring-a-roses' before stooping down on the floor. Emily's eyes lit up as one of the leaders let go of a child's hand and beckoned for her to join in. Immediately, her coat was unzipped and pressed into her mother's arms.

Feeling like a spare part as her daughter jumped up and down and pretended to sneeze, Kelly moved to the side of the room where there were four other women standing in a huddle. The one nearest to her nudged one of the others and they all turned to look. Kelly felt her stomach somersault until one of them smiled at her.

'Hiya, I'm Leah Bradley, Samuel's mum,' she said. Like most of the women in the room, Leah was in her early twenties. She had red hair tied in a ponytail and a freckly complexion. Kelly turned to look at the children, instantly recognising Samuel among the many blondes and brunettes.

'And I'm Sadie, Kurt's mum,' her companion said loudly over the shouting, as the children moved on to other things. On first glance, Kelly couldn't tell which boy would be Kurt. Sadie was at least six foot tall, with three inch heels that made it painful for Kelly to look her in the eye. Her thin arms stuck out from the end of rolled-up sleeves.

Kelly smiled back shyly. 'My daughter's name is Emily and she's four. I'm Kelly.'

'Where are you from?'

'I've moved into Clarence Avenue.' Kelly caught the look of disgust that shot from Leah to Sadie. 'I used to be in Patrick Street, at the bottom of the estate,' she added quickly.

'Did I see you with Jay Kirkwell the other day?' Sadie's bird-like eyes flitted down to Kelly's toes and back up to her face before she nodded, now convinced. 'Yeah, it was you. At the DIY shop – he was carrying some boxes.'

'How come you moved out of Patrick Street?' Leah asked, before Kelly had time to reply to Sadie.

'It's a long story.'

'I'll bet it is.' In a flash, Leah had turned to the others and filled them in on her thoughts. Suddenly, they all turned away. Kelly was left to look awkward again.

'Who do I have to pay my money to?'

'I shouldn't think someone who lives in Clarence Avenue would have the money to pay,' said one of the other women.

'I always pay my way, you cheeky cow!' retorted Kelly.

'Hmm... and how do you manage that, I wonder?' Leah laughed snidely. The other girls laughed with Leah so she continued. 'Did Jay Kirkwell want paying too? What did you do for him in return for a favour?'

Kelly wasn't going to be judged by people who didn't know her. She moved to a chair at the far end of the room. While Emily had a waterproof apron popped over her head, she took off her coat and pretended to be interested in some of the paintings on the walls.

When they left the room an hour later, they stopped at the small coffee bar by the entrance. While they waited for their drinks, Kelly grabbed a prospectus. For the next fifteen minutes, with Emily engrossed in one of the books she'd brought along for her, she sipped her coffee and flicked through the pages. There was so much to choose from.

Basic computer skills – she had those, surely. She knew how to surf the net and navigate around search engines. IT courses – no, she wasn't technical. Cookery courses wouldn't earn her any money. She'd never be able to rustle up anything spectacular on a regular basis and she wouldn't be able to put up with the mess. Maybe she should get a job as a cleaner instead, she mused. Kelly knew she was good at that.

But the course offering secretarial and general office skills was the one that caught her eye. It promised that she would be able to type properly at a fair amount of words per minute, lay out and present documents in a businesslike manner and enhance her chances of getting an office job. Kelly was sold, and her head suddenly filled itself with all kinds of possibilities.

The course was on a Wednesday afternoon through to nine pm. Now that the flat was decorated, Kelly would enquire into a few shifts at Miles' Factory. As long as her mum was still keen to look after Emily, Kelly could fit in four nights a week. While she brought a small amount of money in, it would give her the time she needed to gain some experience. Then, when Emily was at school for most of the day, she'd be able to work in an office with other people, be part of a crowd. Maybe, eventually, she could work as a personal assistant for some bigwig and get paid lots of money. By the time she got to the registration room, Kelly was practically hyperventilating.

Full of renewed vigour, her steps home became lighter. Luckily, the gang of youths had moved on from the health centre to bother someone else. She even stopped off to push Emily on the deserted swings.

'Do you know what, Em? Your mum's going to college to learn how to be an office worker. I'm going to earn lots of pennies to buy nice things.'

'And books,' yelled Emily. 'I'd like my own pink teddy bear books.'

Kelly smiled. 'Yeah, and books.'

She pushed her daughter up towards the sky again and again, watching Emily stretching her little legs out to make herself go higher. She looked as free as Kelly felt. From that moment, she resolved that the sky would be her limit, too. So what if Scott wouldn't approve of either of the things she was about to do? It was her life and she wasn't going to let him live it for her. As well, she vowed to show the likes of all the Leahs and Sadies just what she was capable of.

CHAPTER TEN

Josie pulled the top off her pen with her teeth and wrote the date clearly at the top of her notepad. She was parked a few houses away from Mr Neblin's house, her first call of the day. She needed to see if he had moved the pile of rubbish in his back garden that was in danger of reaching the kitchen windowsill. Bonfire night had gone months before and his excuses for not burning it or getting rid of it were wearing thin.

As she drew level with number 78 Hector Walk, Josie let out a huge sigh in frustration. Even from the pavement, she could see that it was no better than the last time she'd visited. She unlooped the string from the post which was holding the gate in place and walked carefully down the mud-covered pathway. Well, it wasn't a path as such, just an unofficial rut that Mr Neblin had made with the wheels of his car. No matter how many times she told him not to park his car on the garden area, he still left it rotting there.

Josie examined the wreck more closely. The tax disc was two months out of date. She doubted it was insured either, yet only yesterday she had seen him hurtling along Davy Road in it. She reckoned it was time to have a word with Andy. If she couldn't make him shift it, the law could impound it.

When she got closer to the mound of rubbish, Josie noticed the other items added to it since her last visit: a smashed up wardrobe, a small television and more than a dozen rubbish bags.

Josie hammered hard on the back door.

'FUCK OFF!'

Unperturbed, she banged on the door, harder this time. Moments later, it was yanked open and a small man with a prominent belly stood scowling on the doorstep.

'Yes, it's that time again, Mr Neblin,' Josie said bluntly. 'I told you to shift that pile of rubbish by the time I called a week later.'

'Like I care!' Mr Neblin leant on the door frame and folded his arms.

'You will care when I –'

'Yeah, please tell me, Mrs Housing Officer, what are you going to do about it anyway? I'm all ears.'

'No, actually, Mr Neblin, you're all *talk*. I think I've given you enough rope to hang yourself. I'll get the association to remove this pile of crap and recharge it to you. It'll cost you a fortune but at least –'

'You won't get nowt from me. In case you haven't noticed, I haven't worked for years and you can't get blood out of a stone.'

'That isn't a problem. I can get it stopped out of your benefits on a weekly order. I'm sure you won't mind missing a few pints every week.'

Mr Neblin took a step forward, his fists clenched at his sides. 'You can't do that!'

'I can and I will.'

'You're a right fucking bitch, aren't you? You think you're so bleeding clever but you won't get one up on me.'

Mr Neblin looked like he was going to blow up. If he squeezed his cheeks in any more, she could envisage steam coming from his ears. She decided to walk away.

'Do you know that people on this estate hate you?' he shouted after her. 'You haven't got a friend to your name in this place and one day it's going to come back and bite you right on your fucking fancy pants. Then what will you do?'

Josie walked away from the drivel spewing from his mouth. Her job was done there, no need to take any further abuse. If the nicey-nicey approach didn't work then she always had the option to hit him where it would hurt the most: his pocket.

The slam of a door never failed to make her jump, no matter how many times she heard it. She'd thought she'd dealt with everything working as an admin assistant back at the office, but it was nothing like what she sometimes faced out on the estate, with no counter to hide behind and no panic button to press. Out on the patch, if the going got rough, all Josie could do was walk away from the likes of Mr Neblin – and Gina Bradley.

*

Josie decided to call in at the newsagents for a bar of chocolate before heading back to the office. She smiled when she spotted Kelly flicking through a magazine, but wasn't surprised when her expression remained blank.

'Don't worry, I'm not with any of the heavy mob today,' Kelly muttered as she reached the cash desk.

Josie hid a smile: she was definitely not forgiven.

'On your own today?' she asked.

'Yes! Not that it's any of your business.'

'I meant without Emily.'

'Oh, I –'

'How's college?'

'Hey, John,' a loud voice boomed. Josie turned in time to spot Mr Neblin, before he disappeared behind the shelving. 'Do you sell black bin liners? I've got a load of rubbish that needs shifting pretty sharpish.'

The man behind the counter pointed to a shelf. 'They're the only ones we've got, Clive, above the envelopes. Will they do?'

'They'll have to do, especially if they get that stuck-up bitch from the housing office off my back.'

Kelly giggled as Josie's eye's flicked to the ceiling.

'I don't know what her old man must think of her,' Mr Neblin continued. 'She must definitely wear the trousers in that househo– oh, it's you.'

Kelly shoved her face into a magazine in order to stop from roaring with laughter.

'Yes, it's me,' said Josie. 'Glad to hear you're taking my advice, albeit a little late in the day.'

As soon as he'd gone, Kelly finally gave in. 'Did you see his face?' she laughed. Then she snorted. 'It was the colour of beetroot, he was so embarrassed.'

Josie got out her purse. 'I heard and saw everything that would shock me in my first year on this estate. Nothing gets to me now.'

Kelly relaxed a little. Maybe she had judged Josie as well as the other way around. From her actions with the man and the rubbish, it was clear she couldn't care less about his situation.

'College has been great,' she offered. 'And I got a job at Miles' factory.'

'Well done you!'

Kelly nodded and then smiled. Seeing Josie today had made her realise how much she had missed her calling in. She'd only been to see her three times since she'd moved into Clarence Avenue but she'd been the only female company she'd enjoyed for a long time – even if she was a housing officer.

'I do my best,' she replied. 'Now, are you going to add a Kit-Kat to that stash of chocolate you're buying so you can call round some time for a quick break?'

Josie smiled. It had taken a while, but finally she was breaking down the barrier.

Later that afternoon, Josie clock-watched from four o'clock onwards to ensure she left the office bang on five thirty, in order to beat most of the rush hour traffic. When she opened the front door to her home, she could hear noises coming from the kitchen. Unsure of what mood to expect from Stewart, she shrugged off her coat in a desperate attempt to gain more time.

But she needn't have worried. All was clear when she spotted the vase of her favourite flowers on the kitchen table. Propped up by the side of the lilies was a box of milk chocolates. She sniffed garlic in the air.

'I've been shopping,' Stewart informed her. 'I thought we could open a bottle of red, too.'

Josie frowned. Had he used psychic powers to read her mind last month?

'I'm sorry,' he said when she still hadn't moved moments later.

'You accused me of having an affair,' she spoke quietly.

'That's why I'm sorry.'

'You said no one else would want me! Have you any idea how much that hurt?'

Stewart urged her to take a seat. 'I was in a lousy mood. I shouldn't have taken it out on you.'

Josie sat down as Stewart poured her a glass of wine. As he moved to sit opposite her, she struggled to set her emotions straight. She wanted to feel relief that he was out of his dark mood, but she knew that it wouldn't last. She wanted to be content in her home, loved by her husband, but she knew that she never would.

She wanted to believe in Stewart, but something was telling her not to...

After college on Wednesday evening, Kelly walked the ten minute journey home alone. She was so pleased that Emily had wanted to stay over at her nanny's; Emily had been griping for most of the day and Kelly's nerves felt ragged from trying to pacify her. She hadn't been surprised – more faintly amused – to see that Emily had developed the Winterton stubborn streak at such an early age. Verbal battles and grumpiness had been the norm for the past couple of weeks. Emily had started to question when her daddy was coming home. For a child, Kelly assumed that the eight weeks Scott had been inside already must seem like eight years, and Emily's questions were getting more demanding, and upsetting. Everything Kelly had suggested, Emily had given a negative answer in response.

Halfway back, she decided to celebrate the opportunity of a night alone and grab a cheap bottle of wine. As she turned the corner onto Vincent Square, she found herself faced with a gang of teenagers. Two of them ran to block the shop doorway as she drew near.

'Excuse me,' she said, but they ignored her. After a quick dance in the doorway, Kelly pushed past them. The one who had the look of a serial killer followed her in. She walked down the first aisle, sensing his presence behind her. All at once, she imagined she could feel his breath on her neck. She wrapped a fist tightly around the handle of her bag.

'Spare us a quid then, lady,' he said from behind.

Kelly turned quickly, taking him by surprise, and he bumped into her. The smell of ale clung to his breath. She pushed him away aggressively.

'Leave me alone!'

'Ah, come on,' he lurched forward. 'I'm only messing.'

Kelly pushed past him again and marched to the front of the

store, praying that he wouldn't follow. By the time she'd paid for her goods, everything had gone quiet outside – until she stepped out of the door and saw the group reappear from behind the corner of the building.

'What've you got in the bag, then?' a small, plump lad queried.

'Nothing that you'll be allowed. Isn't it past your bedtime?'

The rest of the group laughed loudly but it didn't do Kelly any favours.

'Come on kids, let her past,' the shopkeeper said, in a resigned tone. 'Time you moved on to bother someone else.'

'Fuck off, oldie,' a girl with short red hair shouted, 'or you'll get a brick through your window.'

When they didn't move, Kelly had no choice but to push past them again. 'Stuck up bitch,' she heard one of them say, but she didn't turn around to see who. The lad who had followed her into the shop started to circle around her on a pushbike, each time moving a little closer. Kelly quickened her pace. Luckily, he lost interest as she left them further behind with each step.

A few minutes later, the panic inside her finally began to subside. Looking through the windows of the many houses she passed, Kelly saw family after family settled down for the night and wished she was safe at home too, getting a glass of wine down her neck as quickly as possible so that she could chill out.

She was turning into Davy Road when she heard a noise. Serial killer skidded to a halt on the pavement in front of her. Kelly moved to the side but he followed her. She tried to double back but he was too quick.

'Do you get a kick out of this type of thing or what?' she asked, almost praying that someone would drive past in their car, but knowing full well that no one would stop to help her if they did. 'Because I'm getting a little bit –'

'Give me your bag, bitch.'

'No, I bleeding won't.'

'GIVE ME YOUR FUCKING BAG!'

Kelly clutched it to her chest. At the same time she noticed the sliver of steel in his hand. Instinctively, she moved backwards.

The bike was thrown down onto the pavement. 'Give it to me.

NOW!' he yelled.

Kelly froze with fear. He slapped her face, grabbed her hair and pulled her nearer. 'I'm not fucking messing this time.'

She gave him the bag. He pushed her away and she lost her footing, landing on the pavement with a sickly thud. She looked up at him, half expecting to get his boot in her face, but he got back on his bike. In a flash, he was gone.

Kelly began to retch. She managed to crawl to the kerb where she threw up. Oh god, he had a knife. She could have been killed, all for the sake of a few pounds. Tears streamed down her face when the fear of what could have happened replaced itself with the reality that it hadn't. She tried to remember what was inside her bag. Luckily, her keys and her mobile phone were in her coat pocket. But wait – would he have her address? Kelly sobbed uncontrollably as she tried to recall if anything had her details written on it. She prayed there was nothing in her purse that would lead him to her.

Then she ran.

'Where were you?' Jay asked, when Kelly broke down in his arms. He guided her into the living room and sat her down.

'At the – the – the shops.' Kelly sobbed as she clung on to him.

'Jesus! Don't you know it's mad to go to The Square after dark? It's not just the kids that –'

'I – I thought I'd be okay. It wasn't too late.'

'Did you get a look at him?'

'He was taller than me, really skinny, with horrible beady eyes. He had a black hoodie top... and a tattoo on his neck. Two boxing gloves, hanging down, tied together. And he stunk of booze.'

Jay stiffened. 'That's Ian Newton. He went to juvie about a year ago for assault. I thought he was still inside.'

Kelly pulled away from him in a panic. 'I'm not sure if he has my address! You – you don't think he'll come and find me again, do you?'

Jay shook his head. 'No, he's a smack head. He'll be after a quick fix. Your bag's probably been thrown into someone's garden by now.'

'But he could have stabbed me, Jay, left me to bleed to death! He could have raped me. He could have done anything and I wouldn't have been able to stop him with a knife pointing at me. Emily's lost one parent for the time being, she could have lost both of them. How could I have been so stupid?'

Jay pulled her into his arms again. 'Hey, it's over now. Seeing as I hadn't finished my tea when you rang, do you fancy helping me with a takeaway? I could murder a chop-suey.'

While Jay was gone, Kelly paced up and down the living room waiting for his return. Once she'd got home, she'd flew around in a panic, bolting the door behind her, checking all the windows were secure before shutting the curtains and sitting in the glow of the gas fire. It was only now that she dared put the light on – now that Jay had called round after she'd decided to ring him.

She touched her cheek. The redness was fading but it still felt numb. Stupid, stupid, silly bitch, she cursed herself. Was she the only person brainless enough to assume she was safe to go out alone at night?

When Jay returned, he had not one but two brown bags on his person. Kelly's face momentarily broke into a smile when her fake Louis Vuitton was handed to her. She unzipped the compartment and checked inside. Her purse was still there and so was the ten pound note she'd shoved in earlier, still folded into four behind her gas instalment card.

'Where did you get that?' she asked.

'I spotted Newton – or 'The Newt', as he prefers to be known as, stupid bastard – when I drove past the shops,' said Jay. 'After a little persuading, he told me where the bag was. Everything's there, isn't it?'

'I think so. I can't think of... what do you mean, after a little persuading?' Kelly's eyes bulged. 'You hit him, didn't you?'

Jay shook his head. 'Newton's a pussy. He only goes for women. He didn't put up much of a fight before coming clean.'

'Much of a fight! You said you didn't hit him!'

'It was a figure of speech! And he hit you, didn't he?'

'A slap is a bit different than a thrashing.'

'I didn't do much to him, if that's what you mean.'

All thoughts of the danger Kelly had put herself in went out of the window. As she'd got to know Jay more over the past few weeks, she'd started to think that maybe he was different. She took a step away from him.

'I want you to go,' she said.

'Don't be daft.' He moved past her and into the kitchen. 'The last thing you need is to be on your own.'

'Please, Jay. I've had a rough night. I want to be by myself.'

'Even more reason for me to stay. I'll keep you company while we eat. I'm not going to bite you.'

Kelly stood rooted to the spot.

Jay caught her eye. 'There's no need to look at me like that. I was only trying to help.'

'I don't need that kind of help!'

'Yeah, you do. You don't know who to trust at the moment.'

Kelly stood silent again and he finally got the message. She followed him down the stairs, drawing across the bolts once he'd gone. She slid down the door onto the mat and sat with her head in her hands, Jay's words ringing in her ears.

She should never have taken this flat. She should have moved back in with her mum in Christopher Avenue. But no, Scott was only two months into his sentence and she'd been stupid enough to think that she could cope by herself. The phone call she'd had earlier from him had only added to her confusion. 'I've signed the papers, babe,' Scott had told her. 'No more Patrick Street. I've done it for you – it'll be different this time when I get back. You've got to trust me.'

See it was there again, that word: 'trust'. But how could Kelly trust anyone, let alone Scott? She wasn't even sure if she wanted him to come and live in Clarence Avenue when he was released. Life would only go back to how it was before. Kelly knew he wouldn't change his ways just to suit her. And to top it all, now she'd overreacted with Jay. Was her attempt at independence doomed?

She pulled back her head and banged it on the door three times in quick succession. She knew she could never knock enough sense into her thick skull, but it made her feel better by trying.

One thing was for sure, though. If Jay had spoken a word of truth tonight, it was that she didn't know who to trust anymore. She had never felt so lonely in her life.

CHAPTER ELEVEN

'Right, that's the boring work questions out of the way,' Josie said, as she signed off Kelly's final support questionnaire. 'Is there anything else you'd like to know or can I leave you in the capable hands of Miss Emily?'

It was Wednesday morning, the third one the month of March had seen. Josie had been at Kelly's flat for half an hour now, ensconced far too comfortably in Kelly's settee. The rain lashing at the window gave her no incentive to move whatsoever. Phil and Holly were discussing fruit-shaped figures on daytime television. Emily was playing dressing up, running from room to room and strutting her stuff before running off again. This time she had clattered across the living room floor in a pair of Kelly's high heels, wearing a stripy scarf around her neck like a feather boa and a belt that doubled as a hula hoop, which fell off twice before she got to them.

'Very nice,' Josie nodded her approval before Emily clicked-clacked off again. She turned back to Kelly who was in the middle of a yawn. 'She's so hard to keep up with, she always seems busy.'

The yawn turned into a sigh and Kelly stretched her arms above her head. 'Sometimes she's the only person I speak to during the day. She keeps me sane ... It's been tough for me lately. I – I could really do with an ear, if you don't mind?'

'Go ahead,' Josie said. 'You know I was born to listen.'

Kelly took a deep breath. 'I was mugged a few nights ago and it scared the shit out of me.'

'Mugged?' Josie's eyes searched Kelly's body for injuries but there didn't seem to be any. 'Where did it happen? Were you hurt? Are you okay now?'

'I'm not too bad,' Kelly admitted. 'It takes more than a slap on the face to bring me down. I was scared though.' She began to unburden her tale.

'I know Ian Newton,' Josie broke in when Kelly mentioned his name. 'Lives on Gordon Street – his parents have no control over him. I thought he was still in juvie.'

'He's just got out.'

'Did you lose much?'

Kelly stalled and then decided what the heck. 'No, see, that's the thing. When I got home, I rang Jay.' Josie raised her eyebrows slightly. 'I was petrified that Ian Newton knew my address. Jay went to get a takeaway and came back with my handbag and all of its contents, just like that. He must have picked a fight and I – I lost it with him.'

'Jay's usually the peacekeeper Kirkwell,' Josie came to his defence. 'He might use his reputation to gain control of a situation but I doubt that he would have used his fists unless he was provoked.'

'Two wrongs don't make a right,' Kelly shrugged, feeling embarrassed as she remembered how she had reacted. After her outburst she'd gone to bed and woken up the next day in a better frame of mind. There was no way she would give up her flat. She'd just suffered a setback that night, and knowing that she'd been too hasty jumping to conclusions, she'd sent Jay a text message to apologise. Jay had made her suffer for two days until he'd sent one in return.

'How do you feel about Scott coming out of prison?' Josie dared to question. In recent conversations, just his name had been enough to shut down the barriers.

But Kelly didn't seem to mind this time. She pulled her legs up onto the settee and drew a cushion to her chest. 'He thinks he'll be out soon. I've only been to see him once, which was enough for me.'

'How long have you been with him?'

'He was my first real boyfriend. I met him when I was eighteen and then I was pregnant with Emily the year after.'

Kelly paused but Josie said nothing to ensure the conversation kept going.

'I'm a bit mixed up,' Kelly continued. 'I do miss him, but I don't miss the lifestyle, the constant worrying – whether he's coming home, whether he's been arrested again, who's knocking on the door next. I might have found it hard to start again by myself, but I've done it. I'm going to be earning some money soon – I start this Monday, by the way – and I'm going to college. Both of which Scott will go mad about.'

'You mustn't let him stop you doing anything,' said Josie, feeling guilty as soon as the words came out. Stewart had stopped her from doing lots of things over the years. How could she sit here and preach?

'What do you mean?'

'You can still go to work and complete your college course when he comes out.'

Kelly huffed. 'Yeah, right, and it's as easy as that.'

'Yes, it is. You'll have to think of some good reasons why you should continue, get your ammunition ready. Besides, surely he should want you to try and better yourself? He should be proud of what you've done under the circumstances. You wouldn't have lost your home if it wasn't for him! You need to remember that.'

Kelly nodded. She would never forget how underhand Scott had been regarding the tenancy on Patrick Street – especially the position he'd put Emily in.

'I'm scared he'll want me to be the old Kelly,' she said, 'and I don't want to be her again.'

'No, you don't,' Josie agreed. 'What night is your secretarial course?'

'Tonight, six 'til nine.'

'I'm there every Wednesday too, so I can give you a lift home every week if you like? It's on the estate, before you say that I'm going out of my way.'

'Thanks, but I've managed to sort one out.' Josie didn't need to know that Jay had insisted on taking on the role of chauffeur.

'Fair enough,' said Josie, guessing rightly about what Kelly wasn't telling her. 'Just yell if you need me any time in the future.'

Kelly smiled with gratitude. Despite her job, Josie had turned out to be someone she liked. 'Are you married?' she asked, wanting to know a little more about her.

'Yes, just over five years.'

'Do you have any children?'

'No, we're quite set in our ways at the moment. We're both only children; both sets of parents died when we were young.' Josie knew it was a pathetic excuse. How could they bring a child into their relationship? She checked her watch and jumped up quickly. 'I'd better be on my way. I've promised to cover the phones while some of the girls at the office go to the pub for their lunch.'

At the front door, Kelly thanked Josie for listening to her. 'I've enjoyed talking to you this morning – I hope I haven't said too much though.'

'I don't gossip,' Josie reassured her. 'Nor do I form opinions. What you've told me will stay with me only, if that's what you mean.'

Kelly smiled shyly. 'You change when you take off your coat. You lose your sense of authority.'

Josie was astounded at her perceptiveness. 'In this job, I have to be two different people at the same time. It's one of those things that only individuals who work with the general public face-to-face will understand. It stops you taking the insults personally.'

'You still ask too many questions for my liking,' Kelly continued, rolling her eyes to the ceiling.

'Force of habit, I'm afraid.'

'But I can run to a coffee whenever you can find a free minute in your full day?'

'You mean you'd like to be one of my regular 'tea-stops'?' Josie teased. 'Or 'pee-stops', as we often call them. I'm highly honoured. Most of them are above the age of seventy and only want me to call because they see no one else from week to week. But I suppose I can make an exception for you.'

'How are you getting on with the course?' Brian Walker asked, as he held open the door of Mitchell Academy later that night. He followed Josie out into the drizzle.

'It's great,' said Josie brightly.

Brian was the course lecturer. Although she hadn't known him long, Josie had taken an instant liking to him. He was fair of face and nature and he spoke with a soft pitch.

'Really?' he continued. 'I was certain that tonight's topic had affected you more than you're letting on.'

'It is hard going. I know I'm only in my first month but it's very much like counselling for yourself,' Josie tried to explain. 'The group we have has gelled so quickly, I suppose due to the nature of the course and the things we have to share. It's quite draining actually, but very motivational when you hear what other people have gone through. Especially Tim.'

For part of the night's session, Tim had been talking about his ex-wife and how their marriage had fallen apart from his lack of trust. Sometimes Josie had had to stop her mind from wandering as she tried to listen to him, at the same time listing in her head all the similarities he had with Stewart. Tim explained it was his need for control that eventually drove them apart – he had to be right every time. He found it hard to take criticism, found it hard to trust anyone, and so he pushed them away with his nastiness. Equally, he found it hard to communicate his love.

For Josie, it had been too close for comfort. When she'd met Stewart, she'd thought that her lack of self-belief would disappear, but now that she was married, it was worse than ever. She knew she had let him control her, just like she had let her mother do the same. It was one of the reasons she'd enrolled on the course – to see if she could learn more about herself, as well as to pick up a qualification. She realised she had her limits, but she wanted to gain more confidence.

It had been enough for her to question Tim about it during their break. What Josie had learned had made her heart beat wildly. Eventually, Tim had got help for his problem and now he was much better. He'd lost his wife in the process: they'd divorced a long time ago, but he was with another partner and – for the first time in his forty-nine years – he felt content.

Josie hadn't been able to get the conversation out of her head. Feeling unable to ask him why he'd felt so insecure for the best part of his life, she wondered if Stewart could change if he got help, or perhaps she could find out exactly what was at the root of his problem. If she got him to admit there *was* a problem, she could help him, or try to send him in the right direction.

'That's the trouble with a small group, I'm afraid,' Brian nodded, understanding Josie fully now. 'We can only use ourselves as subject matter and sometimes it gets a little too close. I must admit, it's given me quite a lot of food for thought over the years.'

Josie delved into her handbag for her car keys. 'I thought we were going to learn *how* to be a counsellor, not to *be* counselled.'

Brian held up his hands in mock alarm. 'Hey, don't shoot the lecturer!'

Josie smiled. 'Can I offer you a lift anywhere?'

'I'm supposed to be meeting my son in the George and Dragon. No doubt he'll want some of my hard-earned cash. I don't suppose...'

'It's on my way home. Hop in.'

In the far corner of the car park, Stewart watched from the shadows as Josie stood deep in conversation with a man. He looked in his early fifties, dressed in a smart suit, small and round in stature with a mass of grey hair.

Stewart ground his teeth. Never taking his eyes from them, their laughter made his blood boil. Josie had lied to him last week. She wasn't at a meeting, like she'd told him. Neither had she been tonight. He'd already been into the reception to ask where she was, but they hadn't heard of any council meeting being held. They'd asked him if he had the right night, like he was an idiot. Of course he had the right night: Josie had gone to these so-called meetings for the last three Wednesdays.

It was obvious from what he'd seen – the bitch was having an affair.

As Josie reversed her car out of its space and onto the road, Stewart started up his engine. Not wanting to be spotted, he gave her a moment before pulling out after her. Maybe he could tail her in the dark, see where she was heading.

But then he stopped. He needed to think about this before he did anything too rash. Once he'd found out more details, she'd get his wrath. There was no way he was prepared to lose everything after he had gone this far.

CHAPTER TWELVE

Kelly often wondered how her legs carried her through the gates of Miles Factory on that first Monday afternoon. At quarter to four, Doreen, her supervisor for the shift, showed her to the locker room where she was given a key and some overalls. At five to four, Kelly followed her onto the factory floor with a knot in her stomach and a lump in her throat. The first thing she saw was Sally's welcoming smile. She had shown her what to do at her interview.

'Hi, again,' Sally shouted over the noise. A plump girl with blonde hair and freckles, she placed a cup on the conveyor belt and grabbed for the next one. 'You're sitting across from me – lucky you. Sometimes my talking can be drowned out by the racket in here.' She nodded to the girl who had joined them. 'That's Julia. She's okay for a laugh.'

Julia smiled at Kelly as she sat down behind Sally. She was in her late teens, with huge blue eyes almost hidden by her blonde fringe. Kelly smiled back and then glanced around the room. Women sat at most of the benches along the conveyor belt. There were three men in the far corner making up cardboard boxes and separators and a bunch of men playing air guitars while singing to the track belting out from the radio.

'Can you remember what to do or do you want me to show you again?' Sally offered moments later, when Kelly was sat still.

Kelly's shoulders drooped. 'Would you? Ta. You know how useless I was when I tried.'

'We do the same for everyone who starts – here.' She picked up another cup, gave it to Kelly and walked round to join her. 'Dip your sponge into the water – not too much – and wipe it over one seam. Yes, that's right, not too hard or else you'll have to throw it. Then flick it round like this.' Sally took Kelly's wrist and turned it ninety degrees. 'Right, do the same down that seam. Good, that's much better. Quick, put it on the conveyor belt and grab the next one.'

'How long have you been doing this?' Kelly asked, once they'd finished a few cups together.

'Now, let me see ...' Sally scratched her head in comical fashion. 'Five, maybe six ... years.' She let the facts sink in before she burst into laughter again. 'It's easy once you get the hang of it. Too dry and the seam will still be visible; too wet and the cups will be soggy and have to be thrown. You're doing great,' she enthused.

Just then, Kelly noticed Doreen walking back towards the belt. She saw Sally slide a few of her own cups over towards her. Before Kelly could react, Doreen picked one up and examined it carefully. She ran a finger over the seam and raised a quizzical eyebrow.

'Not bad,' she said. Her eyes landed on Sally. 'I don't suppose you had anything to do with the quality of these?'

Sally feigned hurt. 'You've got the wrong idea of me, Mum.'

Doreen smirked.

'She's not too much of a slave driver, my mother,' Sally enlightened Kelly once Doreen had moved way again. 'You could do a lot worse. Some of the women are right bitches, especially that Estelle over on the day shift. She gets away with murder because her mum works here.'

Kelly stifled laughter and hid her face. Sally was talking about her aunty – who had helped her get the job – and her cousin.

Sally pulled a face. 'They're not family, are they? I should have guessed – everyone's related on here.'

Suddenly a young woman, her face as red as her long hair, rushed over to the bench and plonked herself down on the empty seat behind Kelly.

'Bloody typical, I missed the three forty-five bus again. I got a right bollocking last week for being late, but is it my fault that Samuel won't run for ... oh fuck, don't tell me you're the new girl!'

Kelly looked up into the eyes of Leah, one of the women she'd met at the playgroup.

'You two know each other!' exclaimed Sally.

'Know her?' Leah slipped quickly into her overall and sat down as if she hadn't been twenty minutes late. 'I don't think so – she comes from Clarence Avenue. You know, *the* Clarence Avenue –'

'Yeah, we all know Clarence Avenue, Leah,' Sally interrupted. 'Get to the point, what's wrong with it?'

Leah's eyes shot out as if on stalks. 'Where have you been hiding for the past few years? There are dealers and prostitutes and loads of anti-social behaviour going on. I wouldn't live there if my life depended on it.'

'Like your street is far better, then?' Sally turned to Kelly, who, by this time, had cheeks the same colour as Leah's hair. 'Leah lives in Stanley Avenue, two streets from you. Its tenants are – how shall I put it? – the devil's offspring. Isn't that what you usually call them, Leah?'

Leah huffed. She threw a scowl at Kelly before finally starting to work. Kelly bristled, but chose to ignore it for now.

Once they'd had a tea break at six fifteen, the night started to drag. Kelly lost count of the mugs she made a hash of, and the smirks that Leah threw at her every time she used too much water and the whole thing became too soggy.

At five past eight, she made her way back out of the factory gates with Sally. The young woman had taken an instant liking to her, which was more than she could say for Leah, who had stormed off in front of them. Kelly sighed as she realised that they'd probably be catching the same bus.

Sally said goodbye at the end of the street and Kelly crossed over towards the bus stop. A few minutes later, she rounded the corner to see Leah sitting down in the shelter. Leah folded her arms, then her legs, and threw Kelly a look that said, 'stay well away'.

Kelly was fine with this. She had more pressing things to occupy her mind – the first thing she was going to do when she'd collected Emily was relax in a nice, hot bath to ease her aching shoulders and neck. God knows how those women stooped forward for so long during each shift.

Still, she sighed, while all the time feeling Leah's eyes boring into her head, there's always tomorrow. Maybe things will improve.

*

Josie stood in the middle of Philip Matson's living room for what seemed like a lifetime, but in reality was all of ten minutes. The room was a complete tip; papers, beer cans and takeaway cartons littering any available space – far too much of it for her liking. Three Rottweilers sat at Philip's feet while he stubbed out a roll-up cigarette, before immediately lighting up the next. The thick plume of smoke curling around Josie's head started to make her feel light-headed. She wafted it away in vain.

Philip was a good-looking man – or he could be, if he ever took that scowl off his face. He was in his mid-thirties, with no work in him, no brain in him and no balls. Every time she saw him, he reminded Josie of one of the dirty detectives from any number of police television dramas.

They were in the middle of a standoff. Josie had no time for Matson: Matson had no respect for Josie. The threat of eviction seemed the only weapon left to use, and it would hardly be a threat if he didn't pay something towards his rent in the next few days. She'd been trying for months to get him to understand the seriousness of his impending court hearing. She decided to try one more time.

'Mr Matson, if you can't be bothered to follow the correct procedure to claim your benefits, then how am I supposed to stop the eviction next week?'

Philip's head flipped up at the last moment. 'Eviction?' he frowned.

'I have the revenue team on my case. If you don't comply with the court order set up last month, they'll take you back to court and apply for an eviction order. Seeing as you haven't kept up with the simple repayment scheme of four pounds a week, the judge will grant it for us. You've only yourself to blame. You must understand that –'

Philip stood up abruptly. 'No, *you'd* better understand,' he said. 'I filled in the forms; *you* didn't do your job properly.'

'You didn't provide proof of your bank account,' Josie ticked off with her fingers. 'You didn't provide proof that you're claiming sick pay. We don't check all that out for you – you have to do some things for yourself. One of them is to get that lazy backside of yours out of that chair and to the office with the necessary paperwork.'

Philip scowled but Josie wasn't perturbed.

'You need to clear the account by 4 o'clock on Friday afternoon or we'll be applying for the order first thing on Monday morning. You've really left it late this time.'

Josie stepped back as Philip moved towards her. 'You won't kick me out.'

'If you pay what you owe, then –'

'Fifteen hundred quid!' he screamed. Josie started. One of the dogs jumped onto the floor and began to prowl the room. 'Where the fuck am I going to get fifteen hundred quid?'

'It wouldn't have been anything if you'd taken the time to provide us with what we needed. That's the sad thing. We've been asking you for over six months now to provide proof of your bank details – all you had to do was bring it to the office for me to photocopy. Letter after letter, visit after visit. You've been to court four times and been given chances to co-operate with us. What more could we have done?'

'That's right.' Philip's tone was sarcastic. 'You're doing what you're paid to do, Mrs Jobsworth.'

'Yes, that is right.' Josie nodded. 'I am.'

'You chuck me out on Friday and it's you who I'll come after. It'll only take a few days to follow you around and I'll know where you live. You won't feel safe in your bed because you'll never know when I'll come calling.'

'Don't be ridiculous. If you lay one finger on me, I'll get *you* for it. It certainly won't take me long to find out where –' Josie's phone rang and she reached for it quickly. 'Hi, *PC Baxter*,' she almost shouted the words.

'Josie, it's Charlotte Hatfield,' said Andy. 'The control room have had a call from her every minute or so for the past few minutes, but there's no reply when they talk to her. All they can hear in the background is the kids screaming. I think her partner's got to her.'

Josie took a sharp intake of breath. 'Oh no! I – where are you?'

'I'm in Brian Road. You?'

'I'm in Bernard Place. Do you want to meet me there or do you want to come round to fetch me?'

'I'm on my way,' was all she heard before he disconnected the call.

Josie turned to Philip, who didn't seem to scare her anymore. 'I haven't got time for you, or your games. Pay up by Friday or we'll evict you. It's as simple as that. You've had enough chances now.'

Josie ran through the scratty jungle of a garden and jumped over the low wall. She could hear the police siren coming closer. Andy screeched to a halt beside her moments later.

'Get in!' he yelled.

The living room curtains were drawn when they pulled up outside Charlotte Hatfield's house. Andy banged hard on the front door while Josie ran round to the back. She fiddled in frustration with the bolts on the make-shift gate. Eventually, it gave way and she pushed it open. She could hear the children crying. Through the rear window, she saw Charlotte lying on the floor, blood running from a gash on her head. The twins sat either side of her, Joshua hiding his face behind a cushion.

'Charlotte!' Josie banged on the window to get her attention. Charlotte turned her head slightly. She looked dazed; Josie knew that she wouldn't be able to recognise her. She banged on the window again.

'Callum! Jake! Go to the front door and let the policeman in!'

Callum ran towards the window and held up his hands. His tiny palms were smeared in blood. 'Mummy's bleeding!' he screamed.

'Go to the front door!' Josie urged him, her heart going out to the four-year-old.

Suddenly, she heard a loud bang and Andy appeared in the room. She watched him drop to his feet and switch on his radio before coming to her senses. Quickly, she ran round to join him and stepped into her worst nightmare.

Charlotte's injuries were more severe close up. Blood oozed out of the gash and down her neck. She wore only her underwear, the white cotton bra soaking up her blood. Her arms and torso were covered in cuts, her face a mass of swelling.

Andy spoke into the radio while the kids continued to cry. He threw Josie a latex glove. Josie pulled it on and knelt beside Charlotte.

'Charlotte?' she whispered. 'Charlotte? Can you hear me? Please say something.'

Charlotte's breath came quickly. Her mouth moved but there was no sound.

Josie reached inside herself for the strength she needed to deal with the reality. She picked up two-year-old Joshua, who threw his arms tightly around her neck. The little boy's complexion was white and he was shivering uncontrollably.

Glancing across the room, Josie could see that the baby was safe in her cot. She beckoned the two older boys towards her.

'I'll be back in a minute, Andy.'

If Sharon Watson, the next door neighbour, was amazed to see Josie pushing past her with three small children in tow, she never batted an eyelid.

'I haven't got time to explain what's going on,' Josie told her, 'but I need you to look after the boys from next door. There's been an accident and I don't want them in the room. Will you help me?'

'Of course I will,' Sharon said, following closely behind. 'Come on, boys. I'm sure I have a packet of chocolate biscuits somewhere. Then we can see what's on the telly.'

By the time Josie ran back to the house, half the neighbours were out on the pavement and the paramedics were running in front of her. Andy moved away as they took over. Within minutes, Charlotte was moved onto a stretcher. Two more police officers arrived and Josie sent one of them round to next door while she checked on the baby. Thankfully, Poppy had slept through most of the commotion.

Josie sat down on the settee and put her head in her hands. How many times would she be in this situation, feeling anxious, inadequate, and fearful? There was only so much she could do. She wasn't Wonder Woman, nor did she profess to be, but unlike the views of the Philip Matsons on this estate, sometimes what she did was more than a job. It was a lifeline.

Her mind flipped back to the previous summer when Liz McIntyre, another one of her tenants, had been beaten up by her husband. He'd left her for dead before hanging himself – fortunately, Liz had survived, but it was seeing Charlotte Hatfield in the same state that really upset Josie. Why do some men do this to women?

A tear spilled down her cheek. What the hell was she going to do with four kids under five? Charlotte's injuries couldn't be fully assessed until she got to the hospital, and there was no family near who could look after them. Someone from Children's Services was needed. Until then, she'd be left holding the baby herself.

Andy collapsed into the settee beside her. 'The reason I joined the force was that 'not a single day is the same' they say.' He shook his head. 'But days like these make you want to pack it in on the spot.'

Josie wiped at her eyes. It seemed strange to see Andy's face without his usual trademark grin, but today wasn't a day for smiles.

'There was nothing else we could have done,' she assured him. 'We set up everything, just in case, and it all went as planned: the telephone and pendant system that I fitted served its purpose, the control room staff reacted swiftly and you did your job brilliantly.'

Andy's eyes widened. 'You call that a good result?'

'Yes! We can't stop the bastards from doing what they do, but we can make it easier for the victims. If I hadn't fitted the emergency telephone, if you hadn't responded so quickly, Charlotte could have died.' Josie pointed a wobbly finger at the floor. 'Right there, Andy – she could have died right there. That's the reason we do what we do.'

CHAPTER THIRTEEN

It had taken Josie the rest of that day to deal with the attack on Charlotte Hatfield, and her children. Claire Tatton had arrived from Children's Services and taken all four. She'd arranged for them to be looked after until there was any news on how badly hurt Charlotte was.

Josie got back to the office a few minutes after five, thankful that, at least with the doors closed to the public, there would be no interruptions. She wanted to crack on with the paperwork before she left for the day, get down as much of her report as possible. That way she wouldn't have to go over it again tomorrow, although she knew she'd be thinking about it for a long time to come.

At five thirty, her mobile phone rang again. It would probably be Stewart: he'd called twice already to see where she was.

'I'm still at work,' she told him and then sighed, waiting for his torrent of abuse.

'For God's sake, you said you were finishing up ages ago. How long will you be now?'

'I'll be home soon, I promise. I'll bring something in with me to eat. Is there anything you fancy?'

Once she'd pacified him and made a swift call to Andy to learn that Charlotte was in a stable condition for now, she switched off her computer and headed for home.

As soon as she opened the front door, it was pulled from her grip. Stewart seized her arm, pushed her into the hallway and slammed it behind her with a crash.

'What took you so long? I told you to come home straight away.'

'And *I* told you I'd be home soon,' said Josie. 'Show a little compassion, I've spent most of the day dealing with a domestic violence incident.'

'Bollocks. You've been to college again, haven't you?'

Josie faltered. How had he found that out?

'No, I –'

'Liar! I saw you at Mitchell Academy on Wednesday. I checked at the reception and they said there weren't any residents' meetings that night.'

'Okay, okay. I have started a college course,' she admitted, 'although I haven't been there tonight. I wanted to tell you but I knew you wouldn't want me to go.'

'Too right, I wouldn't. You spend too much time away from the house as it is.'

'Stop saying that to me – you only want me here so I can be at your beck and call, to cook your meals, wash your clothes and clean up your mess.'

'That's what you should –'

'And I'm doing this course for me,' Josie retaliated, pushing him away. 'It has nothing to do with my work.'

Stewart huffed. 'So what's so important that you had to lie to me?'

Josie had already worked out what to say when Stewart eventually found out.

'I'm doing a computer course,' she fibbed. 'Spreadsheets, data input and the likes.'

'I wasn't talking about that,' Stewart answered. 'I was referring to the bloke who you were with when you left.'

Josie cast her mind back to Wednesday evening, then nodded in recognition. 'You mean Brian.' Then, after a moment's pause, 'have you been spying on me?'

'It's true though, isn't it? I can't stand it when you sneak around behind my back and –'

Josie pushed past him and went in to the kitchen. 'I'm hungry. I haven't had anything to eat all day except a bar of chocolate. I managed to get a cooked chicken and a pack of fresh salad on the way home. Shall we eat?'

Stewart quickly followed her through. 'So you're not going to deny it?'

Josie opened the fridge. 'There isn't anything *to* deny. Brian is my course tutor. I gave him a lift to the George and Dragon on

Drury Street. He was meeting up with his son for a drink.'

'I don't believe you.'

Josie turned back to face him. 'Think about the logic of what you're insinuating, even for one minute. When have I ever got time to see anyone else? I'm always pandering to you. And, come to think of it, when was the last time that you did anything around the house?'

Stewart held up his hands. 'Not my problem.'

'It's your mess!'

'It's not my frigging house.'

'For god's sake! You've been saying the same thing now for the past five years. It's obvious this house isn't good enough for you. I'm surprised you find it in yourself to come through the front door at all.'

Stewart's face clouded over again. 'Trying to turn the tables now, are we? Trying to blame me for something instead?'

'Yes, I am,' said Josie, with annoyance. 'I don't want to come home to this every night. You treat this house like a hotel and I'm not having it anymore.'

Stewart moved across the room. Pushing her forcefully down into the chair, he sat opposite her at the table.

'What exactly do you mean by that?'

Josie looked behind him through the kitchen window while she tried to put her thoughts into some kind of order. After no more than a few seconds of silence, Stewart reached across and squeezed her chin.

'Get off.' Josie slapped away his hand. 'Why don't you tell me how you knew I was at college on Wednesday? And why you knew I gave Brian a lift. You followed me, didn't you?'

'Wouldn't you like to know!'

Josie felt disgust building up in her stomach as Stewart started to laugh. Not wanting to be near to him a moment longer, she stood up and walked towards the door. He reached for her arm again but she pulled it away from his grasp at the last second.

'Don't touch me,' she spat.

'Don't walk away from me, then. I'm not finished yet.'

'Not finished ..?' Josie shook her head. 'You think you can treat me badly and I'll stand there and take it? Well, I might have done yesterday, but after what I've seen today, I sure as hell won't. You don't own me!'

For a moment, Stewart recoiled at Josie's raised voice, but it didn't take him long to retaliate. 'You don't know how lucky you are to have me,' he threw back. 'No one else would want you, little miss housing officer.'

'Make up your mind. You've just accused me of having an affair.' Josie moved away again.

'I said don't walk away from me!' This time when Stewart grabbed for her, he didn't miss. He swung Josie round to face him. 'I think you'd better remember who you're talking to.'

'And who exactly *am* I talking to?' she seethed. 'A lazy bastard who can't be bothered to do anything for himself? A selfish bastard who thinks his woman should be his servant? An inconsiderate bastard who never does anything nice for anyone without expecting something back in return? Even worse than that – you're a bully.'

Stewart's grip on her arm tightened but Josie switched off from the pain.

'You've turned your own wife against you with your controlling ways. No – wait! What you're actually thinking is, shit, there goes my free meal ticket. Perhaps your plan was to use me until someone better came along.'

Stewart stared at her before pushing her away roughly. He went back into the kitchen but Josie followed him.

'But guess what, Stewart? I'm not going to do anything for you again until I get something done in return. It's about time someone looked after me for a change.'

'I would if you'd come home early for once.'

'Home to what exactly? You're hardly here to welcome me with open arms.'

'That's because you've always thought more of that fucking job than you have of me! What is it that turns you on, Josie? Do I have to smack you one before you take any notice of me?'

'You sick bastard! Do you think that's funny after what I've seen today? I can't believe –'

Whether it was the picture of an injured Charlotte lying unconscious on her living room floor that wouldn't leave her mind right now, she'd never know, but in that split second, Josie saw red. Stopping suddenly to catch her breath, she was left with a rush of energy as adrenaline sloshed through her veins. With both hands, she pushed him in his chest.

Stewart lurched forward and punched her in the face.

Josie slumped to the floor. Trying hard to focus through watery eyes, she cautiously put her hand to her nose and pulled it back. It was covered in blood.

'Fuck... I...' Stewart's words failed to materialise.

Josie struggled to get to her feet, but her legs had other ideas. Stewart dropped to his knees in front of her, looking distraught as the realisation of what had happened – what he'd done – began to sink in. They sat on the floor for what seemed like hours. Neither of them spoke – how could they possibly put into words what had happened?

Finally, Stewart broke into the silence.

'Josie?' He looked into her eyes, frantic for some sign of reassurance.

'I'll be fine,' she eventually spoke.

'No, you won't. Let me...'

She flinched as he reached out to touch her. 'I can manage.'

'I don't know what came over me. I must have –'

'Leave me alone,' she whispered.

'No, I'm not leaving you like this.'

'Please, Stewart.'

'But, I want to –'

Ignoring his offer of support, Josie managed to get to her feet. One arm stretched out in front, she walked slowly into the conservatory. Stewart joined her again when she sat down in the chair, his face racked with emotion. She couldn't be sure if it was concern for the pain he'd caused her or for the trouble he might be in now that he'd hit her.

'Go away,' she said again.

'At least let me –'

'WILL YOU JUST FUCK OFF AND LEAVE ME ALONE?' Josie

screamed so loud that what blood was left in Stewart's face drained away rapidly. Getting the message at last, he made a swift exit.

CHAPTER FOURTEEN

Josie was still sitting in the conservatory two hours later. The last time she'd tried to get up, the agonizing pain that shot across her forehead had sent her reeling back into the chair. When she'd known for certain that Stewart's car had gone, she'd staggered into the hallway to inspect the damage he'd caused. Peering into the mirror, painful though it was, she'd let the tears fall. Stewart's fist had caught her top lip as well as her nose. Tenderly, she'd touched the swollen mess and winced in pain. How she was going to explain it away at work was beyond her imagination. She might be able to hide the inevitable bruising, but no amount of makeup would get rid of the swelling. She'd have to book some time off.

Josie wasn't sure what hurt the most – her face, her heart or the humiliation. She should have seen that coming, especially after hearing Tim talk about his actions the other night, and how they had escalated. And she knew that if it was someone else with this problem, she'd be able to tell them exactly what to do – but herself? She wouldn't be able to take her own advice. No wonder she sometimes felt inadequate to hand out advice to the likes of Amy and Charlotte. How could she, when she wasn't prepared to practice what she preached?

Was it too much to ask for a show of affection now and then, for him to reaffirm his love? Stewart must have loved her at one time. Josie wanted to be wined and dined. The girls at work were always being treated to things. Only last month, Sonia had stayed in a plush hotel in the Lake District, drinking mugs of hot chocolate in front of a roaring fire. The nearest she'd got to that with Stewart had been a walk around the local reservoir and that had been a very long time ago.

She moved back into the conservatory, wondering when the house had stopped being her home. Had it ever been a home to her? Sure, she'd felt safe when she was younger, but lately it had felt more like a prison, like she'd never be in control. Maybe she'd always feel like a fifteen-year-old here.

Perhaps you should leave.

Oh, what was she thinking? Josie began to cry again. It was okay for her to be brave at work as she wasn't dealing with her own problems. But here, the one and only time she'd stood up for herself, Stewart had lashed out. She couldn't let the incident pass. For once in her life, she would have to take note of the advice that she dished out on a regular basis. Tonight she'd had a warning. She knew there could easily be a next time. Was she sure she wanted to stick around?

With thoughts of Charlotte rushing through her mind again, Josie reached for a cushion and pulled it to her chest. *What a mess you've made.* She wept hot tears through swollen eyes. *You bastard, how could you do this to me?*

Kelly woke up sharply as Emily nudged her arm.

'Mummy, your phone is ringing. I'll get it for you.'

Before she had time to respond, Emily had answered the call.

'Daddy! When are you coming home? I miss you. Yes, I'm being a good girl. I'm always a good girl. No, Mummy's been asleep. I'll give it to her.'

Emily ran over to the settee and gave Kelly the phone.

'Hello, babe. How're you doing?'

'I'm okay,' said Kelly. 'How are you?'

'I'm bearing up. Life isn't easy in here, but I'll cope. Are you missing me?'

'Yeah, of course.' She wasn't entirely sure that was true.

'Ah, but I'll be back soon enough.'

Emily came rushing over to Kelly's side. 'Can I speak to Daddy again?' she asked loudly.

'Wait a minute, Em.' Kelly needed some questions answered first. 'Scott, have you decided what you're going do when you get out yet?'

'But I want to speak to Daddy.' Emily pulled on her arm.

'Wait a minute. Have you thought –?'

'Let me speak to Daddy!'

'Put her back on,' said Scott.

Kelly handed the phone to her daughter with a sigh. Every time she mentioned going on the straight and narrow when Scott was released, he changed the subject.

Emily put down the phone a minute later. 'Daddy had to go but he loves us lots and lots.'

Kelly lay back on the settee again and exhaled noisily. The word 'love' didn't always have the desired effect anymore.

Josie was in bed when she heard Stewart come back around eleven. Her mind in turmoil, with every creak of the stairs her heart skipped a beat. She held her breath as he quietly pushed open the bedroom door. Feigning sleep while he stood in front of her, he finally left. Josie blew out the breath she'd been holding. Minutes later, she heard him settle down in the spare room. At least he hadn't disturbed her.

She struggled to find sleep, switching the bedside lamp on as the still of the room got to her. Her head was pounding but she didn't want to fetch any more painkillers for fear of waking Stewart. Instead she lay alone, thinking alone, feeling alone, and questioning how long had she been feeling that way. Things couldn't go on like this.

The following morning, she sat at the kitchen table waiting for Stewart to come downstairs. Lying awake, she'd had time to make a lot of decisions. She knew he'd want to explain his actions, but she didn't care about him. It was about time she started to live life for herself. She was no one's slave. It was her own fault for allowing him to dominate her. In the forefront of her mind was Charlotte Hatfield; she couldn't let that happen to her.

When he came into the kitchen, Stewart's eyes widened in disbelief when he surveyed the damage he'd caused with one punch. The bruising around her eyes had darkened overnight and the cut on her nose from his ring was more visible as she turned her head towards him.

Stewart took a step closer. 'I'm sorry. I –'

Josie raised a hand and he stopped. 'I don't want to hear your excuses, your apologies or even your despicable lies. Right now, I want you to understand that I don't forgive you for what you've done.'

'I know. I –'

'Don't interrupt me!' Josie flinched, her swollen face making it painful for her to talk. 'I'm not the same Josie as I was this time yesterday. You've made me realise a few things and one of them is that you've had your own way for far too long. It stops right now.'

Stewart frowned. 'It... it won't happen again. You've got to believe me.'

'You're damn right it won't happen again.' Even from where she was sitting, Josie could see beads of sweat forming on Stewart's furrowed brow. With shaking hands, she picked up her mug of coffee. 'I want you to leave.'

'You can't be serious! I've said I'm sorry. What –'

'Sorry isn't enough after the mess you've made of me. Look at me!' She pointed to her face. 'I can't live with a bully and I certainly can't live with a man who punched me.'

Stewart ran a hand through his hair before taking a step nearer. 'But I swear I won't do it again.'

'I know you won't because you won't be here.'

'You can't chuck me out! Where will I go?'

Josie had thought about this, but had come to one conclusion. 'I don't care,' she said. 'I don't want to see you here again.'

There was silence in the room for a few seconds as her words sunk in. Then Stewart shook his head.

'No,' he said. 'I'm not leaving.'

Josie pushed herself up to her feet. She'd thought he'd react like this, try to talk her down into submission. But before she crumpled, she needed to let him know that she wasn't going to be a pushover this time. 'Then I'm going to ring the police,' she said. 'Maybe they can make you –'

'Wait!' Stewart touched her arm as she moved past him. He stared at her before his eyes narrowed. 'You're serious, aren't you?'

'I'm deadly serious,' she told him. 'Gullible Josie has gone forever. It's either the police or you leave – it's your choice.'

Stewart was silent for a few seconds in thought. 'Okay, I'll go for now – give you some time to yourself. I'll find someone at work who'll put me up for a few nights, then we can talk things through again.'

Josie nodded. If she could get him out of the house, then she could decide when she wanted to talk.

It wasn't until he left twenty minutes later with a few of his clothes packed into a holdall that she let her façade slip. Her shoulders dropped with relief that she'd had the courage to do what she'd set out to do, but inside she was breaking.

Was she strong enough to see this through?

As Kelly clocked on at the factory that night, she met Sally in the canteen for a drink before their shift began. It was something they'd quickly got into a routine of doing.

A guy called Robbie was doing his best to sing. He wasn't called Rob: Kelly had been informed by Sally when she'd started. It had to be Robbie because he thought he looked exactly like the real version. It had taken a while before Kelly realised that Sally was being serious (the real Robbie Williams had nothing to worry about). Tonight, this Robbie was giving them a rendition of Angels, even though no one had asked him to.

Phil, one of the packers, covered his ears with his hands and grimaced. 'Jesus, Robbie, you sound like a whale. A whale in pain.'

Robbie threw him a smirk. 'That's not what the ladies tell me.'

'Where do you pick them up? At the deaf club?'

Everyone laughed.

'Maybe you're 'Misunderstood', Robbie,' said another fella Kelly vaguely recognised.

Some of the lads whooped.

'Wow,' said Phil. 'Mummy's boy's up on Robbie Williams' music. I'm stunned. Not many people remember that song from his greatest hits CD.'

'Mummy's boy' threw a screwed up crisp packet at him.

Everyone continued to banter until the clock approached four. Kelly slipped on her overall and sat down at her bench.

'Guess what I found out about little miss perfect, here?' Leah said, as she rushed in, late again. She pointed to Kelly. 'I know your secret now. Your fella's been sent down for thieving.'

Sally sighed loudly as she reached for a mug. 'Tell us something we don't know. That isn't a secret.'

'I didn't know!' Leah glared at Kelly. 'Anyway, what have you got to say about it?'

'There's nothing to say,' Kelly replied. 'He planned a break-in, he got caught and now he's doing his time.'

Leah folded her arms across her chest. 'He's a psycho. I heard it straight from the horse's mouth.'

The usually quiet Julia snorted. 'That's rich, coming from you – you look like a horse, Leah. Are you sure that you didn't tell yourself?'

As some of the other workers began to laugh, Leah reached over the belt, purposefully knocking over a whole batch of mugs.

'Oi!' Kelly cried out. 'It's taken me ages to do those, you bitch!'

Leah's hand covered her mouth but it didn't hide the smirk. 'Oh dear, I *am* sorry. It was an accident.'

'No, you did it on purpose.' Sally dropped to the floor to help Kelly pick up the damaged pieces.

'We'll help you to catch up again,' Julia told Kelly. She stared at Leah. 'We'll *all* help.'

Leah folded her arms. 'Don't count on it.'

'It won't matter much anyway.' Sally threw the pieces she'd collected into the bin. 'Kelly's only been here five minutes and she's far quicker than you anyway.'

'No, she's not!'

'And we don't have to make excuses up because she's never late.'

Kelly began to feel as though she was invisible. 'Come on, now,' she said. 'Let's not argue.'

'Who gave you permission to speak?' Leah barked.

Sally slammed down the bin lid. 'Why don't you shut up for once, Leah? What's the matter? Is your reputation as gossip queen faltering? Grow up or move down the line. You're boring us.'

'Thanks, Sal,' said Kelly, 'but I can hold my own.' She stared back angrily at the woman with the red hair who loathed her so much. 'I do think it's time you backed off, though. I'm getting sick and tired of your comments. You're no better than me. We're both in the same position – single mums doing the best we can for our kids. And at least I know where Emily's father is.'

Leah's face reddened by the second. 'Ooh, get you,' she managed to mutter. She didn't speak for the rest of their shift.

'Thank god that's over,' Kelly said as she left the building with Sally afterwards. 'I can't take much more of Leah's bitchy comments. If she carries on, I'll end up chinning her.'

'Don't worry,' Sally answered. 'She's backing down. Leah can't do much without an audience and even Julia isn't taking any notice of her now. You probably think I'm talking garbage but Leah's okay once you get to know her.'

Kelly smirked.

'It's true. For some reason you got off to a bad start. She'll come –'

A car beeped its horn and pulled up alongside them. Kelly smiled when she saw it was Jay.

'Need a lift?' he offered.

'Ooh, yes ta. See you tomorrow, Sal.'

'Things going well?' he asked as he pulled away from the kerb.

Kelly nodded. 'Getting better, I suppose.'

On the main road, Kelly spotted Leah sitting alone at the bus stop. Theatrically, she waved as they drove past. Leah's face was a picture.

CHAPTER FIFTEEN

Before Scott came out of prison, Kelly wanted to treat Jay to lunch for being so good to her over the past few weeks. That weekend, he drove them to a pub out in the country. Emily had been excited all morning because he'd told her it had a ball pit and a bouncy castle. Kelly knew there would be lots of children for her to play with, too. Once there, she and Jay hardly saw her, although they clearly heard her every now and then.

'I think I should have had more to eat before necking that wine,' Kelly said, taking another sip of her drink regardless of feeling a little tipsy. 'I'm such a lightweight. Two glasses of red and I'm under the table.'

'Got any room left for pudding?' Jay asked, as he grabbed for the dessert menu.

'Not even a tiny space.' She rubbed her stomach. 'Oh, go on then. I might just manage a banana split.'

'Care to share?'

'No! Get your own.' Playfully, Kelly poked him in the shoulder. 'Anyway, have what you want. You always pay for everything so it's my treat today.'

'But I don't mind –'

'What's the use of working if I don't get to spend *any* of it on luxuries? And Scott will be back soon so I won't have chance to thank you if I don't do it now.'

'Do you still miss him, Kel?' Jay questioned.

'Course I do!' Kelly lowered hers eyes, afraid of revealing her ever changing feelings for Scott. 'But you've been a massive help too.'

'Kel, I –'

'Mummy!' Emily shouted as she ran towards them. She stopped at the table and took a quick slurp of her drink through a straw.

'I've been hiding in the balls! Did you see me?'

'Yes,' Kelly fibbed. 'I bet the other children didn't though.'

'I'm going to hide again.'

'Urgh,' Jay shuddered as she ran back. 'Can you imagine what's inside that ball pit? I mean, underneath – jelly and custard, splodges of cream off the cakes, fizzy pop ...'

'Bits of fish fingers.' Kelly giggled, then grabbed Jay's hand. 'Thanks.' She leant on the table with her elbow. 'I wouldn't have survived without your help – even though I didn't want your help at first.'

'I remember only too well! You were nasty to me no matter what I did.'

'I wasn't that bad!' Kelly protested.

'You were, but that's what mates are for. Look Kelly, are you sure that you want –'

'Oops!' Kelly's elbow slipped off the table. She fell forward. 'What is it with me and lunchtime drinking?'

Jay sighed. He glanced over to where Emily was climbing a ladder ready to dive into the balls again. Then he looked at his watch. 'Jesus, have you seen the time? We'll have to go soon, Kel.'

'I suppose you're off to check up on your other woman, aren't you?'

Jay laughed. 'Me? I haven't got *time* for another woman.'

'You must have someone special in your life, though. I wonder what she thinks of all the time you spend with me and Em.' Kelly pointed an unsteady finger at him. 'You are a true... true friend. Scott should be vey – vey proud of you.'

In her inebriated state, Kelly didn't realise that Jay's smile didn't reach his eyes.

Surprisingly, but true to his word, Stewart stayed away from Josie. After a week on her own, she started to get over the initial shock of what had happened. Although the swelling around her nose had gone down in days, the black and blue of the bruising could still be seen. Her emotions had taken a battering too.

Stewart had sent her a few text messages, to which she'd responded with as few words as were appropriate. He'd even rung once, on Friday evening, to see if she would see him yet, but she'd told him it was too soon to start talking. She needed to be clear about what she planned to do next and she was nowhere near that stage yet.

By the time she went back to work, she was all thought out. More so, she needed to catch up with her case notes. It was hard for anyone not to have heard about Charlotte Hatfield over the past week. She'd been local front page news for two nights, her story told in bold, graphic details. Josie had been annoyed to be away from the office at such an important time. She wanted to make sure that all the paperwork was filled out correctly, that every t was crossed and every i was dotted, in case the statement was used as evidence in a court case. She wanted to be sure they'd nail Charlotte's partner for it. After the damage Nathan had caused, he deserved no more than to rot in a ten-by-eight cell. However, reporting to work the next day looking the way she had wouldn't have been ideal.

Charlotte's children had been collected by their grandparents and ferried back to Leeds while Charlotte had spent two days in intensive care. She was now – thankfully – on the road to recovery. It never failed to amaze Josie how much a human body could cope with in difficult situations. Her mind flipped back to her mum's last days. Brenda had hung on for what seemed like forever until her body, unable to take in food, slowly deteriorated and her heart stopped.

Arriving at the office, she boxed up her feelings and headed in. The first thing that greeted her was the report of another burglary.

'What's up?' Debbie asked as she passed over a mug of coffee.

'Mrs Lattimer's been robbed over the weekend,' Josie told her. 'Remember, we visited two weeks ago?'

'Yes, she was really nice to me.' Debbie shook her head in disbelief. 'Is she okay?'

'I'm not sure. We only get the basics on the call-out logs. That's five now in the past couple of months. I'll have to pop in and see her.'

Debbie sighed. 'It makes it more personal when you know the tenant involved, doesn't it?'

'Yes.' Josie grabbed her keys and slipped her mobile phone into her coat pocket. 'It took her family and me ages to get her to move there in the first place. She didn't think she'd cope but she's been much more independent since. This will set her back big style. I'll have to pop round this morning, see if I can catch her in.'

'Send her my love,' Debbie shouted as she marched away. 'Let me know if there's anything I can do.'

After trying her best to console Mrs Lattimer, Josie caught up with some paperwork before heading out again after her lunch. Her first visit was to Clarence Avenue. Rather than enjoying a mug of coffee with Kelly in her tidy, clean living room, she was crawling around the floor while baby Reece kicked his legs infuriatingly next to her. Josie was trying to make him laugh by waving a yellow rabbit in front of his face and then pressing it to his nose. He was niggling: Amy was heating some food for him.

'Has he been like this all morning?' Josie shouted through the open kitchen door, waiting for another loud yell as Reece took another breather. His angry little face was beginning to represent the colour of sun-ripened tomatoes.

Before Amy had time to reply, Josie's mobile started to ring. She rummaged around in her pockets until she found it. It was Craig from the office, wanting to know if she would get Irene's card on her way back. It was Irene's fiftieth birthday at the weekend and they'd had a bit of a collection. Although Irene wasn't particularly liked, it was astounding how much of a conscience people had when a collection went around the office. They'd collected quite a sum for her.

Josie disconnected the call, feeling herself shivering in the small room. Amy had reappeared with Reece's gooey delight and settled him onto her knee.

'It's chilly in here, Amy. Have you any gas credits?'

'Yeah, I took me card to the post office on Monday. It was on my to-do list.'

Josie smiled, watching her spoon in another mouthful, then carefully wipe the remainder from Reece's chin with his bib. She was such a good kid, it grieved her to see how she had been let down by her parents.

'Good. I wondered if the problem with your heating had been sorted.'

Amy looked up quickly. 'There's nowt wrong with my heating.'

'But Ray – you remember Ray, the other housing officer? – he said it wasn't working properly the other week. I thought that you were still having –'

'No, it's okay now.'

Josie wondered why Amy's body had tensed. For some reason, she wouldn't look her in the eye either.

'It's okay if you did something wrong,' she said, hoping to encourage Amy to open up. She decided it was time for a white lie. 'I know when I moved into my house, I was forever switching off things that should stay on or leaving things on that should be turned off.'

Amy began to relax a little but Josie had seen the signs and was worried. Amy seemed to be coping: the house was tidy and Reece, despite his grumbling, was looking well. Maybe there was something Amy was keeping to herself?

'Is there something else that you want to tell me?' Josie questioned, her voice soft.

Amy shook her head vehemently.

'I just wondered, because when I called the other day, I couldn't get an answer when I knocked. You were in, though, weren't you?'

'No, I was at the shops!'

'Are you sure?'

'Yes!'

Amy wouldn't look at Josie. Instead, she wiped Reece's face clean and pulled off his bib. Josie sighed and grabbed her file. There was nothing she could do when Amy was in this frame of mind. She was a stubborn little sod when she wanted to be – and she didn't have to tell Josie anything if she didn't want to.

For now, she'd have to be content that Amy was doing okay, even though there was clearly something on her mind. She'd have to dig deeper during her next visit.

*

The rest of the afternoon was quite successful for Josie, too. She'd been to see Mrs Baker from Russell Close, who had finished decorating the downstairs of her property: only another six months before the upstairs would be to a decent standard, no doubt. The new tenant in Winston Place had moved in on time and six of the eight garden checks had been tidied to a reasonable level.

After having a giggle at some of the extremely rude cards on display in the newsagents, she was making her way back to her car when she spotted a figure in the distance.

'Mrs Middleton!' Josie waved to catch her attention.

Ruth Middleton turned slightly but kept on walking.

'Wait a minute!' Josie had to run to catch her up. Finally as she drew nearer, Ruth stopped.

'How are you?' she asked, a hand held to her chest as she caught her breath.

'I'm fine, thanks,' Ruth smiled tightly.

'Good.' Josie knew instantly that the question was being avoided. Ruth didn't look well at all. A small woman, she was pale and thin, bags under her eyes denoting her lack of sleep. 'And how are things at home?'

The last time Josie had visited Ruth after a neighbour complaint about noise, she hadn't been faring well. Ruth seemed depressed, extremely subdued. It was almost as if she was in a trance. Josie had wondered if she was on strong medication but Ruth hadn't come forward with the information. If it wasn't for the fact that she was living with her partner, she might have tried to get her some help – not that Martin was any use, but Josie did see him out a lot with Ruth's two young boys.

'Everything's fine,' Ruth replied.

'Right.' Josie stepped sideways to allow a woman with a double buggy and a toddler to get past. 'And the boys, are they doing okay? Looking forward to the Easter break coming up?'

'Look, I don't mean to be rude,' Ruth fiddled with the strap on her handbag, 'but I'm not sure that it's any of your business.'

'Sorry.' Josie wasn't taken aback by her tone. 'But you were upset when I last saw you and I thought –'

'You thought you'd come and stick your nose in again where it's not wanted.'

'No! That's not it at all. I'm worried about you.'

Ruth looked away. 'No, you're not. You're doing your job.'

'Maybe, but I'm trying –'

'Leave me be.' Ruth started to walk away. 'I don't need your help. I'm fine on my own.'

'Please, wait!' Josie grabbed her arm and was shocked when Ruth flinched. She pulled her hand away. 'You're not all right, are you?'

Ruth's eyes filled with tears.

'Let me help.' Josie tried desperately to connect with her. 'Please.'

'Sure, you can help. Do you know how? Leave me alone.'

Ruth turned away again. Josie had no choice but to let her go. Even so, she was still thinking of her when she got back to the office. She parked up next to Andy's police vehicle in the car park, wondering what he'd called in for.

'What's all the commotion?' she asked Sonia, who was practically sprinting up the corridor heading for the reception.

'Some dickhead's super-glued himself to the rent counter,' she said with a grin.

Josie pushed open the door into the office and Sonia turned back in astonishment.

'Aren't you coming to see? He's pissed off because his rent benefit has been stopped. One of the fraud officers caught him up a ladder cleaning windows on three separate occasions. He's meant to be incapacitated, unable to walk for ten metres without help.'

'I'm on my way.' Josie grinned: this she had to see. The dickhead in question had to be Derek Maddox from Robert Place. Josie had contacted the fraud department six months ago and they'd been building up a file on him ever since. She plonked her things down on her desk – no surprise to see an empty office – and joined the rest of the staff as the party unfurled.

'That's her!' Derek shrieked as soon as Josie caught his furious eyes. 'That's the evil bitch that shopped me!'

Andy was having difficulty keeping his face straight as he

looked over at Josie coming into view behind several housing staff. 'Mrs Mellor, do you have anything to do with this little incident?'

'Absolutely not, PC Baxter.' Josie shook her head. 'Contrary to popular belief, Mr Maddox, I don't know *everything* that goes on around the Mitchell Estate.'

'THEN WHO THE FUCK WAS IT?' Derek screamed again. 'When I find out who it is, I'll break every bone in their fucking body. I'll rip 'em up into pieces. I'll tear their balls off. I'll –'

'Calm down, Derek.' Andy failed to keep the snigger out of his voice. 'Swearing isn't going to help. It'll only stress you out, and you don't want to come unstuck now, do you?'

Derek's face turned a raspberry colour as laughter erupted from all around the reception area. An old lady Josie recognised from William Precinct pushed past him and handed the cashier her rent card through the slot in the glass. It seemed that she wasn't prepared to wait a minute longer.

'I'll leave you to it,' laughed Josie. She nudged Debbie. 'Get the digital camera.'

'Ooh, yes. We can laugh about him later, too.' Debbie grinned. 'What a knob.'

Josie smiled back. She'd known it would only be a matter of months before the job made Debbie as bitter and twisted as the rest of the staff. Once she'd been threatened a few times on the reception desk and verbally abused on the phone, she'd hardened up pretty sharpish.

She grinned. These were the times when she realised that some days on the Mitchell Estate *were* better than others. The rough was worth it for the smooth.

Just then, she noticed Ray scuttling into the office through the staff entrance.

'The photos aren't to show everyone, Debbie,' Josie told her as she moved towards him. 'It's further evidence that he hasn't got a bad back. Ray, have you got a minute?'

Ray turned towards Josie but continued to walk through into the office. 'Not enough of them in the day with scrotes like Maddox allowed to get away with benefit fraud.'

For once, Josie was in agreement with him. 'We got him in the end,' she said as she drew nearer to him. They walked through together into the main office. 'It's Amy Cartwright that I want to talk to you about.'

Ray stopped at his desk, picking up a message left for him on a notepad. 'Bloody pathetic.' He ripped it from the spine, crunched it into a ball and lobbed it at the waste paper bin. 'They always ring after you've arranged to see them yet there was no one in when I called. Well, no one who'd open the door, anyway. What about Amy Cartwright?'

'I saw her earlier and she was a bit off when I mentioned that you'd been out to sort her heating.'

Ray shrugged his shoulders. 'She caught me on one of my better days. She called in at the office to see Doug but he wasn't in so I went instead. Call me a Good Samaritan, if you want.'

Josie sat down at her desk in front of him. 'So why did she look so awkward when I mentioned your name? You didn't give her a hard time because she'd broken something, did you?'

Ray stretched his arms above his head before flexing his fingers noisily. 'Now, now, Josie, you know me better than that.'

Josie sighed. Yes she did, that was the trouble.

'What did you say to upset her?'

'Nothing.'

'Ray, you seem to forget, I've worked with you for years.'

'Amy's a thicko, she'll tell you anything. The only reason I went round at all was to stop me from having to go and see that Neblin bloke of yours. His son's been causing grief and the last time I called I had the whole street on my back moaning at me. So, if you must know, I went to save myself some aggro. Anyway, it's sorted now, so what's the problem?'

'The problem is you've upset her.' Josie reached for her phone to retrieve her voicemail messages as Irene, Sonia and Debbie burst in through the doors, still laughing about Derek Maddox. 'The next time you go to see her, let me know and I'll come with you. It's taken me ages to build a rapport with her. The last thing I need is for you to break the trust – and don't call her a thicko.'

Ray's chair scraped across the flooring as he stood up abruptly. 'Back off, Josie. Just because you look after all the waifs and strays doesn't mean I have to give the same customer care.'

'I –'

He threw his hands up into the air. 'No, don't worry, miss do-gooder. The next time Amy Cartwright needs something, I'll let you sort it out from the beginning. It's less hassle.'

Josie flicked two fingers up as he walked off. Sometimes it was like working in a nursery, not an office.

CHAPTER SIXTEEN

That Wednesday evening, Kelly slid a thin ham and mushroom pizza into the oven for herself and Emily and a crunchy pepperoni one for Jay. It was her first night off in ages, due to a change of shift with one of the early girls. Jay was due in fifteen minutes and Emily was helping her to arrange the salad in a bowl – or rather, she had been for a minute or so, before rushing off.

'Jay's here!' Emily shouted through the door. 'Can I let him in?'

'Only because I know it's Jay, young lady, else the rule still stands.'

As Emily bounded down the stairs to let him in, Kelly rushed across to the mirror and checked her appearance before he came into the room. He smiled and held out a bottle of wine. 'This calls for a celebration – your first night off.'

'That and the fact that the sun's been shining today. I actually took off my jacket this morning when I went to the shops!'

'We're having pizza,' Emily cried. She put both her tiny feet onto Jay's booted ones and balanced on them as he walked across the room. Laughing as she giggled, Jay lifted her up and threw her playfully onto the settee.

Once the pizza had been demolished, Jay topped up their glasses while Kelly got Emily into bed.

'At last,' Kelly sighed when she eventually joined him again. 'I tell you, that girl has got be the chattiest kid I know. I can't wait for her to start school to give me some peace.'

'Don't give me that, you'll miss her like crazy.'

Kelly sat down. 'I know. I'll – I'll miss you too when Scott gets back. I can't believe he'll be home in a few days.'

'I hope he keeps out of trouble this time. He needs to calm down and think of what he might lose if he gets caught again. I –'

'You think he's shit, don't you?' Kelly clipped. 'You thought he'd serve the full sentence because he wouldn't be able to stay out of trouble. Well, he's not a Kirkwell.'

'Ouch.' Jay turned away from Kelly's fierce stare for a moment. 'I didn't mean it to sound so nasty. It's just that I'm going to miss you.'

'Sorry.' Kelly grinned, instantly friends with him again. 'I was thinking earlier how it won't be the same. There'll be no more pizzas,' she raised her glass in the air, 'no more bottles of wine to share, no more nights watching *Cougar* or *Gossip Girl*. Scott hates that type of thing. He's into serial killers, blood, snot and the likes. It's rare I get to watch girlie things. It's been a pleasure to –'

Without warning, Jay leaned forward. Time seemed to suspend as he stared directly into Kelly's eyes. His face contorted as if in pain. Quickly, he stood up and moved away.

'I can't do this anymore,' he said.

'Why? It's early yet.' Kelly picked up the bottle of wine, indicating that it was still half full.

'No, I mean I can't be with you anymore. This is killing me. I thought I could handle things but everything's gone weird now. I need to keep my wits about me. You're Scott's girl, my *mate's* girl. I've got no right to feel the way I do.'

All at once, the penny dropped for Kelly.

Jay sat back down again. He took her hands in his own. 'I can't help myself, Kel. I think about you all the time. I can't wait to pick you up from work every night, I go crazy over the weekends without you.'

'But you've taken me – us – out for the last two Sundays... Oh.' Kelly pulled her hands away.

'I shouldn't have, but I wanted to be with you. I thought I could handle it, but now I realise that... oh, fuck. I'm just going to come right out and say it. I realise that I love you.'

The last few words came out in a whisper but Kelly heard every one as if Jay had shouted them from the top of the Empire State building.

'I know I can give you so much more than Scott,' he continued. 'You're a great mum, you've started work to earn your keep, to make a difference, and you've *survived*. Most women would have sat cowering in a corner waiting for their partners to come back.'

Kelly sat in silence, unable to speak.

'You deserve far better than him,' Jay added.

She laughed harshly. 'Like you, you mean? Don't beat about the bush, Jay.'

He touched Kelly's cheek again, ever so slightly, like a feather floating past. 'I can't stop thinking about you.'

'But you're Scott's mate!'

Jay grimaced. 'I can't stop thinking about that either.'

'No.' Kelly shook her head. 'And you shouldn't.'

'But have you ever stopped to think about why I'm his mate? It's because I wanted to keep an eye on you. I know what Scott gets up to.'

'But you do it too!' Realising the living room door stood ajar, Kelly quickly closed it for fear of waking Emily. As she came back to stand in front of the fire, she shook her head, trying to rid it of all the confusion. How could Jay sit there and make out that Scott was worse than him, just because he hadn't been caught that night? And why say it now? Was he only doing it to cover up his feelings – his guilt, perhaps? Taking her off the scent by trying to put the blame on Scott?

But it wasn't Scott's fault that his mate had fallen for his woman. And it wasn't Scott's fault that Kelly had led Jay on. Because that's what she'd done, hadn't she?

'You're just like him,' she said, if only to reassure herself.

Jay rubbed his hands over his face before looking up at her. 'But I'm not – you've got to believe me.'

'You've got a reputation on the estate for being a hard bastard! No one wants to start on a Kirkwell.'

'That's because I've had to defend myself because of who my brothers *are*. Men pick fights *because* of who I am. That's all it is. I've never stolen anything, and I've never done a job with Scott either.'

Kelly sat silent for a moment, puzzled by what he'd said. 'I thought you always went with him,' she said eventually.

'No! How many more times do I have to tell you?'

'But you warned him off the last job. I heard you talking in the kitchen – you said it was too risky.'

'That's because it *was* too risky. I didn't want to see you suffer. I warned Stevie and Michael but they never listened either.'

Kelly was confused as she tried to work out the finer details. Scott had done lots of jobs with the Kirkwell brothers. Had she assumed that Jay was involved when he wasn't? She thought back to Josie defending his actions after she'd been attacked.

Had she been wrong?

She sat down next to him again. 'Tell me what's going on.'

'You know I'm the youngest brother,' Jay explained. 'I've had to live in their shadows for years. You're not the first person to think I'd be involved. But I swear to you, I'm not. What they do makes me sick. I haven't got time for petty thieves. They think they don't hurt people, people like you and me, but they do. For every factory they do over, hardworking people lose their jobs. For every car they steal to move on, someone's stranded. It's not as easy as the insurance paying out.

'When I heard about the last job, I tried to warn them all, but they wouldn't listen. I knew they wouldn't pull it off and it'd be up to me to pick up the pieces again. My mum's really upset about it. She never brought up four children for two of them to be drop-outs. Michael's been in the nick so many times, it'll be ages before he gets out.'

Kelly watched as Jay struggled with his emotions.

'You haven't got a clue what it's done to our family over the years. I didn't want that for you.' Jay chanced a quick glance at her. 'Nor Emily.'

For a split second, Kelly understood where Jay was coming from. Then she remembered something else.

'That money,' she said. 'That five hundred pounds – did Scott give it to you or was it yours to start with?'

Jay shook his head. 'It was mine. I thought it'd help you out.'

Kelly groaned. Finally she began to understand what he was talking about. Jay *was* racked with guilt: for what his brothers had brought on his parents, for what Scott had brought on her, and, most of all, for his feelings towards another man's woman. She shuddered involuntarily. How had she not seen this happening, right underneath her nose? Stupidly, she'd enjoyed Jay's company more and more and, in the back of her mind, knew he was spending far too much time with her. Simply doing a favour for a mate wasn't what was happening.

And because she'd missed Scott so much, she'd taken Jay as a substitute, a replacement, until Scott was ready to return. She was entirely to blame for letting it happen, when it clearly shouldn't have.

As Jay pleaded with his eyes, begging her to talk, Kelly didn't know what to say. She couldn't give him what he wanted, yet she couldn't tell him what he didn't want to hear.

But staying silent did it for her. With one last look, Jay stood up and walked out of the room. Tears pouring down her cheeks, Kelly had no choice but to let him.

At nine thirty, Kelly dialled Jay's mobile number again. She had to know that everything was all right. It was the last thing she wanted on Tuesday. Scott was bound to ask Jay to pick him up from prison and she needed no awkwardness between them. She had to make sure there was nothing that would make Scott suspicious, make him wonder what had been going on.

She knew she should be happy that Scott was coming home soon but all she could think about was Jay – how she'd hurt his feelings, betrayed his trust and, in a strange, yet totally unknown way, used him. She hadn't meant to – that had hurt the most.

As the call switched to voicemail yet again, Kelly flung her phone down onto the settee in a fit of anger.

But Jay was no more than a hundred yards away. He was parked a few houses down, on the opposite side of Clarence Avenue. Not for the first time, his thoughts switched to what could be going on behind the closed curtains. Was Kelly making herself nice, ready for Scott to come home?

He waited for his phone to stop ringing before he picked it up. Kelly's messages said that she wanted to talk, to clear the air. Jay wanted to talk to her so badly, even if his words would be empty. Over the last few hours, his feelings had heightened, yet he fought with his conscience. Kelly belonged to Scott. He'd had no right to put her in that predicament, but he hadn't been able to stop himself.

Exasperated, he started the car engine and screeched away from the kerb.

When Josie's manager asked for some paperwork to be taken to their head office, Josie drew the short straw. After an age finding a space on the staff car park, she went into the main building. It hadn't changed much since she'd left it all those years ago, apart from a lick of paint here and there and a different corporate logo.

As she walked through the reception area towards the lifts, she saw someone she hadn't seen in years.

'Livvy?'

'Josie!' Livvy gave her a huge hug, looking genuinely pleased to see her. 'I haven't seen you properly in what, five years?'

Josie nodded. 'Yes, it must be. How are you?'

'Fair. I've split up with my partner but apart from that... How about you?'

'Same here. I've just separated from my husband.'

They both smiled half-heartedly, knowing there was now something else they had in common.

'I'm fine though,' Josie added. 'Apart from never having lived alone and jumping every time I hear a strange noise! Funny thing is, he worked shifts so I was often by myself in the house anyway. What are you doing here, though? It's a bit different from your usual role.'

'It's a long story.' Livvy smiled sadly. 'And one that makes me sound like an idiot. I'll never learn.'

'Tell me about it!' Josie joked.

'Hey, I might do that.' Livvy checked her watch. 'I'm on my way to a meeting so I have to go, but I'd love to catch up.'

'Yes, give me a ring when you're free.'

'How do you fancy pasta and wine with another single – maybe tomorrow after work? If we don't arrange something, you know we'll never act on it and it would be a shame not to after all this time.'

*

At half past five the next evening, Josie pulled into one of two allocated parking spaces Livvy had told her about. Romney Court housed eighteen owner-occupied flats in three separate blocks. Number five was the one she was looking for. She pressed the buzzer on the intercom at the door entrance. After a moment, she heard a voice come through it.

'Come on up. You'll find me on the second floor.'

She went into a small lobby area, painted a welcoming lemon colour. Unlike the flats Josie was used to visiting, the area smelt clean, inviting, and fresh.

'I'm so glad you came.'

Josie looked up to see Livvy leaning over the balcony, her black hair hanging down like a curtain.

'Welcome to my humble abode,' she smiled.

Livvy's flat was so far removed from the style of Josie's house that she instantly felt old-fashioned. With every new room Livvy showed her, she had to stop her mouth from dropping to the floor. The first room off the light hallway was the kitchen, which had a mishmash of stainless steel and beech units standing to attention along each side wall. She gasped when she followed Livvy into the living room; plush cream carpeting mostly covered by a woollen rug barely a shade lighter, and two cream leather settees. The only colour in the room came from the vivid orange cushions and fresh lilies arranged in a vase on the glass-topped coffee table.

'It's beautiful,' said Josie. 'And so stylish!'

'Thanks. I have to warn you that it's much better than my cooking, though.' Livvy pushed her gently into the kitchen and reached for a tartan oven glove. 'But I am a dab hand at putting pasta into a saucepan and a bag of salad into a bowl.'

For a long time, Josie had never felt as relaxed as she did that night in Livvy's kitchen. She and Livvy had met on an induction course when they'd both started at Mitchell Housing Association and had got on well since. They'd done various jobs together before going their separate ways, and only lost touch when Livvy had gone to work in the family business. Their conversation flowed naturally, with no awkward silences as they caught up – despite Josie being in awe of Livvy's fabulous figure and the shine on her poker straight hair. She knew Livvy could easily pass as a supermodel, with legs reaching up to her ears in wide-legged linen trousers, a white vest and an oversized slash-necked baby-pink jumper. She padded around in bare feet, crimson toe nails peeping out every now and then. Josie sighed. She'd love to be that elegant.

'I love it here,' Livvy said over another coffee. 'The neighbours are great, I don't have any trouble from them and they don't mind when I have the occasional party. And that intercom system is a godsend.' She grinned. 'Especially being able to screen who is visiting. Great if you want to stand a guy up – not that I've ever done that. I think it'd be good fun to try though.'

'I bet you must have men falling at your feet.'

Livvy laughed. 'I have no intention of settling down in the near future. And when I do, I'm going to be moving into his palatial palace.'

'And you shouldn't let the last one put you off either. They're not all bad.' Josie couldn't believe she was saying that after her recent time with Stewart. But she knew it was true – and she hoped she wouldn't do the same either. This time she was going to take the advice she dished out to others.

'Honey,' Livvy said in a theatrical style that had Josie practically spitting out her drink, 'there isn't anything I can't deal with. If any man chooses to mess with me, and I see his face on my intercom screen, it'll be my pleasure not to let him in!'

'Oi, you two! Wait for me, will you?'

'God, what does she want?' muttered Sally. She had her arm linked through Kelly's as they made their way to the bus stop at the end of their last shift for that week. 'She's crawling around you lately like she wants to bury the hatchet.'

'More like bury a knife in my back, you mean,' Kelly muttered to her.

Leah drew up beside them with a puff. 'Do you fancy sitting with me on the bus tonight? Might as well, seeing as we're on speaking terms now.'

Sally stifled a laugh; Kelly nudged her sharply with her elbow. Leah's 'speaking terms' referred to the fact that she'd let Kelly join in a whole night's conversation without any type of sarcastic dig coming from her side of the bench.

'Suppose so,' said Kelly, her heart dropping when she noticed that Jay wasn't there to pick her up again. She hadn't seen him at all since Wednesday.

The three of them continued out of the factory gates and on towards the main road.

'I want to know *any* gossip she tells you,' Sally whispered, prompting Kelly to nudge her in the ribs again before she left them at the corner of the street. To her amazement, Leah linked an arm through hers as they continued to walk.

'I'm sorry we got off to a bad start,' she began.

Kelly turned to face her, completely bewildered by her turnaround.

Leah had the decency to look shamefaced. 'I suppose I was jealous of you. Look at you – you're gorgeous. Me, I'm fat and ugly.'

'I wouldn't say –'

'It's right though, isn't it? I hated you when I saw you at the playgroup so when I walked in here and found out you were the new girl – well, I kind of flipped.'

They reached the bus shelter and sat down on the empty bench seat.

'So why have you been so nasty to me?'

'I come from a shit family so I tend to stick up for myself by lashing out.' Leah shrugged. 'But I want you to know, if it's okay with you,' she looked up at Kelly through a heavy fringe, 'I'd like us to be friends.'

Kelly smiled. She knew how much of an effort it would have been for Leah to admit she was wrong.

'You have a deal,' she said, supposing she could give her the benefit of the doubt.

Moments later, as the bus drew up beside them, Leah got on first and turned to Kelly as they sat down. 'So, tell me, what's the story with Jay Kirkwell? Have you shagged him yet or can anyone have a go?'

*

At work on Monday morning, Josie rushed to the reception when she received an internal telephone call from Sonia, saying that Charlotte Hatfield wanted to see her. She was curious to see how she was doing. It had been three weeks since Charlotte's attack and even though she had returned to the house on her release from hospital, now she'd decided to move nearer to her family. She'd come in to return the keys to the property.

'How are the boys coping?' Josie had enquired, after she'd accepted the flowers Charlotte had bought for her. She took her into an interview cubicle for the last time. Charlotte only had baby Poppy with her: she was fast asleep in her buggy.

'They're still with my mum in Leeds.'

Josie noticed that Charlotte's hair had been brushed over the gash that Nathan had left her with. Andy had told her she'd had seven stitches. Her front tooth was missing, but at least she was smiling again. She seemed in a lighter mood now that she had made up her mind to move on.

Charlotte delved into Poppy's carry-all bag and handed Josie a bunch of keys. 'Thanks for everything you've done for me,' she said. 'I don't think I'd be here today if it wasn't for your actions – and that copper as well.'

Josie shook her head. 'It wasn't just us. You played your own part in it.'

'Maybe, but it was you who made me think about the situation. You who made me realise I would be better going back home to my mum.' She paused. 'You who made me think about pressing charges.'

Josie looked up from the paperwork she was filling in.

Charlotte nodded her head. 'I've made a statement against Nathan.'

'Great,' said Josie. 'Me too!'

Charlotte smiled. 'Thanks. Nathan's on remand now anyway. They reckon he'll go down for GBH wounding with intent, but still...'

Josie reached across the desk and squeezed Charlotte's hand. 'That's fantastic news. I'm so pleased for you – and I'm proud of you for sticking up for yourself.'

Charlotte's eyes fell on the buggy. 'It's not only me that I have to look out for. I want my kids to have a better chance in life than I did. Poor Josh won't leave my side at the moment. He's become so clingy.'

Josie felt tears well in her eyes as she remembered the little boy's haunted look as she'd pulled him into her arms. It would stay with her for a long time. She prayed that he'd forget it as he got older.

'You'll all be fine soon.' She nodded her head in encouragement.

As they stood up, Charlotte lurched forward and gave her a hug.

'Thanks for giving me my life back,' she said. 'I know the flowers aren't much.'

Josie hugged her back, pleased that there had been a happy ending to this case, albeit in the hard way.

'Are you kidding?' she laughed. 'Do you realise the forms I'll have to fill in because you've brought me a gift? We're not allowed to take anything from tenants in case it's misconstrued as bribery. I daren't even have a toffee off some people!'

Charlotte faltered. 'But that's pathetic! You do such an amazing job. I know I couldn't do what you do.'

'Stop it, you're making me blush.' Josie cried, feeling her cheeks warming.

'It's true though,' said Charlotte. 'I reckon you should change your job title to 'guardian angel'. It's perfect.'

CHAPTER SEVENTEEN

For Kelly, Tuesday morning came around too quickly. Jay finally sent her a text message but it was only to back up what Scott had told her over the phone – Jay was to pick him up and they were due back around eleven.

She'd been waiting for this day for three months, three months where she had fended for herself and got by. But life had moved on and she wasn't sure if she wanted Scott to come back and insist that it reverted to the way it had been. She knew he'd want her to stop going to work and to college, but she couldn't do that – wouldn't do that.

Jay's revelation last week had sent Kelly's mind into a spin. Their disagreement had made her confused. How could she have been so stupid? How had she not seen the signs that his feelings towards her had changed? Was it because she didn't want to?

She'd really started to enjoy Jay's company, looking forward to the end of her shifts to see if he'd be waiting to take her home. She'd loved the fact that he cared enough to pick her up most nights. She loved the fact that he played with Emily, keeping her company while she prepared supper. The truth was that she loved everything about Jay.

And without meaning to, she'd hurt him. Now she was left to wonder how he'd react when he saw her. She'd missed him so much since they'd fallen out – alarmingly so, considering that Scott was coming home and she should be wondering how she would react when she saw him.

By half past ten, she was pacing up and down in her living room. She'd cleaned the flat from top to bottom. The fridge had been stocked up with as much food as she could afford, and Emily had jumped into the bath with her and they'd washed each other's hair. Everything was perfect.

Trying to contain her nerves as Emily stood on the settee looking through the window for Jay's car, Kelly flipped through the TV channels. She stayed on ITV, as *This Morning* was in full swing. As much as she didn't want to hear about some woman's multiple birth going wrong, she needed to switch off. She was still feeling anxious about seeing Scott. What if they didn't like each other anymore after all their time apart? All too soon, there was no more time to worry.

'He's here!' shouted Emily. 'Daddy's back!'

Kelly jumped at the sound of her daughter's cries of excitement and moved to the spot where Emily had vacated. She saw Jay get out of the car first and then it was Scott's turn. His eyes searched the windows for her and her heart flipped as he spotted her and waved. She raised her hand as Emily threw herself at him.

'Daddy! Daddy! Daddy!' echoed down Clarence Avenue.

For the umpteenth time, Kelly checked her appearance. Her hand was shaking as she pulled at her fringe, her brown eyes energized yet fretful. She blew out a long breath. All of a sudden, she heard someone bounding up the stairs and there he was.

Scott smiled and Kelly's knees started to wobble.

'Hello, babe,' he spoke softly.

Kelly ran into his open arms. The relief of feeling his body close to hers was too much and she began to cry. All those mixed up thoughts instantly vanished. He was home.

Scott sat her down on the settee where she clung to him. 'Neat little place,' he admired, as he looked around. 'I see you haven't lost your flair for decorating.'

Kelly wiped her eyes while Emily showed Scott all of her new books. She smiled as Scott oohed and ahhed at the pink teddy bear series that Emily still read over and over.

Jay hung back in the kitchen doorway. Out of the corner of her eye, Kelly saw him trying to cover his emotions. She couldn't look at him; she felt so ashamed. Now that Scott was here, she felt so... so different. It was as if all the feelings she'd struggled with had never existed. Scott was home. They were a family again – but where did that leave Jay?

Kelly tried to push away the guilt but the tears fell again. Scott pulled her nearer.

'Stop your crying, woman,' he teased, kissing her lightly on the tip of her nose.

Kelly gave him a watery smile.

'Because I'm going to take my two favourite women out for a bite of grub.' Scott pulled Emily onto his knee and looked across at Jay. 'Mate, you couldn't lend us a twenty 'til I get me benefits sorted and give us a lift to the Butcher's Arms, could you, youth?'

With time on her hands now Stewart wasn't there to make so much of a mess, Josie decided to clear out the loft, something she had been putting off for years since her mum died. She also wanted to see what things Stewart had put up there and move them to the spare room for him to collect.

She still hadn't seen him since she'd asked him to leave. He kept asking to meet up but she kept saying no. It seemed too rushed, too raw. It was much easier to keep putting it off. Besides, she didn't want to think too far ahead just yet. Even though she knew she'd never take him back and the marriage was over, at the moment all she wanted to do was get used to being alone, and enjoy that feeling first.

Once she'd sorted out a few things for the charity shop, she took them out to her car.

'Hi, Josie,' a voice spoke to her bottom as she struggled to fit everything in the boot.

Josie pulled herself up to see her neighbour's brother standing by her side. He wore stylish glasses with a thick brown frame. Behind those glasses, Josie saw a pair of friendly blue eyes.

'Oh, hi, James,' she acknowledged. 'Been to visit Louise?'

'Yes, I called in after work. She's fed me to the brim, as usual. Can I help you with anything?'

'Thanks, but I can manage,' Josie declined his offer. She smiled at him, hoping she didn't sound too ungrateful. 'How is she, by the way?'

'She's good thanks. The baby's due next weekend. I can't believe it's gone so quickly.'

'Getting used to the sound of Uncle James, then?'

James laughed, then faltered. 'I – Louise told me that you and Stewart have split up.'

'Oh, yes –'

'I hope you don't mind,' he interrupted. 'I wasn't prying. I was just asking, well, you know.'

'No, not at all. It's fine, I'll get over it.'

'It's over for good, then?'

She nodded.

'Well, if there's anything you ever need a hand with, please, just ask.'

'Thanks, I will.' She smiled warmly.

That awkward silence again.

'Well, I'd better –'

'I must –'

They smiled again and James went on his way. Josie watched him for a moment. That was really sweet of him to offer help if she needed it, she realised. He'd seemed quite friendly over the few times she'd spoken to him, and she got on really well with his sister. She wished Louise lived next door to her. It would be a far cry from Mrs Clancy, joined on to her house now. If Josie so much as sneezed loudly, she'd be banging on the wall about the volume.

Once inside again, she moved Stewart's belongings to the spare room before making herself a well-earned cup of tea. Although it had begun to rain slightly, she threw open the conservatory door. Sipping her drink, she marvelled at her luck. Even though she would have to take the rough with the smooth for a while – especially when she finally decided to talk things out with Stewart – maybe this was the point where her life might start to change for the better.

She smiled again, at nothing in particular.

The next morning, Kelly lay awake in bed. By her side, she could hear Scott breathing. She could just about make out his shape in the morning light – a strange shape she wasn't certain about yet.

Yesterday had been such a traumatic day. Emily had been sick after her dinner. Kelly knew it was bound to happen, she'd been so excited, running around like a puppy. Scott had spent the best part of the day teasing his little girl, kissing her, hugging her, loving her. Once Kelly had finally got her off to sleep, it had been her turn. Awkward fumbles had turned into practiced foreplay and they'd made love on the rug in front of the fire. It had been familiar, like old times, like Scott had never been away. But she hadn't felt comforted as they lay in each other's arms afterwards. It had felt ... strange.

She came up on her elbow and watched him while he slept. Scott had a complexion that only had to catch a ray of sun to deepen three shades. Unlike Jay, with his designer stubble, Scott was clean-shaven. She imagined how he would look with trendy facial hair. Right now, although his stubble made him seem darker, Scott looked pasty. He'd lost weight, she'd noticed: about a stone, he'd told her. It didn't suit him; it made him look gaunt and a little scarier. But Scott liked his food and Kelly knew the weight would return in no time. And he was as tall as Jay, so he could carry it.

She turned back towards the wall and shut her eyes tightly to stop her tears. Why couldn't she get Jay out of her mind? Why did she keep comparing him to Scott? She couldn't help but feel that she'd let them both down. Now that Scott was back, Jay might not want to look out for Kelly anymore. If Jay didn't want to see her, maybe he could move on quicker. Then maybe she could leave her awkwardness behind and concentrate on Scott. There had to be no room in her life for Jay anymore.

Scott turned over and dragged her along the bed towards him. He spooned himself into her back and she felt the stirring of his erection.

'Morning, babe,' Scott whispered sleepily before yawning. 'Or should I say, 'morning glory'?'

Pushing Jay as far to the back of her mind as she could, Kelly reached behind her.

Later that morning, Kelly was sitting with Emily on the floor. Scott was lying on the settee watching the television.

'Where's that box you fetched me from Phil Matson's, Kel?' he asked all of a sudden.

'It's in Em's room, hidden in with her toys,' she replied. 'Are you going to show me what's in it now?'

'It's nowt to worry your pretty head about.' Scott began to channel hop.

'You said that it was money.'

'I was kidding.'

Kelly frowned. 'I don't want anything dodgy in this flat.'

'Kelly, Kelly, Kelly.' Scott sighed loudly as he stretched his body. 'I've only just got back, but don't fret. I'll take care of you now. It'll be business as usual soon, you'll see.'

Kelly didn't want it to be business as usual. That box had been the bane of her life for the past few weeks. At first when she'd fetched it she'd shoved it in the kitchen cupboard under the sink, but then she'd moved it in with Emily's toys and hidden it in the cupboard over the stairs, but still it seemed to call to her. It reminded her of when she was the same age as Emily and she'd tried to peel the sellotape off her Christmas presents while no one was watching. There had been times when she'd felt like ripping the tape off, looking inside and replacing it, but she knew he'd find out.

'Mummy, can I go and see Dot?' said Emily.

Scott turned his head towards Kelly. 'Who?'

'Dot lives downstairs and looks after me when mummy goes to college. She doesn't look after me when Mummy goes to work, though. I stay with nanny then.'

Scott nearly fell to the floor in his speed to sit up.

Kelly grimaced. 'Thanks, little lady,' she muttered.

'College?' Scott frowned. 'Work? What the fuck's she talking about, Kel?'

Emily giggled and covered her mouth.

Kelly tutted. 'Don't swear in front of Emily.'

'Don't tell me what to do,' he snarled, 'and don't change the subject! What's going on?'

Kelly wondered where to start. She supposed the beginning would be the best place.

'I've been learning secretarial and office skills. I've passed my first two assignments and my course tutor says I'll be able to take the next level in summer. Then I'm –'

'Whoa!' Scott held up a hand to silence her. 'What's with all the plans? And when had you planned to tell me about them? Was I even included in them?'

Kelly looked a little sheepish. 'Of course you were. I just wanted to surprise you, make you proud of me.'

'You don't have to go to college for me to be proud of you! Jesus, I'll be the laughing stock at the pub.' Scott moved his fingers in the air as if there was a keyboard in front of him. 'Did you think of that while you were typing your stupid letters?'

'You left me alone and I was bored,' Kelly pouted. 'I've always wanted to go to college but you talked me out of it. Now I'm doing something for myself, I feel better about things. I feel like I'm contributing to society.'

'You don't need to contribute to society. I provide for you!'

'Like you've provided for me over the past three months?'

'That was low.' Scott frowned. 'I've served my time.'

Kelly sighed. 'I know, but I was scared. I didn't think I'd cope with the bills on my own. That's why I've been working at the factory, too. I got a job on the twilight shift and –'

'Jesus fucking Christ!' Scott turned to Emily. 'Em, go to your room for a minute, there's a good girl.'

'But I want to stay here with you.'

'Now!'

Emily shot off the settee.

'Don't shout at her!' Kelly came to her daughter's defence. 'It's not her fault that you're annoyed with me.'

'You told me not to swear in front of her – and don't change the subject. Who the fuck have you turned into while I've been gone? Not only are you going to college behind my back, but now you tell me you're working as well?'

'What's wrong with wanting to make something of myself?' Kelly began to pile up Emily's books. 'I used to work before I met you, remember?'

'But you've not worked since, remember!'

'Only because *you* didn't want me to!'

'That's not the point. You don't work because we can claim

more in benefits.'

Kelly placed her hands on her hips. 'As a single man and woman, you mean? If it wasn't for you and your stupid ideas, we'd still be in Patrick Street, so don't you dare blame that one on me. I would have been allowed to stay if I could prove that I'd been living there for over twelve months. But you saw to that, didn't you?'

'I didn't think I'd lose my house, for fuck's sake!'

'Don't give me that! You knew exactly what you were doing – screwing the benefit agency, as normal. Well, I'm halfway out of the benefit trap now and that's the way I'm staying.'

'Over my dead body.'

'Fine – I'll arrange that, shall I?'

Kelly marched past him but he grabbed her hand. She stopped.

'I've changed since you've been away,' she replied. 'I had to, so don't blame things on me. Maybe you should try working yourself – it might keep you out of trouble.'

'You must be joking! Working doesn't feature in my life plan.'

'I'm not stopping.'

'But you don't need to work now! I told you, I'll provide for you, like I used to. It was good enough before I was nicked. Besides, what am I going to do when you're not here?'

'That's simple. You can clean up; do the washing, a little ironing. Run the hoover around, that kind of thing. Think of it as an investment for our future together.'

It was Scott's turn to sigh, but he did it more dramatically. 'Fuck, I've spent three months locked up. It's been torture without you, but if I knew I was coming back to this I'd rather have stayed inside.'

Suddenly, Kelly felt accountable. She'd expected a little griping while they got used to each other again, but Scott had only been back for a night and already she was nagging.

Seeing the distressed look on her face, Scott drew her into his arms. 'I've missed you, babe,' he told her. 'Don't let's row anymore.'

CHAPTER EIGHTEEN

Because of that argument, Kelly's weekend had been hard to get through. She felt like she was tip-toeing on hot coals, trying to get used to having Scott around again. In such a short space of time, everything had changed so much.

After their disagreement on Saturday morning, Scott had gone on all day about her giving up her job at Miles' factory. He'd sulked more than she would have expected Emily to do at her age, creating a particularly charged atmosphere. The day had been finished for her when he told her he'd invited Jay around for a takeaway on Saturday night. She'd feigned a headache at ten thirty, leaving the two of them to enjoy the rest of the bloodthirsty film they were watching. As ever, Scott seemed too pre-occupied with himself to notice the tense atmosphere between Jay and Kelly.

Sunday lunch had been a solemn affair at her mum's house. Neither of her parents were pleased that Scott had returned to Kelly's life, so the atmosphere was dicey. Things got decidedly worse when, after her Dad questioned what prison life had been like, Scott had been only too happy to talk it up. Kelly heard him sneering about one of the inmates who'd been slashed several times across his back during his first month there. With horror, she realised that he was bragging about his spell behind bars as if he had no problem returning.

After checking with her mum that it would be okay to leave Emily with her rather than with Scott when she was at work, they walked home. Within an hour, Scott's phone rang and he'd gone out to meet some guys in the pub, promising that it was only a little bit of business that he needed to sort out.

Ten minutes after he'd gone, Kelly and Emily sat together on the settee. They were reading the final pages of *Cinderella.*

'Mummy, will Daddy go away again soon?'

Kelly looked down into Emily's innocent brown eyes. She tried to hug away her worries. 'Of course he won't, monster.'

'I like it better when there's you and me.'

Kelly gulped away the tears threatening to fall and quickly turned to the next page of the book.

'Never mind, honey,' she said. 'I'm sure things will settle down again soon.'

Josie had been dreading Monday morning at work because she had an eviction lined up for ten o'clock. Philip Matson hadn't paid any money towards his rent since she'd last warned him on the day that Charlotte Hatfield had clung to life and, although the judge had been lenient that month, she wouldn't be this month when she realised that he hadn't kept to his arrangement again.

The first thing she did when she got to her desk was check that all the necessary paperwork had been completed. The bailiffs and the police had been booked and Doug was on standby to accompany her if the police were called away at the last minute – not that that was much comfort. The joiner had been booked to change the locks if necessary, which she was sure would be the case. She knew Philip wouldn't have surrendered his keys.

The next thing was a cup of tea.

'Mondays always come around too soon, don't they?' Debbie remarked as she joined Josie and Craig in the tiny staff room. 'It doesn't seem a minute since we were leaving on Friday night.'

'My head certainly thinks so,' said Craig, rubbing at his left temple. 'I haven't recovered from Friday night yet, never mind Saturday and Sunday.'

'Tell me about it.' Josie shoved her lunch box into the overloaded fridge. 'Every neighbour and his dog seems to have rung up to complain about something or other and we've only been open for ten minutes. I'm sure our tenants see me as some kind of solicitor, the matters they think I'm responsible for.' She paused and turned to Debbie. 'I might have an eviction later this morning. Do you fancy coming with me?'

'Ooh, yeah.' Debbie's eyes lit up. 'Anything to get out of here for an hour or so.'

'I'll warn you now, though. Things might get a bit rough if the tenant shows up.'

'Rather you than me,' said Craig. He chinked his spoon on the side of his mug before chucking it into the sink. 'Those people out there are rough.'

'I can handle them,' said Debbie. 'Besides, there's nothing more I like than a good mur-der,' she added, *Taggart*-style.

Josie grinned. The young woman standing in front of her had the makings of a good officer when the opportunity arose.

Half an hour later, the call had been made and the curtains had started to twitch in Bernard Place. Their vehicles took up most of the tiny cul-de-sac: Josie's car, the marked Ford Focus belonging to the police, the bailiff's Range Rover and the work van belonging to one of the joiners, bearing the Mitchell Housing Association logo along each side.

Josie knocked loudly twice on the front door before banging on the living room window three times. 'I bet he didn't turn up at court,' she said. She peered through the letter box into an empty hallway. 'I can hear his dogs and there's no sign of any packing. He thinks the eviction isn't going to happen. Most people assume it's an empty threat.'

'What do we do now?' asked Debbie.

Josie gave the joiner the go ahead, as he stood waiting with his drill. 'Remove the lock. If he's in there, he'll be out once he hears that.'

Josie and Debbie sat on the wall chatting to the bailiff and PC Mark White while the joiner did his job. Although Mark was fairly new to the force, Josie had known the bailiff for eight years. She knew that his eldest daughter had gone to university and was doing extremely well. She knew that his son was getting married in October. But before she learned about all the things that had gone wrong so far in the planning, she was distracted by a shout as Philip finally showed up.

Josie turned to Debbie. 'Watch out for yourself. He's likely to kick off, so stay out of the way if anything happens.'

'Be careful!' said Debbie.

'Don't worry about me. This is bound to be the last time I'll have to deal with him anyway. The council are hardly likely to give him a place if we've evicted him for non-payment of his rent.'

Debbie stayed seated on the wall. Josie and Mark met Philip halfway up the path.

'Hello, Philip,' said Josie. 'Glad you could make it.'

Philip looked first at the joiner as he drilled through the lock of his front door, then back to Josie.

'What the fuck are you doing?'

What the fuck does it look like, Josie wanted to reply. Instead she kept calm. 'We're evicting you,' she said. 'I told you this would happen if –'

'You can't do this, you bitch!'

'Whoa there, cowboy, watch your language.' Mark held Philip at arms' length as he moved nearer to Josie. The bailiff handed Philip a copy of the eviction notice, which he promptly screwed into a ball.

Even though Josie had taken a step backwards, she tried not to show concern. Philip was a trouble maker, but he seemed to be all mouth and empty threats, by all accounts. She knew the residents of Bernard Place would be glad to see the back of him.

'I warned you enough times,' Josie told him as she regained her composure.

'But... all me stuff... me dogs are still inside!'

'Then you'll have to remove them. I need vacant possession by the end of the day.'

Philip's eyes widened in disbelief. 'But I've got nowhere to go!'

Josie sighed. Evictions were always the worst part of her job, even if it was low life such as Philip. She should have been able to get through to him – show proof of income or else your housing benefits will be stopped. She should have carried out more than the fortnightly visits she'd made over the past few months, insisting that he brought the items she needed to the office, but there wasn't time to keep on chasing. Philip had hardly ever been at home for any of her pre-arranged visits *and* hadn't contacted her regarding any of her letters. Still, Josie felt like she had failed.

'I can give you until the end of the day,' she repeated. A battle of wills began as the two of them locked eyes.

Josie held out her hand. 'There's no going back now. If you give me the keys, we can stop any more damage and you can start to clear out your stuff.'

Once inside the property, Josie felt more at ease. The joiner and the bailiff had left, their work finished. Philip used his mobile, trying to rally some friends to help him. Mark checked the rooms for stolen goods and Debbie took photographs with a digital camera.

'I still can't believe that tenants make up imaginary items so that they can claim against the association,' she said, when Josie came into the living room.

'It's true, which is why, apart from the obvious safety reasons, there has to be at least two officers present at any eviction. Then they can't say we've nicked their brand new widescreen TV, etcetera.'

Philip finished his call. 'I've got a mate coming over with a van. He'll help me move my stuff, though I don't know where the fuck it's all going to go.' He stared at Josie before pushing past them both into the kitchen.

'The steel doors will be fitted no later than three thirty,' Josie shouted after him. 'I'll leave you to sort things out and come back then.'

Desperate for fresh air, Josie followed Debbie out.

'Has he calmed down any?' Paul asked.

'Enough to get his arse into gear.'

'What if he can't do it all by this afternoon?'

'We'll let him in again by arrangement, but one of us will have to stay with him. We give tenants twenty-eight days to remove their belongings. If they don't, we clear it for them. It's such a shame to see good furniture go to waste, but there you have –'

'About bloody time you got rid of that scummy bastard!' a voice shouted from across the street. The unmistakable bubble of Mrs Myatt leaning on her garden gate opposite them assaulted their eyes. 'He's been causing trouble here since the day he moved in,' she continued. 'I can't believe it took you so long to get rid of him.'

'We'd get rid of a lot more people if we could,' Debbie told her.

'Our jobs aren't as easy as they seem.'

'Not that easy?' Mrs Myatt huffed and pointed to her overgrown lawn. 'If you stopped pestering people about keeping their gardens in pristine condition, you'd have plenty of time to do the important things. I'm surprised at you, Josie Mellor. I always thought you had more about you, but letting the likes of him get the better of you.'

Josie felt anger rising within her. 'Mrs Myatt,' she yelled across the cul-de-sac, 'why don't you –'

'Keep an eye on the situation here,' Debbie interrupted, before Josie could shout out the rest of the damning sentence, 'and ring us if anything kicks off before we call back at three-thirty?'

Mrs Myatt nodded and went inside with a slam of her front door.

'Stupid bitch. And you want to be a housing officer?' Josie shook her head in wonder.

After dropping Debbie back at the office, Josie texted Kelly to check if she was home – and that Scott wasn't.

'I'm not stopping,' she explained as she stood on the doorstep. 'I've got some books for Emily. Is she home?'

'No, she's gone to town with my mum. That girl has more of a social life than me.'

'How are things going?' Josie asked tentatively. 'I wanted to check that you were okay but I haven't liked to call unannounced since Scott's release from prison.'

Kelly shrugged. 'I suppose it'll take time to adjust again.'

A silence followed and Josie took this as her cue not to continue. She opened a bag and pulled out the first book she came to. It still tugged at her heartstrings to give them away, but she knew they were going to a good home.

'Aw.' She ran a finger over the cover. 'Enid Blyton was my favourite author. I've always wanted to write a book, especially about my job. People wouldn't believe what goes on here on the Mitchell Estate.'

'Got anything in there for me?' Kelly picked up another book. *Five go to Dorset.*

'Not unless you're seven. Some of them are going to be too old for now but she'll grow into them. And, I hope, grow to love them like I did.'

Kelly flicked through the pages. A photograph dropped onto the floor. Josie picked it up and pulled a face.

'One of my wedding photos.' She handed it to Kelly. 'God, I look so scared!'

Kelly looked at the photo of Josie and her husband standing on the steps of the registry office. Josie looked like a child next to him. She was right, she did look scared. Then Kelly drew it nearer. She recognised the man.

'I know him.'

'Yes, you probably do,' nodded Josie. 'He works at Miles' Factory too. Do you remember me telling you? We've – we've split up recently.'

'Oh, I'm sorry.'

'No, don't be.' Josie smiled half-heartedly. 'There was nothing there to miss, if I'm honest. I'll get over it.'

'Josie. I –'

'Christ on a bike,' Josie interrupted, noticing the time. 'I have to go – I'll catch you later in the week. Bye.'

Kelly closed the door and made her way back up the stairs. Already she was searching her memory, running through previous conversations with Josie. Hadn't she said that they'd both lost their parents?

So that left one question: why did the men at work call the man in the photograph 'mummy's boy'?

CHAPTER NINETEEN

At half past two, Josie was sorting out the eviction paperwork when she received a phone call to say that Stewart was in the main reception asking for her. A little bit taken aback, she rushed up to see him, but at the sight of him, she felt anger tear through her. She pointed to an interview cubicle and Stewart followed her in.

'I came to see how you were,' he said. 'I haven't seen you since...'

'Since you punched me in the face?'

'Sorry.' Stewart lowered his eyes for a moment. 'I got it into my head that you were seeing someone else.'

'So you thought you'd spy on me?'

'I was worried about you!'

'I don't think you'll ever worry about anyone other than yourself. And I can't see why you're so bothered. You haven't really liked living with me for a while now, have you?'

Stewart shrugged like a spoilt child.

'You've wanted out of this marriage for ages,' Josie continued into the silence that had followed. 'So I've given you the opportunity. Now tell me the real reason that you're here.'

'What do you mean?'

'What do you want, Stewart?'

'I want to know what you're doing about the house.'

'*My* house?'

Stewart looked uncomfortable. 'I paid towards it too.'

The penny clicked and Josie gasped. 'You've come here to talk money?'

'I –'

'That house belongs to me! It was left to me by my mother. Granted, you paid towards its keep in the early years of our marriage, but you've hardly given anything towards the bills lately.

I know you may be entitled to something – I'm not that heartless – but I'll be damned if you think you're getting thousands from me.'

'I'm entitled to half.'

'Oh, no you're not,' Josie raged. She lowered her voice before continuing. 'We need to talk but now isn't the time. I can meet you tonight in the Cat and Fiddle.'

'I'll come to the house.'

'No, you won't.'

'But –'

'I have work to do. I'll meet you in the pub later – six o'clock, take it or leave it.'

Josie let out a breath as she watched Stewart walk away. Tears filled her eyes and her hands began to shake uncontrollably. How dare he show up unannounced? She didn't like mixing her home life with her working days and he knew that.

She sat down for a moment to calm herself. After what they'd discussed, she felt totally let down. Seeing him now made her realise that she had no feelings left for him. She didn't love him; she didn't even like him anymore. Especially when it seemed he was more interested in the house than her welfare.

Finally, she stood up. She couldn't let him get away with treating her like this. If Stewart thought for a minute she was willing to bargain with him, he had another think coming.

At ten to three, Kelly thought she'd given Scott enough time to return home. He'd promised to look after Emily that evening but, no sooner had he walked back into her life, than the meetings of before had started up again. He'd been gone since he'd taken a phone call at eleven that morning.

Kelly grabbed her keys. 'Come on, Em. Let's see if Dot's in. Would you mind staying with her while I go to work, just for today?'

The grateful look on her daughter's face was enough to make Kelly blink away tears. Why had she thought she could leave Emily with Scott as soon as he returned? She'd known things were going to be rough while they got reacquainted but she hadn't thought they would be *this* rough. It was like living with a completely different person. Or maybe he'd always been like this and she'd never noticed.

As she was about to fly down the stairs, Kelly heard the key turn in the door.

'I think she's gone,' she heard Scott say. Putting a finger over her lips, Kelly pulled Emily into the bathroom and quietly closed the door.

'Won't she go mental if you keep them in here?' someone else spoke. Kelly frowned, vaguely recognising the voice.

'She doesn't have any choice.' The bathroom door flew open. Scott freaked when he saw them both.

'What the fuck –'

'I might ask you the same thing.' Kelly pointed to the tank he was holding. 'What is that?'

Emily peeped out from behind Kelly's legs. She let out an ear-piercing scream. 'Spiders! Mummy, I hate spiders!'

'Stop your whining.' Scott placed the tank of creepy crawlies into the bath. 'They won't hurt you – well, most of them won't.'

Kelly stared at the man standing behind Scott. It was that Matson guy she'd fetched Scott's parcel from.

'Get them out of here,' she said, at the same time trying to console Emily by pulling her close.

'No, it's only for a few days. Since that bitch of a housing officer,' Scott turned towards Kelly with a sneer, 'the one you're so friendly with – chucked him out of his house, he's nowhere to put them.'

'They can't stay in here.'

Emily was sniffling uncontrollably now.

'Em, don't be a baby.' Scott delved into the tank, picked up a spider and thrust it into her face. Emily turned away and screamed again. He laughed at her look of dismay.

'Grow up, Scott,' Kelly cried. 'She's frightened, for God's sake. Are you too bloody stupid to see that?'

'But where else can they go?'

'If they must stay, put them in the bin store outside.' Kelly pushed past them. Emily tightened her gip on her hand. 'They'd better not be in here when I get home.'

'Okay, okay! Keep your knickers on. I'll put them outside.'

Kelly managed to get down the stairs with Emily still clinging to her. She checked her watch after she'd pressed the tinny bell on Dot's door frame. It was nearing quarter past three; she was going to be late for work now.

'One minute!'

Kelly's shoulders drooped, thankful for small mercies. At least Dot could keep an eye on Scott to see if anything else unpleasant found its way into her bathroom. God knows what else that creepy guy had with him.

'I'm beginning to wish I'd kept hold of Patrick Street,' Scott muttered as he pushed past her rudely.

'That's funny,' Kelly replied sharply. 'So am I.'

Josie turned the dial up on the shower and stepped under the hot water, hoping to wash her troubles down the plug hole along with her shower gel. Sighing loudly, she stood for what seemed like an age as she recalled the last few hours. What a day. When Philip Matson had eventually vacated the property, he'd also ripped the washing machine away from the wall, leaving damaged pipe-work and water pouring everywhere. Josie had had to call out the emergency plumber. Then there had been the meeting with Stewart that never was, as he hadn't turned up at the Cat and Fiddle. She hoped he'd come to his senses, that he wouldn't turn up unannounced again.

Luckily for her, she'd returned the favour and invited Livvy for something to eat that evening. She was glad to have some company.

'He's a right prick, messing you about like that,' Livvy said, as they sat down in the living room. 'What are you going to do now?'

'I'm not sure.' Josie handed her a glass of red wine. 'It's early days yet. I bet he thinks I won't be able to hack it in the real world without him.'

'Why don't you call his bluff and put the house up for sale?'

Josie stopped with the glass near her lips. 'I don't get you.'

'Let him know that you're moving on regardless.'

'But I don't want to sell it.'

'I'm not saying that you have to, but it might make him realise that you're serious about not taking him back. You won't change your mind about that, will you?'

Josie shook her head. It had been a shock when Stewart had lashed out at her, but even before that she'd known the marriage was dead on its feet. There was no point going back to that.

'Good, it will give him something to worry about for a change.'

But Josie wasn't sure that Stewart would worry about that. She assumed he'd think she was putting the house on the market so that she could pay him his half when it sold. However, if it gave her a bit of time and kept him at bay for a while, she would certainly give it some thought.

'I'll definitely think about it.'

She went to check on the food and came back a few minutes later to find Livvy staring into space. Livvy had been reluctant to open up the first time they'd met – maybe she needed to talk now.

'Want to tell me what's weighing you down?' she asked.

Livvy sighed. 'You remember I left the association to work with my family?'

'Yes, I do.' Libby's parents owned their own franchise of recruitment agencies. 'I thought you were doing well. Did something go wrong?'

'Leyton Goldstraw.'

'Ah.' Josie pulled her legs up beside her. 'A man.'

'I'd been going out with him for six months. My parents and my brother and sister never took to him. They didn't like the way he pestered me for money all the time. So, after one almighty row, I quit.'

'You left the family business!'

Livvy shrugged. 'It was hard, I know, but they were never going to approve. I would have thought twice about it, had I known how Leyton would react.'

'Oh?'

'He was far from impressed. My brother and sister had both been given their own branches to run and, being the youngest, I was in line for mine. My dad had picked out the office space and was just about to sign the lease on the building when we fell out. I managed to find work with an agency before getting back on at head office but the money was nowhere near what I'd been earning before. And then, over the next year, Leyton bled me dry.' Livvy pushed her long hair behind her ears and sighed. 'I was a fool, Josie. I loaned him money towards starting his own business, yet his promises to pay me back never materialised. Eventually he just upped and left, leaving me with all his debts. I couldn't face asking my parents to help me out because I felt so humiliated.'

'I don't believe it.' Josie felt angry about Livvy's quandary. It never failed to amaze her just how similar people were. No matter what beginnings they'd had in life, it only took one event to turn everything upside down. 'So what did you do? I mean, they would have been okay with you, surely?'

'Yes, without a doubt I know they would have bailed me out. But me, being pigheaded Livvy, carried on with life as I did before – a life I could no longer afford, I hasten to add. I don't go out much now but when I do, I still have to spend to keep everyone in the dark. At least the argument with my family blew over almost immediately and I still see them regularly. We're really close and I like that. They do still think I'm seeing Leyton, though.'

'What?' Josie was surprised. 'You haven't told them he's gone?'

Livvy shook her head. 'Maybe I hate the words 'I told you so.' But they'd be right.'

'And what about the flat? Are you behind on your rent?'

Livvy shook her head again. 'I lease it from my parents. I pay hardly anything so I've managed to keep up with those payments. It's the other things I'm having trouble with, like my credit cards and the instalments on my car. I can't let them take away my Bessie.'

'I can help, if you like?' Josie volunteered. 'It's part of my job to offer debt advice.'

'If you can sort me out, I'd be eternally grateful,' Livvy laughed, but it was tinged with sadness.

'Okay.' Josie thought it was time to throw in a compromise. 'Providing you tell your parents about Leyton.'

Livvy paused before speaking. 'Okay, providing you at least think about putting the house up for sale.'

'I'm not sure. I'm not usually any kind of risk taker. I'm more your average Joe, anything for a quiet existence. Does that make sense?'

Livvy nodded slightly. 'It does in a strange kind of way. I think what you're trying to say is that you feel trapped living here. Like a bird with clipped wings – never knowing what's out there, but you're too frightened to take a gamble.'

Josie was impressed. 'Wow. You have me down to a tee. I think I've fused my home life with my job. I always feel the need to be looking after someone.'

'Can't you specialise in that for your work?'

Josie wasn't quite sure what she was getting at. 'My job is specialised,' she said.

'I mean, more dedicated to one subject. You seem good with people. You coaxed all that out of me.' Livvy referred to their earlier conversation. 'I've never told anyone about my debt problem, but you're so easy to talk to. You listen and you don't judge. That's the difference.'

'You won't thank me when I cut up your credit cards,' Josie said with a wicked grin.

Livvy shook her head. 'No I won't, but it has to be done.'

'Right then, you go and get them – all of them – and I'll get the scissors.'

'What?' Livvy shuddered. 'Right now? Can't we do it later?'

Josie raised her eyebrows. 'You see? I said you'd hate me!'

Despite worrying what Scott was getting up to at the flat without her there, the photograph of Stewart was still playing on Kelly's mind. During her tea break that evening, she searched out one particular person in the staff canteen.

'Hey, Robbie,' she pulled out a chair and sat down opposite him, giving him her best smile. 'Where's your friend tonight?'

'You mean Phil? He's on the day shift.'

Kelly shook her head. 'Not him. The one they call Mummy's Boy?'

'You're interested in Mummy's Boy?' Robbie frowned. 'What the fuck for? He's a boring bastard.'

'I'm curious to know where his nickname came from, that's all.'

'It's because he's thirty-nine and still lives with his mum.'

Kelly tried to hide her surprise as she ripped open her chocolate. The guy on the photo was definitely Josie's husband, yet here at work it seemed he was a single man living at home with his mum. It didn't make sense.

Robbie reached across the table and pinched the second bar. She slapped his fingers and he dropped it, moving back and folding his arms.

'So what's his real name?' she asked.

'What's with all the questions?'

Kelly waved to get Sally's attention as she came into the room. She slid across the chocolate that Robbie coveted. He took a bite before continuing.

'All the time he's worked here, no one's ever seen him with a woman. That's not to say that he's gay: no one's seen him with a bloke either. All we could find out was that he's never been married, doesn't go out, he just stays at home. I reckon he's too tight to waste money renting or buying anywhere else.'

'What are you doing with the Robster here?' Sally asked as she took the seat next to her friend.

'She wants to know about Mummy's Boy,' Robbie explained. 'I've just been filling her in.'

'I could have told you about him if you'd asked. I've worked here so long I know everything there is to know.'

'They say he'll be loaded when his old woman meets the grim reaper,' Robbie continued, not one to be dismissed.

'Who will?' queried Sally.

Robbie sighed in exasperation. 'Mummy's Boy!'

'Oh,' Sally nodded in recognition. 'You mean Stewart Mellor.'

CHAPTER TWENTY

The following week, Emily had gone to the shops with Dot, and Kelly had a rare chance to put her feet up and drink her coffee. Scott – well, he'd gone out about an hour ago; Kelly had no idea where to, but she was eternally grateful that he was out from under her feet.

For the past two hours she'd been cleaning. She'd forgotten how untidy Scott was. He'd leave the mug wherever he finished with it, he'd drop soggy towels over the side of the bath thinking they'd miraculously dry themselves and last night she'd come into a tip when she'd eventually got home from work. It was obvious that someone else had visited: two of every dirty dish stacked in the kitchen sink and a pile of empty cans shoved into the pedal bin. Most probably it would have been Philip Matson: Jay would have tidied up.

Needing some unbiased company, she texted Josie to let her know the kettle was on if she was free. Her shoulders sagged spectacularly. Was it really only a week since Scott had been released? It seemed like a life time already – and as if nothing had changed. Life for Scott had gone back to normal, just in another place.

The fiasco with the spiders had caused another problem. This morning, Emily wouldn't take a bath until Kelly had checked every single inch of the bathroom while she stood on the threshold of the door. In her mind, she could still hear Scott's teasing laughter. How could he taunt a four-year-old about her fear of spiders when there were lots of adults who felt the same way?

What annoyed Kelly most was the fact that Scott had agreed to look after Emily while she went to work, yet he'd waited until he thought she'd be gone and sneaked into the flat. Yes, sneaked, she realised, that's what he'd done. But this was *her* flat; *her* name on the tenancy agreement. Was he too stupid to think that nothing would change while he was inside? Because she had – she'd changed into a responsible adult. She went to college and she held down a part time job. She was still reliant on some benefits, but she was enjoying herself as she learned new skills and, once she managed to get a full time job, she'd be laughing.

Or rather Kelly would be, if it weren't for one thing. She missed Jay. Jay had made her smile, made her forget all her troubles, made her feel like she could conquer the world. Oh, God. Was she ever going to think rationally again?

Her mobile phone beeped, breaking into her melancholy mood. With Josie on her way, she went to unlock the front door.

'I was only around the corner when I got your message,' Josie said. 'I have a few phone calls to make during my lunch break so I only have time for a quick cuppa, if that's okay?'

Kelly smiled, still marvelling at their unlikely friendship.

'So how are you getting on now?' Josie asked, once Kelly had made coffee.

Kelly took a sip of her drink. 'Okay, I suppose.'

'What about Emily? Is she coping?'

'She seems okay,' Kelly fibbed, but then thought better of it. 'Actually, she's not okay. At first she was all over him, Daddy's back, but now that the novelty's worn off, she wants to be with me all the time. If I leave the room, she's right behind me. Even if I'm only popping to the loo, she'll go and fetch a toy from her bedroom and wait for me in the hallway.'

'I suppose that's to be expected,' Josie sympathised. 'But hopefully she'll get used to having him around again.'

'I'm not so sure. Before he went inside, they used to get on great. Since he's come back, it's as if he doesn't want to know her – nor me, really. He's continually having a go at me for giving up on Patrick Street. He moans at every opportunity: when I go to work, when I get back from work, when I go to college, when I get back from college. In fact, he's turned into a right nag. I suppose I didn't think it would be this hard.'

'It might not be,' Josie tried to reassure her. 'This time next week you could be feeling much better about things.'

'I know, yet... maybe I hadn't realised how much time I was already spending on my own before he was locked up. Maybe I put him on a pedestal while he wasn't here because I was lonely and not because I missed him. I – I don't want to live like this anymore.'

'Do you think the relationship was over before he was sent to prison?' Josie probed gently.

Kelly nodded. 'Possibly. And now I feel trapped. Because he gave up Patrick Street –'

'Lost it, more like.'

'He's got nowhere else to go. I can't abandon him.'

'No one's asking you to. Despite the fact that I think he's a loser, maybe you need to give yourself time to adjust. If everything is still iffy after another couple of weeks, then that'll be the time to do something about it.'

With the sound of the radio playing in the background, they finished their drinks in a comfortable silence. Josie looked over at Kelly, wishing she could do more for her but knowing that it was up to her what happened next. Kelly had to make her own decision; she wasn't going to influence her in any way.

'How are you doing at college?' Kelly asked.

'I'm finding it hard to fit in,' Josie grimaced. 'I've already missed two weeks but I only have a few sessions left. I'll be back on track soon – though that's only an introduction to counselling. If I want to take it further I have to commit myself to four and half hours a week and it's double the length of this course. I need to think about it – but I would like to go further with it. What about you? Passed any more assignments lately?'

Kelly smiled for the first time that morning. 'Yes, another two. I've only got two more to do and I've finished the course.'

'And then?'

Kelly sighed. 'I haven't got a clue what's going to happen. And I'm not sure I even want to think about it.'

Over the next two weeks, life changed dramatically for Josie and Kelly. Every evening as Josie got home from work, she wondered if she would get a letter from Stewart, or even a solicitor acting on his behalf, but there was nothing. Every night as Kelly got home, she let herself into the flat with a dread in her heart, knowing full well that it would be in a mess and that she'd have to prepare her own supper. That was if Scott was even at home: already he'd slipped into his old routine, often coming home after midnight.

Every day Josie got used to her freedom, being able to go out with friends whenever she liked. Every day, Kelly missed her times with Jay, finding out that it hurt more as time went on. She'd only seen him twice since Scott had come home.

Every morning that Josie woke up alone, Kelly awoke with trepidation, sharing the bed with a loser.

The old Josie had gone; the old Kelly had gone. Josie didn't want to be with Stewart; Kelly didn't want to be with Scott.

Little did these two women realise when their friendship evolved that they would eventually wish for the same things to happen in their lives.

'Hey, Kelly! Wait up!'

Kelly turned to see Lynsey, Jay's sister, wobbling towards her across Vincent Square from the direction of the Post Office. She pushed along a buggy, a child either side of her holding onto the handles. It was Monday, benefit collection day for most of the residents of the Mitchell Estate.

Kelly hadn't seen Lynsey in ages. As ever, she was devoid of make-up, her garish blonde hair tied off her face in a severe pony tail. The warmer weather always brought out strange sights on the Mitchell Estate and Lynsey was no exception. Wearing the shortest denim skirt with a skimpy vest, there was flesh oozing out at every opportunity. But was it still fashionable to have your belly hanging over your waistband? Kelly hid her look of astonishment as she grasped the fact that Lynsey was pregnant.

'Hiya, Lynsey, how are you doing?' Kelly greeted her with a smile.

Lynsey ran a hand over her bulging stomach. 'Up the duff again by the same useless prick that got me pregnant with the first one! You'd think I'd learn my lesson by now. How about you? I heard Scott's out.'

'Yeah, he is.'

Emily tugged at Kelly's hand as Lynsey's two boys ran towards the bench that sat forlornly in what was meant to be a garden area in the middle of the square. Kelly reached in her handbag for the sweets she'd bought earlier.

'Share them out,' she shouted after Emily's little figure as she raced after them.

'It takes some getting used to,' Lynsey added knowingly. 'My Steve has gone down again. He's been ringing cars, got six months – left me holding the baby.' She roared with laughter at her joke. 'Literally!'

Kelly tried to keep her facial expressions impartial. Deep inside she was horrified. There was no way she was sticking around if Scott got sent to prison for the second time.

'Things seem to be getting back to normal,' she decided to say.

In a sad way, it was true. Kelly cast her mind back to yesterday as she watched Emily busy handing out sweets to the boys. Sunday evening, one of only two nights off that she had, and Scott had disappeared again. He'd eaten his tea, grabbed his keys and said he was going to see a man about a dog. No amount of nagging had stopped him. He'd gone out regardless, coming back after midnight when she'd been lying awake in bed. He'd tried to cuddle up to her but the smell of ale had repulsed her and he'd finally got the message.

'Kieran! Gerrof that wall. You'll break your bleeding neck if you fall!' Lynsey screeched at the top of her voice. She turned back to Kelly. 'You should think about dropping another one.'

Kelly managed to stop her head shaking from side to side. Emily was always pleading for a little sister, but there were no plans on her behalf to increase the family.

'How's Jay?' she asked, to change the subject.

Lynsey threw a thumb over her sunburnt shoulder towards the car park. 'Ask him yourself, he's over there waiting for us. He might cheer up when he sees you. Your name always did make his eyes sparkle. He's been a right moody bastard lately, don't know what's got into him. Unless it's something to do with that bird he's been seeing. Frankly, you'd think a few dates would cheer him up.'

'Anyone we know?' Kelly tried to sound casual.

Before Lynsey could reply, the boys came rushing over and Emily followed shortly afterwards.

'Mummy, can we go home now?' she wanted to know.

Lynsey turned the buggy around and started to walk towards the car park. 'Come over with me,' she said. 'Jay will give you a lift.'

Kelly shook her head but it was too late. Lynsey was away before she had time to decline. Quickly, she rubbed a finger underneath both eyes to remove any trace of rogue mascara.

By the time she got to the car, Lynsey was collapsing the buggy and had the baby shoved precariously under her arm as she ushered the boys into the back seats.

'Taxi for Winterton?' Jay said with a smile that made Kelly's insides do something weird. She noticed his sideburns were slightly longer and his hair a little shorter.

Jay clucked Emily under the chin as she hung onto the open window. 'Can we come with you, Jay?' she asked.

'Of course you can, monster, but you'll have to sit on your mum's knee until we drop the kids off.' Jay looked up at Kelly. 'It's only a couple of streets, though. She'll be okay.'

'Kelly's been asking how you are,' Lynsey informed her brother as he reversed out of the parking space once they were all in. 'I told her I've fixed you up and you don't seem very grateful.' She leant forward and nudged Jay's shoulder. 'Lisa's really nice. She'll do until something better comes along, won't she?'

'Although I'm grateful for your help, little sis,' Jay flicked his eyes upwards towards the rear mirror, 'I'm quite capable of finding my own dates, thanks very much.'

'But you've been moping around for ages!'

'I haven't.'

'You have!' Lynsey nudged Kelly this time. 'Want me to tell you what I think? I think someone we don't know about has broken his heart.'

'Lynsey!' Jay cried. 'Do us a favour and shut your mouth.'

'You've only got yourself to blame. You won't tell me what's going on.'

Once the tribe had been dropped off, it was only a few minutes' drive to Clarence Avenue. Almost immediately, the friendly banter that had been present disappeared. Jay turned the radio up to drown out their silence and Kelly concentrated on looking at the passing gardens. Emily was busy singing to some rapper song. Kelly felt slightly alarmed that she knew most of the words.

'So how are tricks?' Jay spoke first.

'Strange,' Kelly admitted. 'I feel like I've been taken over by an alien.'

Jay eyed her with a frown.

'I mean.... it's....' She sighed. How could she explain to Jay, of all people, that she couldn't get used to having Scott around again? 'I mean that it's weird. I suppose things will settle down eventually.'

Jay nodded. 'I thought you seemed low. You don't seem your usual sparkly self.'

Another silence fell between them. Kelly wound down the window to let in some air but it wasn't simply the sun that was making her feel warm. Here she was talking to a man who two weeks previous had told her that he loved her and then picked up his best mate from prison. A man who she now couldn't get off her mind; a man, she was mortified to grasp, who had moved on to someone else to forget her.

Kelly wanted to ask him everything about this new woman. She wanted to know what she looked like, how old she was. Did she have any children? Did she live local; did he share pizzas with her and laugh at episodes of *Hot in Cleveland*? She wanted to know if they had the same tastes in music, if she made him smile.

Kelly wanted to know everything, but she wasn't going to ask – although she couldn't resist asking one question. She kept her tone as even as a friend to a friend would.

'So, this woman you're dating, is she nice?'

'You mean Lisa?' Jay laughed. 'That's my baby sister's way of saying I'm a saddo. As if I'd want to be with anyone at the moment. She's okay, I suppose, but I need to sort my head out first.'

Kelly studied the gardens again, not knowing if she was relieved or jealous. Either way, she had no right to be feeling like that. She was going home to Scott.

Jay pulled up outside the flat and got out of the car.

'Coffee?' Kelly checked her watch to see that it was almost eleven o' clock. 'Scott will probably still be in bed though, but if you come in he's bound to get up.'

Jay shook his head. 'I'd better not. I'm...'

Emily rushed around and threw herself at his legs. 'I miss you!' She squeezed Jay as hard as she could.

Jay picked her up and hugged her back. 'I miss you too, my little angel. I hope you're looking after your mum.'

'When are you coming to see us again?'

Jay glanced at Kelly long enough for her heart to skip a beat.

'Jay's a busy man,' she told her. 'He can't keep calling on us every two minutes.'

Emily shrugged herself down Jay's body. She tugged down her red T-shirt that had risen up to expose her midriff. 'He used to,' she said with a sulk.

As Jay ruffled Emily's hair, Kelly gathered up her shopping bags. 'Come on, Em.' She held out a hand.

Emily huffed. Watching her reach up to Jay for a goodbye kiss, Kelly only wished she could do the same. Jay caught her eye and she felt her cheeks burning.

'I'll see you, then.' She left him standing there, in case the urge to follow through took over.

Across the estate, Josie had other things on her mind as she tried to concentrate during their staff meeting. All the housing team had crammed into one of the tiny cubicles to have their monthly catch up session. It was the one time they'd be guaranteed to see the office manager.

Unlike the others, it wasn't on the tip of her tongue to let Kay know that the staff rota system she'd come up with was pathetic and wouldn't work in a month of Sundays. Josie was thinking about Stewart. She'd finally received contact from him, in the form of a handwritten letter delivered through the post. She fingered it in her skirt pocket as she recalled his words. During the first few paragraphs, he wrote that he was sorry, that he wanted to try again, but then his tone changed. It was as if he knew she wouldn't agree to him coming back so he wanted to turn the knife. Maybe it was time to get in touch with a solicitor.

'Finally, I'm sure you'll all be pleased to hear – especially you, Josie – that the local council have given the go ahead to convert the old sheltered housing block into an enterprise centre.'

Josie sat forward in her chair as she heard the words she'd been longing to hear for ages. 'How many units have they agreed to?'

'Let me see.' Kay flicked noisily through her paperwork. 'Ah, here it is. There will be twenty-seven individual offices. That'll be easy to plan as the building was originally self-contained flats. The designers thought the idea to rip out the interiors was a waste of time. They think the fact that each unit will come with its own tiny bathroom and kitchen area will be a good rental point. I happen to agree. I think people will like that.'

Ray burst into laughter. 'If you're talking about people living on the Mitchell Estate, you must be joking.'

Kay shot him a filthy look. 'As usual, you see the brighter side of things. It will give people on the estate something to work towards, something to aspire to.'

Ray slid further down into his seat. 'You're forgetting one thing. There's no work in anyone who lives on the Mitchell Estate. That's *why* they live here.'

'That's why *you* work here,' Doug mocked. Even Ray laughed at that.

But Josie hadn't been listening to the bickering. She'd wondered why the gates had been open the other day as she'd driven past the site. She'd been meaning to report it to one of the community wardens so that they could check it out but, once back in the throes of the office, she'd forgotten all about it. All of a sudden, her mind had gone into overdrive at the possibilities of things to come.

The Workshop had been something Josie had been passionate to move forward. About six months ago, the local council had approached Mitchell Housing to see if they were interested in helping out with funding or expertise when the centre was open.

Josie had been chosen as a representative to speak on behalf of the association. With every meeting she'd attended, she'd come away more enthusiastic than the last. This could be a perfect chance to get the estate a better name for itself. Never mind what the likes of Ray thought, there were lots of people who wanted to work but, with all the factories and skilled jobs disappearing at a steady rate, there were less opportunities. This centre could be a lifeline for a lot of them, and Josie would see to it that one of her tenants didn't miss out on her big break. This was perfect for Kelly.

'Josie?' Kay clicked her fingers.

Josie shook her head and had a guess at what she'd been asked. 'I'm not sure?' she attempted.

Kay grinned. 'I asked you if you'd like to represent us still. Yes?'

Josie nodded, looking a little sheepish. She checked her watch and made a mental note to try and concentrate on what was being said for the rest of the meeting. It was eleven-thirty: they'd be finished by lunch, and then she could nip around to see Kelly. She had some seeds to plant.

CHAPTER TWENTY-ONE

'Bloody hell, Josie, I thought you were going to bang the door down,' Kelly cried. 'Where's the fire?'

Josie followed her up the stairs. 'I've got some fantastic news.' She paused as she set a foot on the landing. 'Scott isn't in, is he? I forgot to check.'

Kelly huffed. 'I haven't spoken to him since last night. He went out after he'd eaten and I was in bed by the time he came in. He was in bed when I went to the shops this morning and gone by the time I got back. Passing ships we are, but it's better than arguing, I suppose.

'So, what's got you so excited?' she asked, after Josie had shared an imaginary cup of tea with Emily. Kelly swapped it for a mug of coffee and sat down next to her.

'You know the old housing block on Davy Road?'

Kelly shook her head.

'No, I don't suppose you would. Anyway, it's been empty for over a year now. It used to be a sheltered housing block until the local authority deemed it too expensive to maintain. All the residents have moved out now into another purpose built block – Poplar Village, it's a fabulous place – which leaves the whole building for developing. I've just been told that the council have finally agreed to develop the site into business units for the people on the estate. All the units will come with reduced rates and a grant to set up any new business for the first twelve months.'

Josie paused for breath as well as dramatic effect, but it was completely lost on Kelly. She pointed at her.

'You,' she said, 'could open your own secretarial business. There will be room for twenty-seven individual businesses. Those businesses will all need letters typing, telephone calls answering, photocopying, filing etc. You could provide all these things at a low cost. You could do it on a part time basis until all the units are full, which will give you time to learn your skills and gain confidence. You'll be able to –'

Kelly held up a hand for Josie to stop. 'Slow down, will you? Emily, turn the television down for a minute, please?'

'But I'm watching –'

'*Dora the Explorer* will have to wait, sweetheart. Mummy needs to hear this.'

With the volume lowered yet Emily still engrossed, Josie slowed down long enough to explain it all to Kelly again.

'It's a perfect opportunity,' she said afterwards. 'You'll be able to base yourself in one of the rooms. Your clients –' Josie noticed the hint of a smile at the word – 'will come to you. They'll be able to divert their phones to you so that you can take messages for them. It means that they won't miss important calls because they aren't in the office. You can be everyone's personal secretary at the same time.'

'Do you really think I could do that?' Kelly latched on to Josie's enthusiasm. 'Wouldn't it be beyond me?'

'Of course not! I'd help you wherever I could. Once you've set it up, it'll be a doddle, you'll see.'

Kelly certainly did see. Immediately, she pictured herself in her own office typing into a computer. She'd be taking messages for the printing firm, typing letters for the catering business, making up invoices for the plumbers. Maybe she'd need her *own* personal assistant as the business grew and grew. But then reality hit Kelly with a thud.

'I'm not sure I can convince Scott it will be a good idea.'

'Then don't tell him until it's too late. He'll have to deal with it, then.' Josie put down her coffee. 'You can do this. It's a perfect chance for you to get off benefits completely and run your own business. How does that sound?'

'Like a bloody nightmare, if you ask me.' Kelly stood up. 'I can't do it.'

Josie wasn't perturbed as she'd been expecting some resistance. 'Then tell him,' she said. 'Tell him the truth, tell him a lie, tell him anything but don't miss out. This could be your chance.'

Kelly's shoulders drooped.

'I'll be there every step of the way, if you let me,' Josie urged. 'Just tell me you'll think about it.'

But there wasn't time to talk anymore as they heard the front door open and close. Before either of them could react, Scott came bounding into the living room.

'What the fuck's she doing here?' he said, freezing in mid-step as he locked eyes with Josie.

'Morning to you too,' Josie replied sarcastically.

'She came to bring me a new rent card,' Kelly improvised, throwing Josie a warning glare. 'I've lost mine.'

'Daddy,' said Emily. 'I'm watching *Dora the Explorer*.'

Scott ignored his daughter and grabbed the TV remote control. 'You shouldn't have to pay any rent.' The room erupted with the sound of music. Emily folded her arms and frowned.

Josie stood up. 'Some people like to earn their keep, Mr Johnstone. What have you done towards yours today?'

Kelly groaned inwardly. The last thing she needed was Josie antagonising Scott. She could tell by his face that he was after a fight and, by the colour of his skin, he looked like he was still in hangover mode.

'Josie was just leaving.' Kelly nodded towards the door.

'More likely she's checking up on me.' Scott threw Josie a look of revulsion. 'I'm surprised to see you here at this time of day. I have housing officers for dinner.'

'I'd spit the likes of you out if I had to eat you,' Josie threw back. 'I'm sure you'd be bitter to your core.'

'Are you mad?' Kelly whispered loudly once they were out of the room. 'Don't make it worse for me than it already is.'

Josie coloured. The sight of Scott Johnstone alone was enough to make her blood boil but she hadn't for one moment thought how her actions could affect Kelly.

'I'm sorry.' She gave a half-smile in apology. 'But sometimes I wonder what you're doing with the likes of him. You're far too good for him. Surely you can see that?'

'That's rich, coming from you. You ought to try getting your own house in order before you start telling me what to do.'

'What's that supposed to mean?'

'Oh, go, will you. I've got enough problems of my own to deal with at the moment.'

'Call me, if you need me!' were the last words Josie said but Kelly had already closed the door.

For a moment, Josie stood on the step. What a waste of an opportunity if Kelly didn't think about what she'd said. She was intelligent and determined; she had absolute faith in her. Still, she could just need a bit of time to think it over. Kelly might deduce that it was a good idea and that she did have the necessary skills to follow it through. It was only her job to plant the seed.

Suddenly she stopped as she went back over Kelly's words. What did she mean by getting her own house in order?

'What the fuck was she doing here?'

'I told you before,' said Kelly. 'I needed a new rent card. Where have you been this morning?'

Scott grabbed her wrist as she bent to pick up Josie's mug. 'Don't change the subject. I don't want her calling again. Do you hear?'

'Yes, I hear you but it isn't going to happen.' Kelly shrugged her arm loose. 'This is my flat, remember?'

'No, it's *our* flat. I let you stay at my house for years, now you can do the same.'

'I stayed at *your* house to look after our daughter! A daughter you seem to have conveniently forgotten since you've got back.'

Scott slouched down onto the settee. 'Don't bring that up again. I told you, I don't like how she's wary of me. It's taking me time to adjust, too. Everything's changed since I went inside.' He pointed at her with the remote control. 'You, for starters. You used to be so... so –'

'Gullible?' Kelly finished the sentence for him.

'I was going to say trusting.'

'Isn't that the same thing?'

Scott pursed his lips. 'You're pushing me away with all this namby-pamby, goody-goody talk. I hardly know you now.'

'That's because I've had to fend for myself for three months,'

Kelly snapped. 'Where were you then? And if you're so bothered about looking after me and Em, where do you keep disappearing to?'

Scott refused to look at her as she continued.

'How the hell do you think I felt when I was told I had to leave Patrick Street? I saw this place and thought my life was over. But do you know what spurred me on? I wanted to make it nice for when you got back. I was hoping things would be okay again.'

'You put the dampers on that when you started working.' Scott spit out the word as if it were a disease. 'Do you know how many years it's taken me to get the social off my back and stop sending me to job interviews?'

Kelly shook her head in frustration. 'What's wrong with getting a job?' she said. 'What's so wrong with having a bit of spare money?'

Scott stared at her, wide-eyed. 'Have you ever gone without when I was here?'

'No, but –'

'You had new clothes, a nice house, furniture, a flat-screen TV. Half the people on this estate will never have as much.'

'I went without you! Why can't you get that into your thick skull? I went without you for three months. I don't want to do that again.'

Emily's face appeared around the door frame, her bottom lip trembling. Kelly ushered her over, sat down and pulled her daughter onto her lap. Emily sunk into her chest and began to suck her thumb.

'Look at her,' Kelly urged Scott. 'The only reason she won't get close to you is because she's frightened you might leave again – and so am I.'

'I won't get caught next time.'

'And that's supposed to make me feel better?' Kelly eyed him with disdain. 'There will always be one more job, and one more after that. You know there will.'

'I don't know why you keep moaning, you'll both benefit from them.'

'I don't want your kind of handouts,' Kelly hissed.

'It's never stopped you before.'

'I had no choice then.'

Suddenly, Scott leaned forward. 'What's up? Lost your faith in me?'

Kelly wanted to tell him she'd lost faith in him a long time ago, but knew it would do more harm than good. She knew no matter what she said, he'd bite back. Instead, she stared at him. It was like looking at a stranger. How could two people change so much in three months?

Scott stood up. 'Fine!' he said. 'Have it your own fucking way.' He glared at her for a moment before storming out of the flat.

Only then did Kelly feel Emily relax in her arms.

That evening, most of the Mitchell Housing Association staff had been out for a meal to celebrate Debbie's birthday. It had been pleasant with lots of light-hearted banter, and exactly what Josie needed. She'd laughed so much that her cheeks had ached. By the time, she'd dropped Debbie and Irene off at their homes, it was past midnight.

It had felt so good to have a night out on her own without all the feelings of guilt, knowing that she wouldn't be coming home to Stewart's miserable face, even though she knew she had that to contend with tomorrow. Earlier, on the way to the restaurant, Josie had called at Miles' Factory and left a letter with his foreman to give to him. Rather than get a solicitor involved straightaway, she'd decided to offer him a lump sum.

As she got to the front door, Stewart stepped out from the side of the garage.

'Jesus, you idiot!' Josie pressed her hand to her chest. 'You nearly gave me a heart attack.'

In two more strides, Stewart stood in front of her. 'What the fuck is this?' He held up the letter.

Josie took another step towards the door while she gained her composure. 'If you're referring to the amount,' she said, 'it's all I'm prepared to offer.'

'Ten grand? It's not enough.' Stewart's fists clenched and unclenched. 'Five fucking years I stayed with you. I want my half.'

'Don't be ridiculous,' she told him. 'You may have contributed a little but the house was *mine* to begin with.'

'I want my half!'

'You're not entitled to half.'

'I'm going to sue you for every penny.'

'Fine, you'll have to find the money to fight me for it. I am not giving *you* half of what my parents worked for because you happened to see another opportunity to exploit me.'

Stewart's chin nearly hit the tarmac. 'I never exploited you,' he said.

'You never loved me, either,' Josie muttered. An uneasy silence descended between them. 'Did you?'

Stewart slowly shook his head from side to side. 'Do you think *I'd* love someone like *you*?' He picked up a mound of Josie's hair, and then let it go. 'Your hair's like straw.' He stepped back and looked at her from top to toe. 'Your body's like a twelve-year-old and your sense of style – well, let's say you haven't got one. Face it, Josie, you're a dowdy bitch.'

Josie faltered. It was all right for her to think these things, *know* these things, but never, ever, had Stewart voiced his abhorrence. What made it worse was the fact that she thought she'd dressed accordingly for a night out. She wore faded jeans, black shoes with a small block heel and a plain red t-shirt. Her hair, although she had tried to do something with it, hung loose and forlorn. She'd attempted to wear make-up, but knew she didn't have the know-how to make a good job.

'Well,' she spoke shakily in her defence, 'you haven't got that much to offer yourself. Look at *you*.'

Josie knew she'd lost the fight even as she pointed at him. Stewart had obviously been spending some of his money because he was wearing jeans she hadn't seen before, his shoes were the most wanted brand of many a teenager and his T-shirt bore the name of a well-known designer. Even his hair had been cut recently.

'Yes, look at me,' Stewart smirked. 'You thought I'd shrivel up and die but I'm doing all right without you.' In one quick movement, he screwed up the letter and threw it at her feet. 'So, there's no way I'm leaving you alone until I get what I deserve. I hope you've got that!'

Josie's tears fell as soon as she closed the front door behind her. Her breath coming in huge gulps, she ran into the living room and flung herself onto the settee. What had she done to deserve this treatment? All she'd ever wanted was to be loved and to give that love back in return. Even her huge heart couldn't bat away Stewart's insults – and because she knew he was right, they hurt all the more.

She knew she was a mess. Meeting up with Livvy again had made her more aware of that. And if Livvy wasn't enough, there was always Kelly to look at: Kelly with her stylish hair, her curvy figure and her youthful complexion. Josie had never looked that good, no matter what her age – and at thirty-seven she was never going to.

On a whim, she decided to ring Livvy.

'I'm sorry,' she sobbed. 'I know it's late but I needed to talk to someone.'

'What's the matter, hun?

At the sound of Livvy's comforting tone, Josie started to cry again. It was some time before she'd calmed down long enough to explain what had happened.

'He's trying to wind you up,' Livvy comforted. 'You shouldn't take him so seriously.'

Josie sniffed. 'So you think I look okay, then? My hair looks wonderful and shiny? My clothes don't hang off my body? I never wear make-up for fear of looking like Coco the Clown.'

Livvy pooh-poohed her thoughts. 'You have so much else, though. Number one, you have a fantastic way with people. Number two, you have a heart – that's always a good thing. Number three, you have personality. You've a knack for making me feel happier since we got back in touch, which leads me to number four: you are a caring person.'

Josie smiled at Livvy's efforts to cheer her up. It didn't alter the fact that she had scarecrow hair, but what the heck.

'And number five, you have me. I can give you a makeover, if you like? You could try a new hairstyle. I think a little shorter would suit you, perhaps stopping at your shoulders, and a fringe, maybe? And you need to make the most of your figure. So what if you're only five-foot and a fag end? That's what heels are for. You need to buy the highest pair you can find and totter around indoors until you feel comfortable in them. Believe me, there is nothing that can give you more of a confidence boost than a pair of 'fuck-off' heels. And I have plenty of tops and shirts that will fit you.' She laughed a little. 'I won't be able to help you in the trouser department, unless I can find some cropped ones. I have boxes of spare make-up, too. Luckily you're dark, like me. Well, you will be once you've visited my hair stylist.'

Josie's eyes filled with tears again. Livvy had changed into her fairy godmother.

'You need to stick up for yourself, show that useless bastard what you're made of.'

Josie nodded, even though Livvy couldn't see her. 'He caught me off guard. He's never been so... so personal.'

'He's beginning to realise that little old Josie is stronger than he thought she'd be. You'll be fine. Did you think any more about selling the house?'

'I did look into it but I'm not sure it would stop him, if I'm honest.'

'It would mean closure though if you did move. He wouldn't know where you were.'

'He'd find me.' Josie recalled how she had seen Charlotte after Nathan had attacked her; he'd found her easily enough. And it wouldn't be hard to follow her to somewhere else once she dropped her guard. Still, the idea to sell the house was one that she'd been thinking about.

'Supposing I did put it up for sale, what if it takes a long time to sell?'

'I don't think it will. It's in a good area and you have it lovely inside. Do you think he means what he says when he wants half of everything?'

Josie wiped away the tears that had escaped. 'No, I think once he sees a cheque, he'll take it and run. He won't want to wait around. He'll want to find another pathetic woman to look after his welfare.'

'Hey, less of the 'pathetic woman',' Livvy cautioned. 'You're a survivor. Don't let the likes of him get you down. I'm surprised you've stuck with him for so long, though. You're far too good for him.'

Left with her thoughts as they hung up, Josie remembered saying something similar to Kelly last week. She wondered if she was feeling any better yet. Although she'd probably made it unbearable the other day by provoking Scott, Josie genuinely hadn't thought of the consequences. She hoped that Kelly was okay and made a mental note to text her later that night.

Kelly was okay. As Josie predicted, she'd thought of nothing else but setting up her own business – so much so that it was heading for three thirty in the morning and she was tackling the ironing. Not bothering to toss and turn like she'd done for the past two nights, she'd decided to do something productive to take her mind off things. As she plodded through Emily's vast pile of T-shirts, trousers and skirts, she ran through the things she could do and the things that were stopping her.

Her own business: it sounded so cool. She'd have to design a logo to display on paperwork and business cards. She'd have to practice speaking on the phone in a professional manner. She'd have to send out invoices for the work she'd carried out and, hopefully, cash up the huge amounts of money that she'd earn every week.

She could take minutes at meetings. Later, if she continued to go to night classes, she could provide a book-keeping service; do weekly, monthly accounts. She could offer a complete business service for the small business entrepreneur. 'You do the hard work: I'll do the sums.' Eventually she could take on her own staff and loan them out to work in the other units. They could provide a portable office service by saving everything on a laptop. The options were endless.

Suddenly, she lay down the iron and reached for last week's copy of *Heat* magazine. She tore a scrap off it and wrote on it.

OFFICE OPTIONS – that could be the name of her business. Her stomach flipped over and she sat down on the settee with a thump.

But then the problems started to break through her optimism. Who would look after Emily during the day if she was working now that she couldn't trust Scott? Kelly wouldn't take liberties with her mum and even though Dot and Emily were firm friends, it was hardly fair to put on the elderly woman's good nature. An odd hour here and there to keep Dot company was one thing, but anything else would be taking advantage.

But Emily was due to start school in September. If everything was up and running with the units by July as planned, Emily's child minding would only be a problem for a few weeks at the most. She could always set her up in the centre with a colouring book. Emily would love that.

No, the biggest hurdle to overcome would be Scott. Kelly sighed. She could almost hear his mocking laughter, his look of disdain, if she as much as mentioned that the thought had even crossed her mind. He'd be convinced that *she* was the one to have gone mad. But surely she could dream?

Why couldn't he be more sympathetic towards her feelings? Since their argument last week, he'd hardly looked after Emily while she was at work anyway, but as soon as she'd got back he'd had his coat on in minutes and was out of the door. Hard habits died slowly, she surmised. Had she really let him go out this much before he'd gone to prison? Had it taken a spell inside for her to realise that she didn't like what he did, but was used to it regardless? From the moment he'd returned, all she'd wanted him to do was stay in with her and watch a DVD; share a bottle of wine and a pizza; laugh with her at some stupid sitcom.

No, no, no. Kelly shook her head to rid it of the thought that had suddenly wedged itself there, but it stayed lodged firmly in place. It wasn't Scott that she wanted to do these things with – it was Jay.

CHAPTER TWENTY-TWO

Despite her nocturnal ironing session, Kelly was still up early the next morning. While Emily was messing around in the bath, surprisingly Scott was up too.

'Don't forget I'm doing that job today.' He slurped up the leftover milk from his cornflakes. 'You'll have to stay in this morning. Jay's calling round for some gear.'

Kelly picked up Emily's pyjama top that she'd left on the settee before snapping at him. 'What gear?'

Scott sighed dramatically. 'Chill out, woman, it's only some tins of paint I got from Fosters. I had a job lot for fifty quid, sold it on for a ton.'

Kelly eyed him in disbelief. 'You sold it on to Jay and charged him *more?*'

'Don't be stupid. Jay's just dropping it off for me.' Scott dived into Emily's bedroom. Moments later, he came out tucking something into the pockets of his jeans.

'But I've got to go to the shops this morning!'

'He isn't coming 'til eleven. You'll be back by then.'

Before Kelly could complain any more, Scott had gone on his way.

As she checked her diary ready for her next appointment, Josie noticed a familiar car parked at the bottom of Clarence Avenue. She shook her head in frustration and sighed loudly. Her first call that morning had been to Martin Smith, one of the troublemakers on the estate who hated any type of authority and had a mouth like a sewer. He always made out that she was scum. His wife was no better and ever since the couple had accused Josie of being rude and abusive towards them, she'd long ago stopped going on her own. Yesterday, she'd asked Doug if he'd come with her, but he was going to the dentist first thing so wouldn't be around. So when Ray had come in this morning, she'd asked him to go with her, but he'd told her that he was too busy.

'But you know how he was with me last time,' Josie had protested as he sat down with his coffee. 'I'll make it quick, fifteen at the most. I need to sort out an alleged complaint that his youngest son's getting involved in the vandalism at the health centre.'

Ray shook his head. 'No can do. My diary's full this morning and I'm working at the bottom of the estate for most of it.'

'Ah, come on Ray. I'm not asking you to do a thousand miles, turn round for half an hour and do a thousand miles again,' Josie persisted. 'I just need you first thing, then you can shoot off.'

But Ray wasn't having any of it. Try as she might, he wouldn't be swayed. Hence Josie's annoyance at seeing his car on her patch. He'd gone out of his way for something. She started her engine and moved away from the kerb.

Ray's car was outside Amy Cartwright's flat. Glancing around as she drove past, Josie couldn't spot him anywhere, so assumed he must be in someone's home. When she rounded the bend into Penelope Drive, curiosity got the better of her. She decided to go back.

Something was going on: why would he be around here? Amy had been really off with Josie whenever she mentioned his name. She'd thought it was because Amy had done something wrong, but now she wondered if there was more to it. She'd always thought Ray was a creep but...

Oh no. He couldn't be capable of ...

Goosebumps rose all over Josie's body. She quickly locked up her car, ran up the path and knocked on the door. Her intuition had been right as she could hear shouting from inside.

'Amy?' she cried. 'Are you there?'

Josie tried the door handle and, finding it unlocked, faced a dilemma. She hadn't been invited into the property but she couldn't stand there and let something happen to Amy. The shouting became louder and, as she recognised Ray's voice, she knocked again, but this time she opened the door and went in.

The commotion was coming from inside the living room but the door was shut. To her left, Amy's bedroom door was wide open. Baby Reece was screaming but Josie couldn't see him anywhere. Amy was sitting at the top of the bed, a blank expression on her face. Her knees were drawn up to her chest and she'd pulled her nightie over them.

Josie's heart went out to her. Whatever had happened, Amy was trying to blank it out of her mind.

'Amy?' she asked gently, sitting down beside her. 'It's Josie, sweetheart. What's going on?'

Amy shook her head. Josie could still hear voices from the other room. She popped her head back into the hallway but the living room door was still shut.

'Who's in there with Ray?'

Amy shook her head again. Josie moved back to her.

'Has Ray hurt you?'

Amy's head went from side to side and she began to cry. 'Where's Reece? I want Reece.' She looked up at Josie. 'Get me Reece.'

Josie gulped. She couldn't go into the living room unless she knew what she was going in to. As hard as it was, she had to question Amy to find out more.

'Why is Reece in there, Amy? And why are you in here?'

Amy's face crumbled again. She fell into Josie's arms as the living room door flew open.

'Come here, you little bastard!' Ray shouted. Josie moved to the doorway again, just as a young lad ran past it, but Ray was quick on his tail. He jumped on his back and they both went down onto the floor.

'Ray!' Josie shouted.

Ray turned to her, a look of relief on his face. 'You have to help me out here. This bastard was –'

'He's gone mental,' the lad shouted, turning his face towards Josie. 'He's a fucking nutter, get him off me.'

As Amy pushed past her to go to Reece, Ray shouted again. 'For fuck's sake, Josie, give me a hand.'

Josie suddenly came to her senses. Even though she hadn't got a lot of time for Ray, intuition told her that he was trying to help. She pressed her knee into the lad's back and grabbed his arm.

'Call the police!' said Ray. He moved out of the way as booted feet flailed around, his captive struggling and kicking in his efforts to get away.

'No, I'll stop. Don't get the cops involved.'

'What's going on, Ray?' Josie demanded. She'd recognised Sam Pearson the minute he'd turned his head. He hung around with Amy's younger brother, Ricky.

'Ray!'

But Ray was in a different zone. 'Lock the door,' he ordered her.

'But –'

'LOCK THE FUCKING DOOR!'

Shocked into action, Josie did as she was told.

Ray grabbed the back of Sam's neck. 'Now are you going to calm down long enough to talk?'

Sam nodded and Ray's grip lessened. He fought to catch his breath and it was then that Josie noticed he was bleeding.

'Your mouth,' she said. 'Are you okay?'

Ray wiped away the blood with the sleeve of his shirt. A nudge of his knee in the side of Sam's ribs got the lad to his feet. He pointed to the living room door.

'In there, you, and this time no funny business.'

Sam did as he was told. Amy was sitting on the settee with Reece, who now that he'd been given a teething biscuit was quietly munching away, his feet bobbing up and down as he sat with his mum.

Amy, however, wasn't happy. Her body stiffened as they came into the room.

Ray pointed to the chair in the window. 'Sit there,' he said to Sam. 'That way you can't do a runner again.'

Josie noticed bruising appearing around Sam's right eye. For all of his big man attitude, and the large amount of meat he had on his frame, Sam was barely seventeen. The fight had gone. He was like a shrinking violet.

She sat down on the settee next to Amy and took Reece from her. Amy immediately pulled up her knees again, pushing her nightie over them.

Josie looked at Ray, then Sam, then back to Ray again.

'Is someone going to tell me what's going on?' she said.

'This evil little bastard has been making Amy have sex with him.'

Sam was looking scared now. Underneath his pock-marked skin, it was clear to see that the colour on his face had faded. His right hand was tapping away on the arm of the chair.

'I didn't force her, if that's what you're getting at!'

'So Amy looking away while you're pumping into her isn't forcing yourself on her?' Ray scorned.

'That isn't what happened.' Sam looked at Josie. 'I swear I didn't force her. She was up for it all the time.'

'Is this true?' Josie asked Amy. 'Did you want to have sex with Sam?'

Amy wouldn't look at anyone but she did nod her head.

'How long have you been calling around, Sam?'

Sam shrugged.

Ray tutted and folded his arms. 'I've caught him here before, once or twice. I said the last time that if I caught him here again, I'd lamp him one.'

'But Amy likes it, don't you, Amy?' said Sam.

Amy saw all eyes on her and nodded again.

Josie sighed. 'I think you'd better go,' she said to the men. 'Both of you.'

Ray sat down on the arm of the settee. 'You must be joking. I'm not –'

'Ray!' Josie motioned her head in Amy's direction. 'Can't you see she's distressed? Leave me to sort her out.'

Sam stood up pretty sharpish and moved to the door.

'And don't think you're getting away with this,' Josie told him sharply. 'I'll deal with you later.'

When Jay arrived, Kelly was in the back garden. It wasn't looking too bad now, even if it did consist of a rectangular lawn with a border. She'd done her best to add some colour by planting mixed lobelias around its perimeter but not a lot of them had flowered yet. She sat on a checked picnic rug that Dot had given to her. The weather had been good for over a week now, making Kelly's skin a golden flash of colour. Her charity shop halter-neck top looked far more inviting with a push-up bra and she'd teamed it with a skimpy pair of cut-off jeans.

'Hiya,' she greeted Jay with a wave. 'Hot enough for you?'

Jay wiped a hand across his brow. 'Yeah, I love it when it's like this.'

'Em's inside. She's been running up and down the path like a blue-arsed fly waiting for you. Her thing at the moment is making ice cubes. The second she saw your car, she dashed to fetch you a cold drink, though I'm not sure how much will be left in the glass when she gets down the stairs.'

Jay sat down next to Kelly on the rug. She flinched, his bare legs inches away from hers, and waved a hand in front of her face. Was it her or had it gone hotter all of a sudden?

'Yoo-hoo,' shouted Dot from behind them. 'I was wondering if a certain young lady would like to nip into town with me. I need to pay a few bills and I think ice-cream will be on order.'

'Ooh, yeah, that would be great,' smiled Kelly, getting up. Now she'd be able to relax in peace for a couple of hours and top up her tan. Emily never sat for longer than two minutes at a time when it was hot.

Jay was lying on the rug with his hands behind his head and his long legs crossed at the ankles when she got back. He'd slipped off his shoes, his toes busy waggling back and forth in the grass.

'Where's Scott gone?' he asked.

Kelly dropped down beside him on the rug. 'He's doing some kind of job, painting I think. I haven't seen that much of him really. He's been out more than he's been in since he came out of prison.'

Jay rested on his elbow. 'I think you're amazing,' he said.

Kelly blushed. 'Jay, please. I don't –'

'Oh, no,' Jay cut in. 'I wasn't talking about... you know. I was talking about Stephanie and Luke. I think it's great how you've accepted it.'

'Accepted what?'

'Well, you never mention them, especially Luke, so you must be cool with everything.'

Kelly frowned. 'You've lost me, Jay. Who the hell is Luke?'

Even though Jay's skin had tanned rapidly during the hot spell, Kelly watched him pale.

'Fuck,' he said at last. 'I thought you knew.'

'Stop talking in riddles. *What* did you think I knew?'

Jay looked away, knowing he'd never find the right words to articulate what he'd started. Kelly, deep in thought, was adding some of her own.

'You mean there's another reason why Scott keeps disappearing? That he isn't always at the pub so he can get away from me? That –' She broke off suddenly. 'Who the hell is Stephanie?'

'I – I –' Jay stammered.

Kelly wrapped her arms around her knees. Despite the heat of the day, she'd suddenly gone cold. 'Tell me,' she demanded. 'Tell me everything and don't miss anything out.'

For the next few minutes, Jay told Kelly about Stephanie, Scott's eight-year-old daughter and Luke, his three-year-old son.

'You're lying,' she said when Jay had finished. She eyed him with suspicion: Jay, who she thought would never hurt her; Jay, who had said he loved her – Jay, who had every reason to break them up.

'I thought you knew! I'm sorry!'

Kelly stopped, tears pouring down her face. 'You think you know me but you have no idea. If you did, you'd never think I'd be happy about my bloke having kids with someone else. A kid from a previous relationship I could handle but...' she gulped, 'but a kid who's a year younger than Emily? What do you take me for – a fucking mug?'

'I'm sorry,' Jay said again.

'And why tell me now? You could have told me when Scott was inside so I could deal with it before he got out.'

'Until five minutes ago, I wasn't aware that you *didn't* know,' he replied. 'You never mentioned them so I thought you weren't comfortable talking about them. But when you said he'd started staying out again, I thought you meant he was with Anne-Marie and the kids.'

Kelly backed away as his words sunk in. *Anne-Marie and the kids*. No, there couldn't be another woman as well. Could there?

'No... NO! For fuck's sake, Jay, what are you trying to do to me?'

Jay held up his hands. 'Whoa, don't take it out on me. I'm not the one who's got another family stashed away.'

Kelly could see from the look of anguish on his face that Jay regretted saying that as soon as the words were out, but she couldn't let him get away with it. If he wanted to get his own back on her for letting him down, then he'd done it in style. Her body started to shake as shock began to set in.

'No,' she spoke quietly. 'You're the bastard that let it slip for your own means.'

Kelly got up and ran inside. She could still hear Jay's cries as she slammed the front door shut behind her.

While Kelly's life was falling apart, Josie made two cups of tea, settled Reece down on the floor with a few toy building bricks and then sat down next to Amy on the settee.

'Do you want to tell me what's been going on?' she asked gently.

Amy shrugged. 'Nothing.'

'It certainly doesn't seem like nothing. What did Ray see when he came to your front door?'

'I wasn't doing anything wrong,' Amy spoke out immediately. 'Sam calls every day, sometimes twice a day. We have sex and then he goes.'

Josie flinched. Amy didn't seem bothered by what had happened. This was going to take some working out. Ray had seen something to make him react the way he did, but what was it?

'Do you like having sex with Sam?' she asked next.

Amy wouldn't look at her.

'It's okay. All I want to know is if you enjoy it. If you do, then that's really good. It's nothing to be ashamed of, if that's what you're thinking. Sex is good, it should be fun.'

When Amy stayed quiet, Josie wondered if she'd got the wrong end of the stick. Maybe she should try a different tack.

'But when it isn't fun, that's when it's bad. Do you understand?'

Amy nodded.

'So is sex for you good or bad?'

Amy looked up and Josie's heart lurched. Would she trust her enough to tell her the truth?

'I don't like it. Sam's not nasty to me but sometimes it hurts.'

'Did it hurt today?'

Amy nodded again.

Josie kept her anger locked deep inside. 'Now, Amy, listen to me very carefully. You don't have to have sex with Sam. You mustn't let him in again, unless you want to. Can you do that for me?'

Amy smiled then.

Moments later, tears brimmed in Josie's eyes as she watched her playing with Reece, seemingly forgetting the past hour. She wondered what to do. She'd never be able to prove that Sam had raped Amy because she wasn't sure that he had. Amy was nineteen with a mental age of a young teenager. Sam Pearson was seventeen: he wasn't much better, granted, but he was more capable of bending the truth than Amy was of telling it.

No, there was nothing legally Josie could threaten him with. But when she collared him, he wouldn't know that, would he?

CHAPTER TWENTY-THREE

When Josie left Amy's flat, she felt emotionally drained. She knew her job meant that she was there to sort out problems, but when it involved such intense episodes, sometimes it was more than she could take.

As she made her way to the shops to pick up some lunch, she thought about Amy, sitting on her bed, huddled up like a five-year-old who had lost her favourite doll. The image would stay with her for some time. She hoped Sam Pearson would leave her alone now that he'd been caught out. He was only a chancer on the estate, low enough down on the criminal hierarchy to not worry about his features after a kicking, but high enough not to want to ruin his street credibility.

And, for once, Josie was so proud of Ray. Ray had really gone up in her books today. Surprisingly, he did seem to have a heart; he'd gone out of his way to help Amy. Lord knows how she'd be able to thank him for that.

She parked her car and walked across Vincent Square towards the sandwich shop. Out of the corner of her eye, she spotted Debbie with Scott Johnstone. They looked like they were having a heated conversation. Josie waved to get her attention and pointed in the direction of the shop. Debbie joined her moments later.

'Sometimes I wish tenants would remember that we're off duty when we come across here,' Josie remarked, as she waited for her order to be wrapped. 'What's he giving you grief for this time?'

Debbie grabbed a can of coke and a bag of crisps. 'Oh, he's moaning about his benefits. Apparently he thinks he should be on more money than he is.'

'He would be if he'd signed Patrick Street over straight away.'

Debbie sighed. 'I've told him that already but you know he won't listen. He thinks he should be able to pay off fifty pence a bloody week rather than the few pounds he is paying. If it was left to me, I'd make him pay the lot in one go or take away his benefits until it was paid in full.'

Josie saw Debbie's hands shaking as she paid for her lunch.

'Hey,' she touched her arm lightly. 'Don't let him get to you. He's a piece of nothing.'

Debbie lifted her head and smiled. 'I'm fine, really.'

'I know, but sometimes it's hard not to take things personally.' Josie pointed to the glassed counter. 'Do you fancy one of those jammy, creamy doughnut things? Something gooey is always good for the soul.'

At half past three, Kelly rang and spoke to her supervisor, explaining that she wasn't feeling well enough to complete her shift that night. Like a robot, she bundled Emily off to her mum's before returning to the flat to wait for Scott. By the time he finally arrived home at quarter to eight, Kelly's suspicions were beyond question. He looked flustered when he found her sitting on the settee.

'What are you doing back?' he asked. 'You're not normally home yet.'

'Where have you been?' she demanded, ignoring his comment.

'I told you this morning I was doing a job. Then I grabbed some food at the pub.'

'And which pub would that be? The Cat and Fiddle, by any chance? I suppose that's close enough for you to visit Anne-Marie afterwards, isn't it?'

Kelly couldn't even take satisfaction from the look of incredulity on his face.

'I'm right, aren't I?' she continued. 'And we mustn't forget Stephanie and little Luke.'

'Kel, I –'

'Don't try and deny it! I know it's true.'

Kelly thumped Scott on his chest, then again and again. But Scott was too strong for her. He pushed her arms forcefully back down to her side.

'Stop it, for fuck's sake, or I'll –'

'How could you?' she sobbed, her legs barely able to take her weight. 'All I ever did was love you, look after you. Did you think of me when you were fucking her and then coming home afterwards? Unless you don't think of this as home now you're with her too.'

Scott let go of her hands and moved away. 'I was fucked up. You know I was using when I met you.'

'Did you ever stop?'

'You know I did, when Perry died.' Perry Hedley had been friends with Scott since they'd met in nursery school, right through to him dying of an overdose aged twenty-three. 'But when Em was born,' Scott carried on, 'you hardly took any notice of me.'

Kelly's face reddened. 'Don't you dare blame this on me! I was twenty-years-old with a new baby. And you treated Emily as if she was the apple of your eye.'

'She was.'

'Until Luke came along, the baby boy that every man dreams of. God, I bet you thought you were so wonderful.'

Scott pushed past her and into the kitchen. He came back moments later with a can of lager and sat down. As he took a sip, Kelly hit the can with so much force that it flew across the room, landing on its side by the window. Neither of them stopped to straighten it up as its contents oozed into a fizzy puddle on the floor.

'Back off,' Scott warned, flashing dangerous eyes her way.

But Kelly wasn't listening. 'Are you shagging her?' she wanted to know.

Scott shook his head.

'Liar! You stay away for hours on end and you expect me to believe that?'

'What do you want me to say?' he cried. 'Yeah, I have a daughter; yeah, I have a son; yeah, there is an Anne-Marie.'

Kelly wanted to hit him again. She wanted to squeeze every last breath out of his body. In the space of ten hours, her life had taken a dramatic turn for the worse. Yesterday, she'd been dreaming of setting up her own business. Today, she'd found out that her partner had set up another family.

The more she glared at him, the more bile rose in her throat.

She ran through to the bathroom where she threw up. In desperation, she grasped the rim of the toilet as all her hopes and dreams went down the pan with the vomit. Afterwards, she sat back against the wall. How could she have been so stupid? The bongo drums on the Mitchell Estate had certainly let her down this time. Scott hadn't even denied what he'd done.

Minutes later, she heard him go into their bedroom. She listened closely, then heard him opening a drawer. Then another. She got to her feet and raced through to the bedroom.

'What are you doing?' she said.

'It's obvious that you don't want me to stay here.' Scott didn't even look at her as he threw balled-up socks into a sports bag. 'I'm just getting a few things and then I'll be back for the rest.'

'You don't get to finish this.' Kelly prodded herself in the chest and screamed. 'I DO! You're a cheating bastard and I hate you. How could you do this to me? Maybe shagging someone else I could get over in time, but to have children with her? And that boy was born a year after Emily, which means... which means...' She paused for a moment. 'Oh, I get it now. That's why you were offered a house in Patrick Street – because you had access to a child.'

Scott shrugged.

'It's the oldest trick in the book. Single men don't want flats because of the stigma attached – single bloke equals druggie slash trouble-maker – so they say they need more room because they have access rights to their kids three or four times a week. You got that because of Stephanie before I met you, didn't you? You wouldn't have been offered a house so quickly any other way. You would have stayed on the waiting list or had to take a flat.'

'So what if I did? You still had it good while you were with me.'

Kelly was crying openly now but she was damned if she was letting him get away with humiliating her. She moved towards the door.

'Where are you going?' he said.

'I'm coming with you to Anne-Marie's. She needs to hear about this. And I hope she throws you out, because you deserve it. Then where will you go?'

Scott grabbed her arm and threw her down onto the bed. 'Don't fucking threaten me!'

'You're a loser,' she shouted at him. 'A fucking LOSER! Don't ever think you're coming back.'

'I wouldn't want to come back to you.' It was the last thing he said before slamming the bedroom door on his way out.

Moments later, Kelly heard the front door open and close. She pinched herself and it hurt, prompting yet more tears to fall, not just for the way he'd treated her, but for the chance of happiness she had given up with Jay. Covering her face with her hands, she sobbed.

After checking up on Amy first thing, it took Josie over half an hour to find Sam Pearson the next morning. She'd driven around all the usual haunts and hang outs before realising it was probably too early for a creature like him to be out of his pit. But just as she was about to give up, she spotted him walking towards the shops. He was alone, a skateboard under his arm. Josie tutted: he couldn't even be bothered to skate, the idle bastard. What a generation was being raised.

Like a scene from a bad cop movie, Josie slammed on her brakes, parked up her car and raced over to him.

'Hey!' She shouted to him. 'I want a word with you!'

'Fucking hell!' Sam cried, jumping away from her. 'You scared the shit out of me, you lunatic.'

'I'll do more than scare you if you go anywhere near Amy Cartwright again, you little creep.'

Sam laughed, even if it was a little uneasy. 'You haven't got a thing on me,' he said. 'Amy was gagging for it. You can't prove anything else.'

'I don't need to prove it. I've got Amy's night-dress with your DNA all over it.' Josie tried to stop herself from grinning. She sounded like a Crime Scene Investigator: Gil Grissolm would be proud of her.

'That doesn't mean owt,' Sam spat out quickly. 'I'll say she's up for it with everyone. Loads of me mates will vouch for me.'

'Even Ricky Cartwright?'

At the mention of Amy's older brother, Sam's cocky demeanour changed. Ricky Cartwright was a fighter: they both knew he'd go mad if he found out what had been happening.

'Is Reece your son?' Josie asked next. The thought had been running through her mind all morning.

'No, he's fucking not!' And with that, Sam was off. 'You're not landing me with that one,' he threw over his shoulder. 'I'll say I never touched her at all.'

'But you used that as an excuse to get her knickers off.' Josie ran to catch up with him and yanked hold of his arm. 'She'd done it once, she'd do it again? Is that what you thought?'

Sam shrugged her arm away. 'Gerrof me, you mad woman. Look, I told you it wasn't like that.'

'No, rape never is from the rapist's point of view.'

'Rape?' Sam cowered. He looked up and down the street, as if the word had been shouted, but apart from a car in the distance, there was no one around. 'I never did that! You can't say –'

'Then what would you call it?' Josie prodded a finger into his chest. 'Making mad, passionate love?'

Sam's eyes went to the floor.

'You used her. She's vulnerable and you used that for your own means.'

'I won't go round again!'

'You'll have to think of something better than that to stop me going to the police.'

Josie walked off, but Sam was quick on her tail.

'Wait! Please, I promise I'll leave her alone – I swear!'

Josie opened her car door. 'You've just told me there's no point in threatening you so I don't have a choice, do I?'

'What are you doing?' If it were possible for Sam to go any paler, it happened then as Josie reached for her mobile phone. 'Don't call the pigs!'

'But if I let you off, you'll be round Amy's like a shot.'

'I won't! I swear – please, I'll do anything.'

His words were like music to Josie's ears, but what could she do to make him understand his predicament? Her mind went blank, but she'd think of something in time. For now though, she'd let the hard-man-come-mardy-arse stew.

R u ok, Kel? Heard what happened. Text me if u want to talk. J. xx

Although they'd been out separately on their morning calls, Josie and Ray got back to the office at the same time. After they'd parked up, Ray asked how Amy was doing.

Josie locked her car and shoved her files underneath her arm. 'She seems okay, thanks. More to the point – how are you?'

Ray's hand automatically rose to the split in his lip. 'I'm okay,' he said.

'What happened to make you flip like that?'

Ray shrugged uncomfortably. He moved aside as a car pulled into the space beside him.

'I'd seen Pearson's scooter parked outside Amy's flat quite often when I'd been on my rounds.'

'That's funny,' said Josie. 'I never saw it.'

'It changed on a regular basis. Pearson would have a different one every few weeks or so. They were hot, I reckon. When Amy's heating broke down a while ago, I suppose I started to feel sorry for her. She came into reception in such a panic, as if she was going to get into trouble, so I told her I'd call round later that afternoon. When I got there, Pearson came to the door, I could see Amy was uncomfortable around him, but when I suggested that Pearson leave while I sort everything out, he grabbed Amy's arm and told me to go instead. I just saw red. That little bastard was up to no good but what I didn't know was whether Amy was okay with it. So I barged in –'

'You didn't!' Josie was shocked.

Ray looked uncomfortable again. 'They weren't, you know, exactly having sex, but I still told him to sling his hook. He told me to mind my own business, in so many words, so he felt the back of my boot up his arse.'

Josie smiled. That was more like the Ray she knew.

'I meant metaphorically,' he said, clocking her expression. 'A job's a job and I'm not losing mine over scum like him. I tried to talk to Amy about it and she froze up. And when I next collared Pearson, he practically laughed me off the shops. There were too many witnesses for me to have gone at him.'

'So how did you know when he'd be there again?'

'I kept an eye on those scooters. When I drove past last week, he'd just parked it up and was going up the path. He saw me looking and gave me the finger. That was all I needed.'

'Ray –'

'That bloody kid's not mine,' Ray joked, 'if that's what you're thinking.'

Josie smiled. 'That's the furthest thing from my mind, I just wanted to know why. You always have this big macho attitude about you. Why help Amy?'

Ray looked away for a moment. He seemed to be concentrating on a rose bush popping through the railings, hell bent on pulling the petals off one poor flower.

'She really got under my skin,' he said. 'Her face... it was so... empty. Void of any feeling. She reminded me of a lump of meat. Even prostitutes get paid for it.'

'Amy's not a prostitute!' retorted Josie, annoyed at his insinuation. An elderly man getting into his car turned his head, wondering if he'd heard her correctly.

Ray held up his hand. 'I was comparing, that's all. But you know what I mean. She's just a kid.'

Josie nodded. 'I hope Sam keeps away now. I've got nothing to use on him, except reminding him what Ricky would do if he found out. If that doesn't work, then –'

'It'll work,' Ray said, with a nod of his head.

Josie frowned. 'You seem very sure about yourself.'

They began to walk towards the staff entrance. 'I've been checking into our Mr Pearson,' Ray explained. 'He's been doing a bit of work with Scott Johnstone. Word has it he's trying to get in with the Kirkwells when they get out, stupid bastard. He thinks he's one of the main men around the estate because of it – but he's only a kid. It's a shame to see that he's taking the usual route, but maybe we can catch him early. Or maybe he'll end up in prison. At least he'll be out of our hair then. And you certainly scared him.'

'Oh?' Josie looked on in perplexity.

'He didn't give me any lip when I saw him yesterday. In fact, he looked the other way, which is unlike him. Usually he mouths off, no matter how far away he is. But yesterday he kept his head down, as if he wanted to be invisible.'

'Funny what power a word like 'rape' can have,' said Josie, feeling better about her little episode with Sam. If it kept him away from Amy, then it had been worth it. Sometimes it was okay to move down a level.

'You'll have to be very careful, Mr Harman,' she continued, wagging her finger at him. 'You're going a long way to ruining your miserable bastard reputation.'

'Don't worry,' Ray assured her with a grin as he took the steps. 'I'll be back to normal tomorrow.'

Kelly pulled herself together and went into work the following night. Now that Scott had gone, she couldn't afford to miss a shift. When Sally heard what had been going on, she threw her arms around her, causing Kelly to burst into tears again. Sally beckoned Leah over to the bench.

'I can't believe that!' Leah was shaking her head after she'd told them everything. 'I know Anne-Marie; she isn't a slag. I wouldn't be surprised if Scott hadn't told her about you either. The sneaky bastard.'

'But all this time?' Kelly sniffed. 'What an idiot I've been.'

'Don't say that,' said Sally. 'This isn't your doing, you've got to remember that. How's Emily?'

'That's the sad thing,' Kelly replied, as Julia came over with mugs of tea for them all. 'She doesn't seem bothered. In fact, if I'm honest, she seems better now that he's gone.'

'That's good then, isn't it? With him having to pick her up for visits, it means you'll be tied to him, so it might work out better if they don't see each other.'

Kelly looked on in dismay. She hadn't thought that far ahead.

'I can't deprive Em of her father,' she said. 'I'd rather be dead than see him on a regular basis but I would do it, for Emily's sake.'

Sally touched her lightly on her arm. 'You know that's not what

I mean. If Scott really is a loser, then he probably won't want to fetch her. You've got to prepare for that.'

'So what happens now?' Leah asked quietly.

Kelly sighed and blew her nose. 'I don't know. I haven't heard from him since he pissed off last night. I suppose he'll be in touch soon.'

It was then she remembered something. In his rush to get out, she wondered if Scott had remembered it too.

As soon as she got home, Kelly popped Emily into her pyjamas and they settled down together on the settee. It wasn't long before Emily was sleep. Careful not to wake her, she moved her carefully to one side and went through to her bedroom. In the cupboard over the stairs, she moved some of Emily's toys and looked to where she had last seen the box that she'd collected for Scott. To her surprise, it was still there. She pulled it out.

Scott must have been in it because some of the tape had come away now, making it easier to get her hand inside. She searched around, stretching into all four corners but there was nothing in it. Typical Scott, she thought, leaving me to tidy up his mess. She put the lid back on. Taking the box with her, she stepped backwards into Emily's room.

It was then that she saw a small plastic bag shoved inside a game that her daughter didn't use anymore. She pulled it out and looked inside. Then she gasped. Inside it were an old gentleman's watch, two gold bands slipped through a gold-link chain, and three wallets. They weren't the only items in the bag. They were on top of piles of twenty pound notes.

She sat on Emily's bed and counted the money. Once she'd finished, her hand rose to her mouth.

The total came to six thousand, two hundred and eighty pounds.

CHAPTER TWENTY-FOUR

Kelly sat on her settee in a daze. Where the hell had all of that money come from? This was more than the odd knock off bargain or earning a bit on the side that she was used to Scott doing. He must have done more than a burglary here and there to have thousands stashed away.

Then another thought struck her. Had the money come from more than one job? And if so, how long had he been keeping it away from her? And why the hell had he left it behind? Surely he still didn't think she trusted him? Not after what he'd done.

She was desperate for someone to talk to, but there was no one she could trust. She couldn't say anything about this to her parents. She couldn't ring Jay. He probably knew about it, although he hadn't mentioned anything to make her suspicious of him. She'd definitely have to keep it a secret from Josie. If Kelly was right and the money was from lots of jobs, then she might have given him an alibi. She used to cover for him all the time, say he was home with her when he'd been out until all hours.

Before she could think herself into a sleepless night, she hid the bag under the sink unit in the kitchen.

After a quiet weekend, Josie started off the week at a planner's meeting discussing The Workshop. Her head, fit to bursting full of facts and figures, dates for completion and unit sizes, couldn't spare any room to think of Kelly until lunchtime. It had shocked her to hear what Scott had been up to. She really wanted to call to see how Kelly was doing, but instead she sent a text message, reiterating that she'd be right over if she needed her.

Her mobile phone beeped moments later. Kelly had replied to say that she was holding it together for Emily's sake and that she'd be in touch soon. Josie felt relieved. She'd always thought that

Johnstone was a creep, but what he'd done to Kelly was far worse than she could put into words.

Yet, even if it had been terrible to hear Kelly so upset when she'd last visited, inside Josie had been jumping up and down with glee. If Scott did stay away for good, she was sure she'd be able to keep her on the straight and narrow. It could be the best thing that had happened. Josie felt so proud of her: she wasn't even the Kelly *she'd* met in January, never mind who Scott had made her into over the years, resigned to her lot and not prepared to fight for anything else because she felt she didn't deserve any better. Josie knew she'd have a hard job to get rid of Scott – you don't get rid of scum like him without a fight. She only hoped that Kelly would be strong enough to stand her ground, whatever she decided. She made a note on her pad to check out the benefits he was getting. He wasn't going to get away with anything if she could help it.

Her office phone rang next. It was one of the revenue officers asking her to visit a tenant who had rent arrears. Before she knew it, Josie was thrust into her work again. She had another eviction pending, one that she didn't want to happen and was going to do her best to stop – the family had been torn apart by the death of their six-year-old son from leukaemia and, since then, everything had gone to pot. Josie hoped they would see her first. Maybe she could make things more comfortable for them over time.

Next, she conducted an interview with the Bradley twins. They were acting as if they owned Stanley Avenue again. Neighbours had been complaining about the teenagers' shouting foul language, throwing bricks and bottles, scratching cars. Luckily for her, getting Gina Bradley onto her turf always subdued her, so it hadn't been too much of an ordeal.

Then she gave Amy a quick call. She hadn't seen her for a couple of days and wanted to know if she was okay. Amy had surprised her by answering the phone in a chirpy manner, letting her know instantly that she was feeling happier. It seemed like Sam Pearson was keeping his promise.

It was four thirty when Josie next checked her watch and she gasped at the lateness. Livvy had made an appointment for her at the hairdressers for five fifteen. She switched off her computer –

stuff the groaning in tray and the overflowing desk; she'd better get a move on.

Despite the initial shock of being handed her own fairy godmother, Josie had been pleasantly surprised to find that Livvy hadn't wanted to railroad her into anything she didn't want to do. 'One step at a time', she'd said to her when she'd told her about the appointment. 'First it's a good cut and colour and then I'll take you shopping.' Josie felt nervous about it, but trusted Livvy not to fit her out like a teenager. Besides that, she had never shown an interest in what was fashionable, so she wouldn't know where to start.

Home at last a few hours later, she retrieved her things from the back seat of her car before messing with her new fringe for the umpteenth time. The stylist had done wonders with her thick matt of straw. After telling him exactly what she didn't want, Josie had left him to decide on a longer version of a geometric bob with a short fringe and, after straightening and smoothing for quite some time, she'd been left with a shine that would compete with any supermodel on any television advert. Add to that an all-over chocolate colour strewn with honey highlights, and her transformation was complete.

She ran a hand down the side – it felt really peculiar to stop at her shoulder – and grinned. Now all she needed were the rude heels that Livvy talked about.

There was a whistle from behind her. Josie turned to see James at the end of her driveway.

'Wow, you look amazing!' he said.

Josie's hand shot up to her hair again. 'Do you think so?'

James nodded.

'Thank you.' Not used to compliments, she felt the colour rising to her cheeks.

'I think I might have to take you out to celebrate.' James threw her a flirty smile.

Josie blushed even more when she caught a whiff of his aftershave in the slight breeze. Because she was drawn to the twinkle in his eyes, she noticed a different pair of glasses, this time with a thicker frame in navy blue. A recent television advert sprang to her mind and she grinned. He must have gone to...

'What's so funny?' James asked.

'Nothing,' she told him. 'I was just admiring your glasses.'

'And I thought you were admiring me. Hey, I don't suppose you fancy joining me tonight?' he questioned. 'I'm going out with a few friends for something to eat. It's a kind of farewell meal as I'm off to America tomorrow for a while. I'm overseeing a project there – bit annoyed that I'll miss the birth of my first nephew or niece as Louise shows no signs of having the baby yet. I'm sure one more bum on a seat wouldn't make a difference.'

Josie was taken aback. It would be so easy to say yes. She hadn't eaten since dinner time and she felt as if she wanted to show off her new image. But to go out with someone she barely knew, in the company of his friends? She'd feel like a fish out of water.

'I've got a lot to do tonight,' she smiled, hoping that he wouldn't be offended by her refusal. 'Some other time, perhaps?'

James nodded. 'I'll hold you to that – in exactly two months.' He pulled out his wallet and handed her a business card. 'Maybe we could keep in touch via email? Do you have a card with your details too?'

Josie stood rooted to the spot long after James had gone. She ran a finger over his name on the card. There might not be anything in it, and she might not want to go out with another man so soon after separating from Stewart but it was certainly nice to be asked to join him.

A huge grin erupted across her face as she went into the house.

The following morning, Kelly flung open a wardrobe door and dumped the remainder of Scott's belongings on to their bed. It had been a few days since he'd left and, after badgering him with text messages telling him to pick up his things, he'd finally agreed to call round. If she packed all his stuff now, at least he wouldn't have to stay there longer than was necessary. And she knew it would be show time over the money. Even though she wasn't surprised he hadn't come back for it – she realised now that he was using the flat as a safe place to keep it – she knew he'd want it eventually.

But she wanted answers first.

She pulled out a drawer and sat down on the edge of the bed next to it all. Tears pricked her eyes again. Pants and socks were one thing but what else would he want to take with him? The television? The fridge, the microwave, the settees; even the bed she was sitting on Scott had provided. She wouldn't put it past him right now to make things as awkward as possible – even though she knew Anne-Marie would probably have it all too.

Emily chose her moment to bring out the devil. She wouldn't eat her breakfast and the cereal in her bowl ended up in a clutter on the floor. Then she refused to eat the toast that she'd wanted instead. Kelly nibbled her bottom lip to stop from yelling at her.

Scott knocked on the door less than an hour later. He bounded past her and up the stairs, leaving a sheepish-looking Jay standing on the doorstep.

'Thought I'd come as the peacekeeper,' he forced a smile.

Kelly forced a smile too as she held open the door. They could hear Scott banging drawers and opening wardrobe doors from where they were standing.

'I don't know what he's doing up there,' she said. 'I've already packed up his things.'

They went upstairs into the living room.

'Do you want to show Jay your new books, Emily?' Kelly asked. She wanted her out of the room for a moment so she could talk to him.

As Emily raced off, Jay sat down on the settee. 'I'm sorry, Kel,' he said, looking troubled. 'I wouldn't have said a word if I thought you didn't know what was going on.'

Kelly sat down too. 'I'm glad you did tell me,' she admitted. 'I wish it had been earlier.'

'I never did it for my own purposes.'

'I realise that now. It was just such a shock, but I'll get over it.' Kelly placed her hand over his and then drew it away, surprised by the intensity of their touch.

'Of course you will,' Jay replied. 'You're one of life's fighters.'

'Why do you stick with him, Jay?'

The question had plagued Kelly for some time now. Jay seemed nothing like Scott and certainly nothing resembling the reputation of his brothers. It didn't make sense. She wondered if he knew about the money.

'Jay, did you know anything about –'

'I want to watch Pingu!' Emily rushed back in with a DVD instead of the book she'd been asked to fetch. She pushed herself onto Jay's knee. 'Pingu... Pingu... Pingu. Can I, Mummy?'

The door opened and Scott came into the room.

'Daddy, where are you living now?' Emily chirped.

'Nowhere that you need to worry your head about, Em.'

'Can I come and see you?'

'Maybe when I've settled in.'

'When will that be?'

Kelly hid a smirk as her little girl played detective for her. Without being prompted, Emily asked him all the questions she wanted to know.

'Mummy says –'

'Mummy says lots of things, Emily,' Scott cut in. 'It doesn't mean they're all true.'

Kelly's eyes bore into Scott's. 'I'm not the liar in this family,' she said.

His look was cold but she held his stare. Eventually, his eyes moved around the room.

'Take what you want,' Kelly motioned with a flick of her wrist. 'If you want to deprive your child, that is.'

'I don't need any stuff.'

'Yeah, of course,' Kelly acknowledged. 'You've got it all at Anne-Marie's house. I suppose you kitted that out as well. What did you do, steal one and get one for me?'

Scott ignored her.

'Where does she live?'

'What's it got to do with you?'

'I obviously need somewhere to send your giro on to.'

'Don't worry. I'm changing my address as soon as I get out of this dump.'

'Come on, guys. Give the arguing a break, hmm?' Jay nodded his chin towards Emily, even though she seemed oblivious to anything other than the antics of the penguins.

Kelly turned towards Jay. 'He started it.'

Jay sighed. 'I can pick your giro up, if you like.'

Scott nodded. 'I can see I'm not wanted here.' Before he got to the door, he turned back. 'Don't think you're getting a penny of maintenance out of me.'

Kelly gasped in disbelief. 'She's your daughter, too!'

'What's maintenance?' Emily asked Jay. Jay shushed her.

'Your point being?' said Scott.

'You're a creep, a pathetic loser! You'd use Emily to get back at me?'

'I'm just saying, don't come running to me when you haven't got a penny to your name.'

'I managed when you were sent down!' Kelly paused, lowering her voice. 'I can manage again. And you haven't given me any money since you got out.'

'I shouldn't have come back at all,' Scott retaliated. 'It would have saved me a load of bother if I hadn't.'

Kelly pointed a finger at him. 'You came back because you thought I'd be the pushover you left behind.'

'No, I –'

'Come on, youth, let's go.' Jay put Emily on to the floor. 'I'll see you on Thursday, Kelly.'

Scott was already out of the flat when Kelly and Jay reached the bottom of the stairs.

'Call me later,' Jay insisted. 'I'm here if you need me.'

Funny, thought Kelly, that's what Josie had said, Sally too. Altogether it made Kelly realise that she didn't have to be alone. She had friends she could turn to, friends that cared about her wellbeing. It was such a wonderful feeling. But right now wasn't the time to keep contact with Jay. Emotions were running high.

'No strings attached,' Jay added into the silence.

Kelly watched him walk away, her heart hurting to see him so wounded. She pushed her hands deep into the pockets of her jeans to stop them reaching out to him. She wanted to hug him but knew he'd read more into it than he should. She might not let him go either.

As she was shutting the door, Scott reappeared. 'Now Jay's out of the way, I'll get what I really came for.' He pushed past her and ran back up the stairs.

Kelly quickly followed him. When she reached the landing, she knew he'd be in Emily's room. It was show time. She stood in the doorway with her arms folded.

'Looking for something?' she asked.

Scott threw a pile of Emily's toys across the room. 'You know bloody well what I'm after. Where the fuck's my money?'

'Tell me where it came from and I'll tell you where it is.'

Scott took a step towards her. 'Don't fuck me about. Where is it?'

'What did you do to get it?'

'That's none of your business.'

'You must have done something major to get that much. You said you'd changed your ways.'

'I had it before I went inside, remember?'

'Yeah, when I was still weak and vulnerable Kelly.'

In an instant, Scott pushed her up against the wall. His face inches from hers, he clasped her chin tightly with his right hand. Her arms flailed as his pressure intensified. Scott's eyes locked with hers and, for the first time ever, she saw what everyone else saw. Scott Johnstone, the good for nothing, the thief – not fit to be scraped off the bottom of her shoes. But she also saw Scott Johnstone the maniac, who could really hurt her if he wanted to.

'Get. Off. Me!'

Kelly tried to push him away but he was too strong. He held her there with the weight of his torso.

'You think you're the only one who's changed since I've been inside? You're not and if you know what's good for you, you'll keep your mouth shut about what's in the bag. If I hear anyone' – he squeezed Kelly's chin harder – '*anyone* talking about it, I'll rip your fucking head off. Do you hear me?'

Kelly felt tears burning her eyes. She knew she shouldn't cry and give away her weakness but she didn't know how to stop. She nodded slightly and Scott released his grip.

'Right, then. I'll ask you again, where's the bag?'

'Under the sink in the kitchen.'

Scott swiped the back of his hand across her face. Crying out in pain, Kelly dropped to her knees.

'Good answer,' he said as he left the room.

Kelly gasped for air. She cradled her cheek as she fought to gain her composure.

'Mummy, what've you done with my toys?' Emily wailed from behind her. She picked up a doll that had landed on its head in the corner of the room.

'I tripped over the box and everything fell out,' Kelly fibbed, knowing that if Emily had been older the logic of the lie wouldn't have worked. She stood up quickly. Through the window, she could see Jay sitting in his car, saw him check his watch before glancing upwards. Kelly moved back quickly. She didn't want him to see her. This was nothing to do with him, this was her fault.

Scott appeared in the doorway again, holding the bag. 'I've put it inside another bag. I'll tell Jay it's stuff for Emily.' He sneered at her. 'Now keep your nose out of my business or next time you'll find out exactly how much I've changed. That was for starters. If –'

'Everything okay up there?' Jay shouted from the bottom of the stairs.

'Yeah, I'll be down in a sec,' Scott shouted back. Then he glared at Kelly. 'See you around, babe. And remember,' he tapped the side of his nose, 'keep this out in future.'

As soon as he'd gone, Kelly ran down the stairs and locked the door. She slammed the bolts across top and bottom. Sure that she was safe, she sat down on the stairs and stared ahead at the brick wall. She wanted to bang her head against it to rid herself of all the frustration.

What the hell had gone on between them during the last ten minutes? She'd thought he'd leave her alone now that she knew about the money but her plan had backfired. And now he had the upper hand, he would use it against her.

Soft footsteps and tiny legs enveloping her body alerted her to Emily's presence.

'I love you,' she whispered as she cuddled into Kelly's back.

Kelly pulled her around to sit on her lap. 'I love you too,

monster.' Through her pain and tears, she smiled. If there was one thing guaranteed to make a parent cheerful again, it was the love of a child. Kelly would protect Emily from anything and anyone, even if that included her father, so if staying safe meant keeping her mouth shut about the money, then she would play ball.

What she needed to do now was to concentrate on a life without Scott Johnstone. Now that he wouldn't be there to stop her following her dreams, making a future for her and Emily, she could do as she pleased. And that meant talking to Josie.

Josie, meanwhile, was up to her ears in paperwork. She'd been updating her case files all morning. Now she was catching up with her emails. She scanned down the list of new ones to see if there was anything demanding her immediate attention, praying that everything could wait until another day.

Suddenly her eyes caught a benefit officer's name. Philip Matson was the subject heading. She opened the email right away. It could mean only one thing: they had a new address for him after his recent eviction. Now she could get on with his re-charge for the water damage.

As she read, Josie gasped and her hand shot to her mouth. She glanced around the office quickly to see if anyone had noticed her reaction but everyone was going about as they were before. She read the email again, thinking there must be some mistake. But she'd known that particular benefits officer for years now. Between them they had a great reputation for tying up lots of outstanding debts. Josie knew that she wouldn't be wrong. She just didn't want to believe what she was reading – because the new address she had for Philip Matson was somewhere that she had visited recently. It was where she had collected and dropped off Debbie when they'd been out for her birthday meal.

CHAPTER TWENTY-FIVE

As soon as Kelly opened her eyes the next day, she got out of bed on a mission. Papers, pens and files were spread over the living room carpet. All the thoughts swirling around in her head were written down and being worked out, if only to keep Scott away from her mind. So far she had some kind of business plan, an advertising leaflet and a price list – none of which may be viable, but she had tried. She'd drawn a huge idea for a logo, so that Emily could be kept busy colouring it in. Kelly smiled as she watched her daughter, absorbed in what she was doing, tongue sticking out as she concentrated. Two hours later, they were sat in the reception area of Mitchell Housing Association.

'Kelly, Emily! Hello,' Josie greeted her in the reception. 'To what do I owe this pleasure?'

Kelly's look was comical. 'Your hair!' she cried with wide eyes. 'It looks amazing!'

Josie ran her fingers over it again, still not used to the reaction that it got.

'You should have told me that I looked like a scarecrow,' she teased. 'Do you like it?'

'Oh, I do. It's taken years off...'

Josie grinned. 'It's okay. Everyone's put their foot in it, but I don't mind. I feel like a different person.'

They sat down in an interview cubicle. Emily was engrossed in a box of toys in the reception area.

'How are you anyway?' Josie asked, wondering if Kelly would want to talk about Scott yet.

'Okay, I suppose.'

Kelly looked a little awkward as she spoke so Josie didn't push the matter. 'Is this a social call or a business one?' she asked instead. 'I can return the favour and make you a cup of coffee, but it won't be the same.'

Kelly emptied the contents of her carrier bag on the desk. 'I've been thinking about what you said, about the business.' A look of panic crossed her face. 'I'm not too late, am I?'

Josie shook her head, pleased that her earlier seeds had been fertilised.

Kelly slid the file across to Josie.

'Office Options?' Josie raised her eyebrows. 'What a brilliant name.' She flicked through the pages in silence, every now and then catching Kelly's intense stare.

Kelly's hands felt clammy. It was like being back at school again, hoping for a good mark for an essay.

'Wow,' Josie exclaimed once she'd gone through every page. 'You've obviously thought things through.'

Kelly nodded. 'I needed something else to concentrate on. Scott's gone for good. I reckon he's moved in with that Anne-Marie, not that I care. All I'm bothered about is Emily.' Through the glassed-walls, she eyed her daughter sitting cross-legged on the floor, happily playing with an abacus. 'I don't want it to affect her.'

Josie nodded knowingly. A lot of her tenants were single parents; a lot of their children had been tearaways by the time they hit their teens.

She reached across the table and squeezed Kelly's hand. 'Emily's a good girl because you've brought her up right. If parents stay together but are always arguing, I think it does more harm than good. She settled in well when Scott left before.'

'I know, but I don't want him to forget her.'

Josie snorted. 'And you think that's a bad thing?'

'Honestly?' Kelly sighed long and loud. 'I don't know. I do think she should see her dad but, on the other hand, I don't want him to use her to get at me. I'll have to play things by ear until everything's settled down.'

'You'll work it out,' Josie assured her. 'You're one of life's fighters.'

Kelly gasped. That was exactly what Jay had said. Were her friends telepathic? Or were they simply looking out for her? She felt that warm feeling rise in her stomach again.

Josie got up as she spotted one of the workmen standing at the reception desk. 'Wait here.'

She was gone less than two minutes. When she came back into the room, she jangled a huge set of keys. 'The keys to your future. Would you be able to leave Emily at your mum's a bit earlier this afternoon? I have a few things to do first but then I can show you what I mean.'

For the first time in a long while, Kelly felt optimistic. 'Thanks,' she said sincerely. 'I couldn't have done all this without you.'

Josie batted the comment away with her hand. 'I'm sure you could.'

'No, seriously, I couldn't. You and me, we come from different backgrounds, yet, in some ways, you were right before, we're exactly the same. You didn't have to help me. I know what people think of me.'

'No,' Josie corrected her. 'You have a preconceived idea of what people think of you. That's different. In my line of work, I never judge a book by its cover. And with you, my girl, I'm following through until I get to The End.'

While there weren't many people in the office, Josie took the opportunity to grab a coffee and sit down with some case files. Something had been bugging her since she'd received the email about Philip Matson's address. She logged on to the computer system and opened her electronic calendar. Then she wrote a list of all the tenant support calls she'd carried out over the last few months. Next she opened Debbie's calendar and wrote down the dates she'd been along to visits with her. Then she began to cross reference them. She had to be sure before she decided what to do next.

Finally, she checked the list of burglaries and cross referenced those dates also. When she got to Mrs Lattimer, Josie's blood ran cold. She and Debbie had visited her two days before she was burgled. But then she remembered the conversation she'd had with Debbie the day after it had happened. '*Send her my love,*' Debbie had shouted to her as she'd left the building. Maybe she was reading too much into this notion of hers.

Yet, was it too much of a coincidence that four other tenants had been burgled shortly after she'd taken Debbie out on calls with her? Josie held her head in her hands and sighed. It couldn't be anything to do with her, could it? Not Debbie, who she'd taken under her wing? Because if it was, she wouldn't be able to live with the guilt that she had taken her into their homes.

A few hours later, Josie pulled up in front of a long building. It stood behind a grassed area, overgrown and neglected. Metal sheeting covered the windows and doors on each of its three floors, graffiti slapped across the ones on the ground floor.

'This is it?' Kelly turned to Josie with a grimace.

'Yes. Don't look so worried. It will be great when it's spruced up. It doesn't need much doing to it. All this grass,' Josie pointed in front of her, 'is coming up and it's going to be made into a car park. Access will probably have to be from Brendan Street, around the corner, as long as we don't have any objections from its residents about the extra traffic. We're consulting with them at the moment.'

Kelly followed Josie up the weed-ridden path to the entrance. Once the locks were undone, they went through double doors into a large room. With their eyes refocusing amongst the gloom, Josie walked over and flicked on a switch. The tiny strip light barely made an impact.

'I hate this vandaglaze but it does serve its purpose,' said Josie. 'I suggested that it went on the minute the building was empty, but the council said it'd be too costly – they have to pay weekly rental for it. You won't believe the amount of times they were called out because another window had been broken. In the end, it would have been cheaper to go with the original idea. They've been boarded up for six months now and the council have had hardly any problems.'

Kelly cast an eye around the depressing room. The walls were painted some kind of pale pink colour, with occasional chunks of plaster missing and black scratches around the room at knee level. The cord carpet underfoot was so thin that it felt as though it wasn't there. There was a serving hatch covered by a metal shutter on the far wall.

Kelly followed Josie through the doorway into another room similar to the one they had left.

Josie pointed at one of the walls. 'This is coming down to make the area into one huge reception. There'll be a receptionist on duty to man the desk, employed by the local council.' She pointed again. 'This will be a seating area where prospective clients can wait, with a coffee machine and a few comfy chairs, a bit more relaxing. And there'll be leaflet racks on the walls, over here, and a floor plan showing where everything is.'

They made their way down a long corridor, which seemed to have a door every five yards. Josie opened the first one and walked in.

'They used to be one-bed, self-contained flats,' she explained as she watched Kelly's face light up. 'Perfect, aren't they? They come at a fixed price, no matter what the size, and will be let on a first come first served basis. They each have their own bathroom and kitchen. We're going to leave in the loos and take out the baths – some of them are pretty disgusting – and add a partition to make a storage cupboard. The living room and bedroom are going to be converted into one room.' She pushed open another door. 'I thought you'd like to see the room that's perfect for Office Options.'

Although inside was dark because of the metal sheeting outside, Kelly turned her head to the right and, all at once, could see herself sat at a desk by the window. She turned to the left where she saw herself sat with a client, having made them coffee in her kitchen. The walls would be painted white for extra light and she could imagine the perfect pictures to decorate them. And a rug and ...

'It's right next to the main reception area,' Josie's voice broke into Kelly's thoughts. 'Outside, we're going to have small signs erected in a uniformed place on each window, which will be another form of advertising. There's also going to be a walkway directly underneath your window, so your sign will be the last one they remember as they walk in.'

Kelly smiled, daring to feel a little hope. 'It's amazing,' she said.

Josie smiled too. 'I was so pleased when I was let loose with the architect. He toured the building with me for two hours and noted down everything I said. More to the point – he acted on most of it.'

'No wonder they asked you to the meetings. I can't imagine planning anything like this. It's really cool.'

'You should give yourself more credit. I've studied your paperwork again. By the look of all the sample work in there, you've part of a marketing strategy already.'

Kelly nodded. 'After you first told me about the centre, I couldn't stop thinking about it. I really wanted to do it – believe that I could do it, rather – but Scott was in my way.'

'And now he's out of the equation?'

'Most definitely.'

'That was said with conviction.'

'I want to show him I can survive on my own but I want a dream too. So I went to the library and borrowed some books. There are so many things to look into. Do you really think I can do it?'

Josie guided her back out into the main corridor. 'Of course you can do it. I can be your mentor if you like. And I've found a grant that you can apply for. Once I have everything sorted out, I'll have even more time. It will be like a home from home.'

Kelly paused. Maybe now she could slip in a subtle question.

'Talking of home, how's that going?' she asked.

Josie shook her head. 'You don't want to know and I don't want to ruin my day by talking about it.'

Subj: Hey there
Date: 15/05/2013 20:10
From: Americanboy@bluememory.com
To: J.Mellor@MitchellHousingAssociation.co.uk

Hi Josie,
I hope you're well. Thought I'd pop you a quick line. New York is a fabulous place, even though I'm working. I'm staying with a guy called Darwin who works for the same company. I feel like I've been here for far longer than ten days. It has such a buzz

about it: no wonder they say it's addictive.
I have had time for a little sightseeing too. I've been to Central Park – it's huge: 843 acres, covering 51 blocks. It's awesome (oh my god, I'm getting the lingo already)! We also went on a 9/11 Memorial Walking Tour. They're provided by people directly affected by 9/11. It was really eerie, I can tell you.
Anyway, enough of me and my love affair with New York. How's that project of yours coming along? I would love to hear all about it, if you have the time.
PS I hope you like the photos. My favourite is the Wall Street Bull, but I'm not going to go boring you with the history of how it first arrived without a permit...
Bye for now, James

Subj: Hello
Date: 16/06/2013 10:21
From: J.Mellor@MitchellHousingAssociation.co.uk
To: Americanboy@bluememory.com

Hi James,
Thank you for the photos. Central Park looks amazing! I'd love to see the Big Apple, maybe one day. I'd also like to visit Ground Zero, morbid I know, but that's life.
Hope you enjoy the rest of your visit.
Bye for now, Josie

Josie's index finger hovered over the send button as she pondered whether to let it go into the ether or not. Only last week, Louise had mentioned that James was asking for information about her – not that he was being obsessive or anything. Louise said she'd known that he had a soft spot for Josie for some time. So it had been quite a thrill to get James' email but Josie didn't know what to make of it, nor how much to write to seem sociable but not too friendly.

She reread her reply again. Had she been too forthcoming or not open enough? There was hardly any meaning to it. She didn't know why she was worrying really. It was a message from a friend to a friend. But...

Should she send it? Should she leave it?

Should she send it? Should she leave it?

Oh what the heck. Josie pressed the send button.

CHAPTER TWENTY-SIX

On Friday morning, Kelly answered the door to find Jay standing on her doorstep.

'Great timing,' she commented. 'Scott's coming to fetch Em. I've rung him three times and he's finally agreed to make an effort.'

'That's good, isn't it?' said Jay.

Kelly shrugged. 'I'm not sure. I suppose time will tell.'

'Do you want me to stay until he's gone?'

Kelly nodded appreciatively. Jay followed Kelly into the living room where Emily lay on the settee. He ruffled her hair but she batted his hand away, too busy watching the television.

They'd had two mugs of coffee each by the time Scott finally arrived, over an hour late. Immediately, he turned on Jay.

'What are you doing here?'

'Fixing my knackered iron,' Kelly said quickly. 'You never had time, remember?'

'I was busy, remember?'

'Don't seem to recall that.'

'I only came to pick up Em, so don't start your nit-picking again.'

Jay sighed. 'Come on, Em,' he said. 'Let's get your bag while the grown-ups act like kids.'

Emily shook her head. 'I don't want to go with Daddy. He smells of beer.'

'Don't be stupid,' said Scott, unaware that he'd filled the room with his rancid breath. 'Come on, get your things. We're going.'

Emily rushed to Kelly and pushed herself between her knees. 'No, I want to stay here with Mummy and Jay. Please don't make me go, Mummy!'

Kelly's eyes filled with tears as her daughter clung to her. Exasperated, Scott grabbed for Emily's rucksack but Emily snatched it back.

'That's mine,' she sobbed and then ran to Jay. 'Can I stay here with you, Jay? We can play dominoes – you can win again.'

Scott's eyes narrowed. He looked at Jay, who by this time had Emily on his knee. Then he looked at Kelly. 'Oh, I get the picture. Quite the happy family, aren't we?'

Kelly shook her head. 'I don't know what you mean.'

'Don't deny it! I can see it in your eyes.' Scott looked back at Jay. 'You back-stabbing bastard! You're supposed to be my mate!'

Jay put Emily onto the floor but she still clung to him. He bent down and tilted her chin up.

'Em, go and play in your room for a bit, there's a good girl.'

'I... I don't have go with Daddy?'

'You don't have to do anything if you don't want to.'

Emily wiped her nose on the back of her hand before giving Scott an extremely wide berth as she left. Jay closed the door behind her.

Scott moved towards him. 'You'd better tell me what the fuck's going on, youth, or I'll –'

'Or you'll what?' Jay interrupted. 'Come on, Johnstone. I'm sick of you and your empty threats. What are you going to do?'

Kelly watched anxiously as they squared up to one another in the middle of her living room.

'You've been screwing my lady, haven't you?' Scott's face creased with rage.

'That's not true,' said Kelly.

'She's right,' said Jay. 'I've wanted to, but Kelly wasn't interested. She waited for you – fuck knows why. I've tried to persuade her otherwise but she stayed loyal to you. And what did you do? Go off and shag someone else.'

'That's got fuck all to do with you.'

'Do you know what she's gone through these past few months? I've had to watch her suffer while her whole life collapsed at her feet. She lost her home, she lost you, you dickhead, and she had no money. But did you see it break her?'

Jay looked at Kelly with such love in his eyes that she was momentarily breathless. Gulping back tears, she stood up, but Jay indicated with his hand for her to sit again.

'She stood by you!' Jay pulled back his head and laughed. 'Yes, you, you scummy bastard. I don't have a clue why the hell she'd have you when she can have me.'

Scott's top lip curled. 'You'd better back off, *mate*, or I'll kick your face all around the estate.'

'Will you two calm down?' Kelly tried, but again she went unheard.

'You think you're so fucking smart, don't you?' Scott goaded Jay.

Jay nodded. 'Yeah, I am, because I get to spend time with Kelly. I'm not sure she'll have me yet, but I'll wait.'

Scott turned once again on his friend. 'Haven't you forgotten something? Something I know about you that she doesn't? What about *your* little secret, Kirkwell? What will she think when she finds out about the other woman in *your* life?'

Jay's fist connected with the corner of Scott's right eye. It knocked him back but he stayed on his feet.

'Stop it!' Kelly shouted as Scott lunged back, scarcely missing Jay's jaw.

A fury erupted inside Jay and he caught Scott full in the face before landing a blow in his stomach. As Scott bent double, Jay drew his elbows down onto his back and, along with the cups on the coffee table, watched as he went crashing to the floor.

'Stop it!' Kelly screamed, as Jay went to punch him again. She pulled him back. 'He's not worth it!'

Jay stood for a moment while his breathing calmed. On all fours, Scott wheezed and held onto his stomach. He wiped the blood away from his top lip and spat onto the laminate flooring before getting to his feet.

Kelly felt bile rise in her throat. She stood behind Jay, knowing that he would protect her.

'I'd watch your back if I was you,' Scott threatened. 'I'll have my day.'

'Yeah, yeah, I've heard the rumours, big boy. Let's see how tough you are next month when Stevie gets out. My brother will be more than pissed off when he hears what you've been up to. So I'd watch *your* back if I were you.'

A staring competition began but it only lasted for a few seconds before Scott sloped to the door. He turned one last time to Kelly.

'You think you're something special now that you're involved with him, don't you? And that Mellor woman, that stupid housing officer that put all these pathetic ideas into your head. But you can't get away from your roots. You might think you've changed but you're nothing but scum really – you always were and you always will be.'

Before Jay could catch him again, Scott was out of the door.

Back at the office, as Josie waited for her computer to load up the system, she noticed Debbie at her desk. As she watched her, she still couldn't understand how she would be involved with Matson. Were they in a relationship or had Debbie just taken him in when he had nowhere to go? He certainly didn't seem partner material to her.

A thought crossed her mind as her eyes travelled around the office. Ray and Doug were out on the patch. Irene was covering the reception. Craig and Sonia were deep in conversation about last night's television. Josie realised it was now or never. She might not get another opportunity like this for a while.

'Debbie,' she shouted over. 'You wouldn't be a darling and make me a drink, would you, please? I'm parched.'

Debbie came over to Josie's desk. 'I'll do anything to stop the monotony of this bloody spreadsheet I'm working on.' She picked up Josie's mug. 'Coffee?'

'Thanks.' Josie nodded, trying to avoid eye contact for fear of blushing with embarrassment.

The second she was out of the room, Josie picked up a file from her desk and sidled over to Debbie's. She grabbed her mobile phone and slid it inside the file on the pretext of scanning the paperwork. As quick as she could, she navigated to the contacts screen.

Suddenly the office door opened and Irene popped her head around the frame. Josie threw down the phone as if it were a hot piece of coal.

'Mrs Summers is asking for you in reception,' said Irene. 'Shall I say that you're in or out?'

'I'll be there in a minute. She'll probably only want some form or other.'

'She won't let me get anything for her. She only wants to see you, I don't know why. I'm capable of doing that for the old –'

'I'll be there in a minute!' Josie reiterated.

With a melodramatic sigh, Irene retreated. Knowing she was running out of time, Josie grabbed the phone again, pressed a few buttons and wrote down a number. She put the phone back in its original place and sat down at her desk.

Moments later, Debbie came in with two drinks. Once they, and Josie's heartbeat, had settled down again, Josie opened Matson's file on computer. She queried a search for his contact details – and there it was.

Philip's telephone number was stored on Debbie's mobile phone.

Kelly glanced at Jay as she flipped through a magazine casually. She'd been trying to read an article about the reasoning behind plastic surgery but her mind had been elsewhere. It was eight thirty, the rain of a summer storm had recently stopped and the sky promised another warm day tomorrow.

They sat either end of the settee sharing a bottle of wine, Kelly with her legs along most of its length. Emily had gone to bed less than half an hour ago. The soulful tones of Adele played in the background: a favourite of them both, Jay had bought Kelly the CD when he'd found out.

'The other woman Scott was talking about ...' Jay began.

Kelly looked up immediately.

'My mum's not well. She suffers from bronchial asthma and is riddled with arthritis. Her hands are the worst. Her fingers are twisted and they won't go back to normal now. She sleeps downstairs in the living room so she doesn't have to tackle the stairs. I help her out as much as I can. I do all her meals, I clean the house, I do the shopping, that kind of thing, and she has carers come in twice a day to help with personal stuff. If we didn't have those women she'd have to go in a home, and I can't let that happen.'

Kelly sighed. 'So that's why you don't go to work. But I –'

Jay shook his head. 'That's why I have to leave in a rush sometimes. I'm a carer too. That's why I had to go this afternoon, to check if she's okay. I don't like to be away for too long. And that's the reason why I still live at home. My dad died when I was fifteen. Mum's sixty-eight this year and most of her life she's lived in fear of my brothers. It's better for her – for both of us, really – when they're away.'

Kelly's brow furrowed. 'So why hang around with Scott? I always thought you looked out for him.'

'He tricked me into helping him out one night. It was ages ago – I know he'd only recently met you. He'd arranged to do over a cash and carry. A guy who worked there told him where the money was kept and what time to hit the place – for a cut, of course. Nobody does something for nothing around here. Anyway, it wasn't a big place so there had hardly been any security on the site. Scott rang, asking if I'd pick him up from Daniel Street in twenty minutes.

'I was waiting for him on the road outside. I thought he'd been in the Black Horse around the corner to get an early start.' Jay pointed to his half empty glass. 'As you know, I'm not a big drinker, so I was everyone's taxi. I didn't mind so much, I suppose. I got there, with time to spare. Good old Jay, always reliable. A few minutes later, Scott walked out of the place as calm as anything. He said he wanted to go home first to get changed. On the way back, I worked out what had happened. I flipped and swung for him but Scott threatened to tell my mum that I was involved.' Jay looked on in anguish. 'Call me what you like, but I couldn't let that happen. I didn't want her to think that I was turning out to be like my brothers. It would have killed her.'

Kelly finally realised what had been troubling her for ages, the reason why everything hadn't slotted into place.

'He blackmailed you!'

Jay shrugged. 'Emotionally, I suppose. Scott said he'd tell my mum I was into everything, the same as Stevie and Michael. I didn't want her to find out I'd been a stupid prick. She felt safe with me. I'd never lie to my mum, so if she'd asked me about it, I'd have told her the truth.'

'But she would have believed you'd been conned!'

'Probably, but I couldn't chance it. I love my mum, I feel responsible for her. Lynsey doesn't go to see her unless she wants something. I'm all she has.'

'Why didn't you just deck him one and have done with it?'

'Stevie and Michael have always looked out for Scott. He'd do anything they asked him. Oh, he thinks he's one of the boys, but you should hear what they say about him when he's not there. They call him their 'lackey lad', 'the fetch-and-carrier'. So I thought I'd be better off if I stuck with him. I know Stevie and Michael look out for me but there's a fine line to tread between keeping them happy and showing my true feelings.'

'So that's why every time I've mentioned her, you've never opened up?'

'Don't be daft, that's because I'm a bloke.'

Jay's attempt at a joke was feeble. All at once, shame washed over Kelly. She remembered when Scott had first been sent to prison and Jay had been there for her. She'd thought that he lived off benefits and handouts from lucrative jobs his brothers carried out, even though he told her he couldn't stand what they did. But why would she think any different? Jay was Scott's friend, his partner in crime, surely?

It wasn't until Kelly started to spend more time with him that things hadn't tallied. What was it Josie had said to her – never judge a book by its cover? How could she have done that to Jay?

'I'm sorry,' she said. 'I put Scott up on a pedestal, settled for the life he had in mind. I had a roof over my head, a beautiful baby girl, someone to be around. Until I had to move from Patrick Street, I had stability. But he changed.' Kelly thought better of telling Jay how Scott had lashed out at her when he'd come back for his money. 'I don't like him that much now. I certainly don't feel safe with him anymore.'

They sat in silence as Adele sang of love and hurt and happiness and moving on.

'When Scott was here, I was silently screaming at you to carry on punching his lights out,' Kelly admitted.

Jay gave Kelly's toes a squeeze. 'I wish you'd yelled it out.'

'What exactly did you hear going around the estate?'

'Nothing,' sniggered Jay. 'But he looked worried about something or other, didn't he?'

Kelly smiled and shuffled along to him. Jay's eyes were telling her all she needed to know, but all the same she needed to hear it.

'Did you really mean all those things you said about me?'

Jay kissed Kelly's forehead, a light yet tender flutter of his lips. 'Do you know what, Kel? I think we've had enough surprises for tonight.'

CHAPTER TWENTY-SEVEN

'Push me higher, mummy. I'm going to fly!'

Emily had been on the swings for several minutes now. Kelly wanted to talk to her about Scott but her plan had gone wrong. For starters, the hot weather at the weekend had brought everyone out. There were kids everywhere: all six swings were full, both seesaws were in use and there were numerous kids hanging upside down on the monkey-bar frame.

Because it took her so long to get onto the swings, she decided to let Emily stay until she'd had enough. Then she would sit her down and explain things. Once Jay had left the other night, Kelly had stayed up late, trying to get her life into some sort of order. It hurt her deeply that Scott had been sleeping with someone else but it hurt her even more to think that because of it, she'd missed her chance with Jay. Jay Kirkwell was worth a million Scott Johnstones – why had she been the last to see that?

However, the most important thing for her at the moment was to reassure Emily. Kelly could only guess at how traumatic this had been for her daughter. She was only four-years-old after all, no matter how grown up she pretended to be.

Kelly pushed Emily a little higher, enjoying listening to her screams of joy. When do children start to gain their inhibitions? She wondered, was it life that took over and made things rough, got in the way of the good times, making every pleasurable memory disappear in a puff of smoke with one dreadful act?

Kelly didn't find the words to tell Emily while she played in the sandpit for ten minutes; while she skipped all the way home holding onto her hand; while they made jam sandwiches for lunch. In the end, Emily brought up the subject for her.

'Mummy, is Daddy ever coming back to live here?' she asked, spreading the gooey mess across a slice of bread.

'Would you be upset if he wasn't?' said Kelly.

Emily raised her head and frowned as if deep in thought. 'No, I like it better when there's just you and me.'

'That's good, monster, because Daddy's never coming back to live with us.'

'Where will Daddy live now?'

'He's staying with a friend of his. But don't you worry, you'll be able to see him whenever you like.'

Emily's bottom lip started to tremble. 'You won't send me to live with him, will you?'

Kelly shook her head. 'Of course I won't!'

'Not even when I'm naughty?'

Kelly bent to Emily's level and drew her tiny body into the comfort of her arms. If she squeezed a little hard, Emily didn't protest.

'Mummy and Daddy don't love each other anymore, Em, but it doesn't mean that we don't love you. You'll still be able to see Daddy, but you'll always come home to me.'

'I like it when Jay comes to see us, Mummy,' Emily seemed to be through with the subject of her father. 'You do too, don't you?'

Kelly swallowed. 'Yeah, monster, I do.'

'Jay won't stop coming to see us, will he?'

Kelly squeezed her tight again and let out a huge sigh. 'Now that I don't know the answer to.'

Josie had worried about finding Matson's phone number stored on Debbie's mobile all weekend. She'd gone over and over the details until, unable to sleep on Saturday evening, she'd got up and began to write things out. She couldn't make her mind up whether it was circumstantial evidence or the real deal. Each time she came up with the same scenario: she wasn't being stupid. She needed to speak to Andy.

As soon as she got to work on Monday morning she called him. He was there within half an hour. She led him into an interview cubicle and they sat down across the table from each other. She handed him the list of addresses that she felt suspicious about and told him everything she had found out regarding Debbie.

'This doesn't look good,' Andy said with a shake of his head.

'I'm right, aren't I?'

Andy scanned over the paperwork again. He sighed loudly before shaking his head. 'But *Debbie*?'

'I was fooled, too.' Josie lowered her eyes briefly in embarrassment. 'She's such a devious cow. I'm struggling to look at her at the moment, never mind speak to her. All the people they've hurt. I want to slap her.'

'You need to stay calm for now. Keep this to yourself and I'll do a bit of digging, see if we can link it all up. We haven't got a scrap of evidence from any of the burglaries, nor any fingerprints or sightings.'

Josie decided to tell him what she had been thinking about at the weekend. 'I'm not sure if this will work, but maybe we could set something up. If it is down to Matson, we've never known where he's going to strike next, until now. I have a bungalow that's come empty over in Ryan place. It's quiet there. How about I set it up as if someone has moved in and give Debbie clues when I'm in the office?'

Andy gnawed on his bottom lip. 'Go on,' he said.

'You know how we have a few weeks to collar tenants if they don't move in right away?'

'Because they claim benefits and then sometimes don't move in at all?'

'Yeah, or they use the address to apply for loans, white-goods and the likes – no matter how much we've pre-checked them beforehand.'

Andy nodded.

'I could say something to Debbie like, 'I've just called to see Mrs Marley but she hasn't moved in yet. I'll have to get in touch with her daughter. She hasn't put curtains up and there's a bloody TV and a microwave all still boxed up. She's asking for trouble with all these burglaries lately.' Something like that – what do you reckon?'

'Don't mention the burglaries because it might be too obvious,' Andy suggested. 'Say that she's asking for trouble or something similar.'

'Right,' said Josie. 'Then if Debbie tells Philip, it will be over to you then. Would your lot be able to set up some sort of surveillance? Catch them in the act?'

'Yeah, it's worth a shot. I'll speak to my sergeant. It would be great to clear up this case. People are so frightened on the estate.'

Josie gave him a half smile, glad she had finally got the weight off her shoulders. 'So you don't think I'm mad, then?' she asked.

Andy shook his head. 'Sadly, I don't. Though I do think you should become a police community support officer. With your mind, we'd solve far more crimes.'

Josie smiled properly this time, even though she hadn't thought of how to solve her own problems yet. 'Not for me, Andy,' she told him. 'I like to stop the crimes on the estate *before* they happen.'

But as Andy stood up to go, Josie thought of something else.

'Oh, God, you don't think he could have had anything to do with Edie Rutter's murder, do you?'

Andy sighed. 'It's highly likely, given what you've just told me.'

'But you don't have evidence from that either.'

'Not yet.' Andy shook his head. 'But leave that with me.'

As Andy left, Josie shuddered at the thought of Debbie being involved in all this – because if she was and Josie hadn't reacted quickly enough, not only would she have Edie's death on her conscience but, she realised, she could have stopped the rest of the burglaries and assaults on the estate too.

Even though the transformation of The Workshop wouldn't take many weeks to complete as most of the layout of the building would remain unchanged, fascinated by the on-going makeover, Josie took it upon herself to visit the site every day. Since she'd had a word with the project manager from the local authority and found out he was up to his ears with other work, Josie had volunteered to oversee most things. Every now and then he'd ring in to check on something, but other than that, it had been pretty much left up to her. It felt like her project now, and she'd had more input because of it – a fact that she loved. She decided to invite Kelly around to see how things were progressing.

'You'll need to wear this,' Josie handed her a yellow hard-hat before they set foot inside the building.

Kelly gazed around in awe, shocked by the amount of work that had been done already. Now that the wall had been removed in the reception area and the metal sheeting taken down from the windows, it was easier to picture a bright and airy reception area. The stained burgundy carpet had gone and there were three men plastering the walls, ready for decoration. In the main corridor, workmen walked its length and breadth, carrying all sorts of tools and accessories.

Kelly beamed at Josie. 'It's amazing,' she said. 'It looks much bigger than before.'

Josie nodded. 'It's really coming on but I've spent so much time here that I've hardly been into the office. Lord knows how much work will have piled up on my desk. Still, do you know what? I've enjoyed every minute of it. Can I get you a coffee for a change?'

Kelly rummaged inside her bag and pulled out a thermos flask and a packet of biscuits. 'I bought some, just in case.'

They made room for two little ones in the makeshift kitchen.

'So what do you think?' Josie asked, as she dunked a digestive into her drink. 'Are you pleased so far?'

Kelly nodded enthusiastically. 'But I'm still worried that I won't be up to doing it.'

'You'll be okay,' said Josie. 'And I'm sure your business grant will be approved.'

'How many applications have you had so far?'

'Fourteen at the last count.'

Kelly clapped her hands eagerly. 'Great! That means fourteen possibilities for me to work my charms on, too.'

Josie smiled. 'It's good to see you excited. So come on then, tell me what's been happening with you lately. It seems ages since I saw you. Last week flew by.'

Kelly explained the falling out between Scott and Jay and about Jay's mum and the predicament he found himself in.

Josie was flabbergasted. 'It goes to show, doesn't it? Gut feelings can be right. I always thought more of Jay. There was something I couldn't quite put my finger on.'

Kelly thought back to the conversation. 'It shocked me too at first but once I knew, everything started to make sense. Is there any way you can help them out?'

Josie nodded. 'The hardest part will be persuading Mrs Kirkwell to accept it. People are so proud. But the trick I use is to suggest a solution, plant a seed – I usually hear a ton of excuses – and then I wait for the idea to sink in. Sometimes it takes a matter of hours, sometimes days, but it always comes out in my favour.' Josie waved a hand around the room. 'I did the same with you about this place.'

Kelly laughed at her audacity. Josie was a mastermind: she *had* come round to her way of thinking eventually.

'If you ever need a favour you know where I am,' she volunteered.

'Now that you mention it, I've put you down as a member of the task and finish group to get this place right from the very beginning.' Josie rushed for her mobile as it vibrated across the worktop. 'There's a meeting to attend, once a week for the next month, until we open. You're the perfect person to put forward an idea for a crèche or after school club. It'd be great for clients and unit holders alike. Hello, Josie Mellor speaking.'

Kelly smiled as Josie moved away to take the call. Josie was so full of confidence at the moment. She seemed happy, more positive. Surely it couldn't only be a haircut and a change of environment. Although she was working in dusty, messy rooms, Josie was dressed in new clothes. She wore black tailored trousers and a fitted blouse, the jacket to the suit draped carefully over the back of her chair. Kelly had also spotted a pair of heels in the corner by the window. Josie had her work boots on now but she must have brought them here to change into whenever necessary.

Josie, however, wasn't looking happy when she disconnected the call. Momentarily, she gazed out of the tiny window to her right. It overlooked a brick wall, something she thought she might hit again and again over the coming days.

'Bad news?' Kelly questioned, noticing her distress.

'Just another nasty phone call from my bloody husband. He's now threatening to move back into my house until he gets half of everything – *half* of everything, idiot. I don't know where he got that notion from.'

'But...' Kelly was confused, 'it's your house, isn't it?'

Josie nodded.

'So he can't do that!'

'He's intent on fighting me for every penny. Stewart's really tight where money is concerned. He's told me he's willing to pay a solicitor to get what is rightly his, so I know he's serious.'

'But what about his mother?' Kelly had to bring the subject up now.

'His mother died a few years ago. I'm sure I've told you that already.'

Kelly watched as Josie stared ahead deep in thought, a frown on her face. In a matter of seconds she was faced with her worst nightmare. Should she tell Josie what she knew about Stewart? Was it really any of her business to interfere?

But how *could* she tell her?

Then again, how could she *not* tell her? How would she feel if it was kept from her?

Josie turned to her with a smile but she could see her eyes brimming with tears. Before she gave herself time to bottle out, Kelly spoke out.

'Josie, I have something to tell you.'

'When did you find this out? More to the point, *how* did you find this out? You're telling me that his mother is alive? That he pretends he isn't married to me, like I don't exist? They think he's a single bloke at the factory?'

The questions all came out at once. Kelly hardly had time to answer one before Josie fired another at her. She watched the colour fading from her face.

'It can't be true.' Josie clasped her hands together to stop them shaking. She sat down with a thump.

'I wouldn't have told you without checking everything out first,' Kelly said.

'It's not that I don't believe you.' Josie shook her head. 'Quite frankly, I wouldn't put it past Stewart to do such a thing the more I've seen of him lately. It's just that I don't want to believe he would do it to *me*.'

'I'm sorry, but I couldn't let you give away half of your house to a fuckwit like him.'

'How long have you known?'

'Since I saw that photo, the one that fell out of the books you gave to Emily.' Kelly gulped. This was the moment of truth, the moment where she'd find out if Josie hated her for not telling her sooner.

Josie's right eye twitched. 'But that was weeks ago! Why didn't you tell me then?'

'I... I... didn't know how to.'

Josie was lost for words. Her mind formed question after question. What Kelly had told her would make perfect sense to anyone who knew Stewart. He was sneaky enough, she knew that. But would even he do something as bitter and twisted as this? And why, what would be his reasoning?

'I'm sorry,' said Kelly.

But Josie didn't blame her. 'This isn't your fault. I'd have done the same thing in your predicament.'

'Really?' Kelly didn't sound convinced.

'Absolutely. Besides, knowing this allows me to be one step ahead for a while until I figure out what the hell is going on.'

As soon as Josie got home that evening, she raced up to the spare room where she had stored all of Stewart's belongings. He hadn't collected them, no matter how many times she had asked. She wondered if he thought that the longer he left them there, the more chance there was of him coming back, when in actual fact there was no chance at all. If what Kelly had told her earlier turned out to be true, his stuff would be thrown at the gates of Miles' Factory.

She checked through the things she'd bagged up for him, and inside the boxes that she had filled with items from the drawers of his desk: lots of papers, magazines, notepads and car brochures, old bill reminders. Then she paused for a moment before dashing downstairs to the hallway. Rummaging through the recent pile of mail that had accumulated in Stewart's name, she found the envelope she was after. With shaking hands, she reached inside it and pulled out the letter.

For what seemed like forever, she stood in the hallway. Still in denial, she read the salutation again.

Dear Mrs Sarah Mellor. *Mrs* S Mellor.

Was it any wonder the bank hadn't stopped sending the statements out after she'd complained? There hadn't been any mistake in their wording. The letter shouldn't have been addressed to Mr S Mellor.

Stewart's mother was called Sarah.

Mrs Sarah Mellor.

Mrs S Mellor.

Josie looked down to the bottom of the letter. The balance on the enclosed statement was twenty-two thousand, seven hundred and twenty-nine pounds. And twenty-one pence; mustn't forget the pennies.

She stared at her reflection in the full-length mirror. A deflated Josie stared back at her. A destroyed, disillusioned Josie. A bruised, a battered Josie.

An enraged Josie that was ready to erupt at any second. She went through to the living room, put on a CD and switched the volume up high. Then she screamed.

Stewart had lied to her. He'd told her his parents had died, how despicable was that! He'd used the 'death' of her mother to find common territory to play his little game. He'd conned – there could be no other word for it – his way into her life, pretending to love her. Josie couldn't work out the whys and wherefores yet, but there had to be some reason behind what he'd done.

Her mind flipped back to the night when Stewart had accused her of having an affair. He hadn't been jealous at all – just simply worried that he'd lose his place to live. How had she let him get away with it?

Josie threw herself onto the settee. Her marriage had been a sham, bogus – a set-up, if you like. And she'd fallen for it. She felt humiliated, hurt, angry and upset. Still the tears came.

Suddenly remembering their wedding album, she ran into the kitchen, pulled the photos from their cheap-plastic coverings and slashed at every one of them with a pair of scissors. Twenty six-by-fours from a disposable camera. She often wondered why she'd kept them: they'd been cheap and nasty, a reminder of the day itself. It hadn't been what she'd wanted; the marriage had been no better.

Ten minutes later, Josie pulled herself tall and turned down the CD before Mrs Clancy next door complained. From a bottle that had been open for some time, she poured a large brandy, allowing herself a moment's pleasure as it made its way down her throat. Then she gathered up her wits and sat down. She needed to think about what to do next.

CHAPTER TWENTY-EIGHT

Poplar Village was on the outskirts of the Mitchell Estate, nearly into the city centre of Stockleigh itself. The building was a little over four-years-old and set up into self-contained flats, one hundred and ten of them to be precise. Josie stood in the entrance with Kelly. They were waiting to meet Jay and his mum.

'There's an electronic door system,' Josie explained as she pressed buttons marked 'reception' and 'call' consecutively at the entrance. 'You can't get in unless you're invited or with an electronic key fob.'

Josie had found that she hadn't needed to plant a seed in Cynthia Kirkwell's mind when she'd called round to see her. Once Cynthia had seen the colour brochure that advertised Poplar Village, she'd practically packed her bags there and then.

'She's driven Jay mad going on about it,' Kelly told her, while they waited to be let in. 'It does look great, though, doesn't it?'

'Yes,' agreed Josie. 'I'm tempted to add my name to the waiting list every time I visit, ready for when I retire. I think it's the most practical use of space under one roof that I've ever seen.'

A buzzer went off and Josie grabbed for the door. 'I've found out that three people have died over the past month – sounds harsh but it's the only reason flats become empty. There's a pretty high turnover here, as you'd expect. I've blagged my way into viewing two of them. Unfortunately, it's taken me three days to get the necessary transfer paperwork filled in. I've had to put other work on hold and go back to the office to do this so you owe me big time.'

Josie had arranged to borrow a wheelchair from reception. She told Kelly to wait by the door with it while she checked her mobile to see if she had a message or an email from her solicitor. After her recent discovery plus the fiasco when she'd sent the letter by herself, she wanted to see where she legally stood before she decided what to do next about Stewart. But there was nothing yet. Looking up, she spotted Cynthia being wheeled over by Jay and went to meet them.

Cynthia waved her welcome. 'Hello, Josie. Have you got the keys? I can't wait to see them.'

'She hasn't shut up about it since you came to see her,' Jay muttered to Josie through clenched teeth.

The first flat was decorated throughout with curtains and carpets left behind too. Josie always marvelled at the way residents looked after new-build properties far better than older ones. She couldn't smell a single bad odour in here.

Cynthia touched Jay's arm. 'Help me out of this chair, son. I want to see everything standing up.'

They spent ten minutes there before moving onto the next flat. While Jay wheeled his mother along the brightly lit corridor, Josie held back and grabbed Kelly's arm.

'You and Jay seem a little close,' she said.

'He's helped me through a lot lately.' Kelly shook her head. 'We're just mates.'

'Hmm.'

'What's that supposed to mean?'

'Correct me if I'm wrong, but I thought fleeting glances were shooting across the room?'

Jay looked back over his shoulder and they both quickened their pace – but not before Josie spotted Kelly blushing.

'Tell him,' she urged, nudging Kelly a little harsher than she'd intended.

'Tell him what?'

'That you *love* him, you want to *kiss* him, you want to *marry* him.'

'You sound like a teenager.'

'You're acting like one.'

Kelly licked her tongue out at her before flouncing off dramatically.

Josie hurried ahead too; she had the keys to the next flat. 'Right, Cynthia, wait until you see the décor in *this* one.'

This flat was slightly larger than the first one. The kitchen units were a pale lemon and the walls had been painted a peach colour. The living room had a picture window at its far end and the view out of the bedroom window was of so far undeveloped fields.

'I can see cows out of the window!' Cynthia clapped her hands in delight. With Jay's help, she got out of the wheelchair again. 'It certainly beats looking at old Mrs Morrison's huge knickers on the washing line next door.'

Josie smiled. 'Old Mrs Morrison' was sixty-two, six years younger than Cynthia.

'Everything's so new,' Cynthia exclaimed next. 'Are you sure I can afford to live here? It looks pretty pricey to me.'

'Your housing benefit will cover most of it,' Josie explained. 'And the money from your allowances that you save on personal care now that it's provided here will go towards the rest.'

With a huge effort on the part of her knees, Cynthia sat down in the wheelchair again. She watched Jay, who was checking over the bathroom facilities. 'I'll be able to have a shower by myself,' she sighed.

'I think she'll have this one,' Kelly whispered to Josie. 'I know I would. It's nicer than my flat. And that indoor garden is amazing.'

'What do you think, Mum?' Jay shouted over to Cynthia.

'I love it, son,' Cynthia answered. 'When can I move my stuff in?'

'Don't you want to think about it first?' said Josie. 'It's a big decision.'

Cynthia shook her head. She reached for Jay's hand as he walked past. He stooped down to her level.

'I don't know how I would have survived this long if it wasn't for your help, Jay. At least I have one good son.'

Josie noticed Kelly and Jay sharing that look again and sniggered. Kelly threw her the evil eye before sniggering herself.

'But it's about time you lived a little,' Cynthia continued, oblivious to any goings-on. 'You deserve it after looking out for me for so long. And there are people here that I can mix with.' She winked at him. 'I'll be able to fend for myself. It's not right for me to burden myself on you. You've got your own life.'

'Are you sure, though, Mum?' asked Jay.

Cynthia smiled up at her youngest son. 'You're a good boy, Jay. I'm so lucky to have you.'

Tears glistened in Jay's eyes as Cynthia's face lit up. Josie went into the kitchen to stop her tears from falling. For so long she'd been in Jay's position being a carer, taking the rough days with the smooth. It ate at your soul every day they deteriorated. At least Josie could make things better for Cynthia – and for Jay.

Cynthia looked up at Josie expectantly when she'd gathered herself together and rejoined the group.

'He will be able to stay at the house?' she wanted to know. 'Because if he can't, I'm not moving.'

Josie nodded. 'Yes, he can stay. I can transfer the tenancy over into Jay's name once you've moved in here. He's been living there far longer than necessary.'

'Then I'll take it,' Cynthia said firmly. She pinched Jay's chin; this time, he knocked her hand away in jest.

Kelly hung back to wait for Josie while she locked the door once they were all out in the corridor.

'Do you want me to come with you?' she asked.

Josie turned towards her with a frown. 'What?'

'To see Stewart's mum. I'll come with you, if you like. That's what you want to do, isn't it?'

Josie was amazed at Kelly's insight.

'I'm not sure it would make any difference.' She sighed.

'Me neither.' Kelly shrugged. 'But it might put your mind at rest, for one thing. And it would give you more evidence to use against him. I know I'd want to know.'

Subj: It's me again!
Date: 30/05/2013 19:07
From: Americanboy@bluememory.com
To: J.Mellor@MitchellHousingAssociation.co.uk

Hi Josie,
I thought I'd let you know where I've been on my latest excursion.

I was taken on the Staten Island Ferry, where I had a perfect view of The Statue of Liberty and Ellis Island. The weather was so hot though! Last weekend we barbequed with some of their friends and also some of the people I've been working with. I've met some really lovely people. Darwin and Jorja have adopted me – they've made me feel so welcome.
Tata for now, James.
PS I've attached more photos, this place is so picturesque. The one with me and the two boys in the park - that's the twins, Warwick and Caleb. What great names aren't they?

By the middle of the week, Josie was kept busy as she surveyed the work continuing at the Workshop. Most of the sub-contractors had finished but there were still the odd painting and decorating jobs to be done before all the flooring could be fitted. Kelly was helping out too. It was good to get another opinion on how things were progressing. Eddie, the architect who had been overseeing the building work, had a great eye for walls and wood and window frames, but he had no idea on colour schemes and desk shapes, storage units and comfortable chairs.

Josie's mind, however, was buzzing with other things. There was the visit planned for Friday – she felt anxious about it already but everything at the bungalow was ready to go: empty electrical boxes on display looking as though they were still full, the odd bits of furniture but no curtains. Andy had told her that the police were setting up a 'capture house' – putting cameras in place at the bungalow for all of next weekend rather than having to keep watch. All she needed to do now was give Debbie a few subtle clues – and hope that she took the bait. Or, perhaps, hope that she didn't. She'd already arranged to take her out on a few visits on the pretext of closing as many cases as possible before The Workshop opened. Her intention was to show Debbie the goods clearly on display through the window and tell her that Mrs Marley was definitely moving in on the following Monday. It would mean that Philip Matson would have to do the robbery that weekend or miss out.

She also still had Stewart to deal with. Her solicitor had

returned her call, urging her to refer him back to them if he came to the house or sent any more letters. But she still needed to see for herself. An hour later, she picked Kelly up during her lunch break. In less than ten minutes, they were driving along a road, looking out for a number to indicate whereabouts Stewart's mum lived. Kelly had managed to find out her address pretty easily: Leah Bradley's current boyfriend was a postman.

'What if she knows all about it?' Josie said, peering at the houses. She spotted a plaque with a brass number nine on it and drove on, realising she needed the other side. 'What if there's a reason why he's kept her a secret from me? That they're in this together somehow?'

'Although I wish that was true for your sake, I very much doubt it,' Kelly said. 'Twenty-six, twenty-eight... Oh my god, she's there! I can see her.'

Josie pulled into the kerb quickly. She turned to look again just as Kelly wriggled down her seat.

'What are you doing?'

'She's in the garden. I don't want her to see me.'

'Why?'

Kelly thought about it and then pulled herself up again. 'I'm not sure, really.'

'Look, we aren't on a surveillance job for *Scott and Bailey*. Where is she? Oh shit, she's there!'

Josie wriggled down in her seat.

When she had got over the initial shock and sat upright again, for the next few minutes Josie watched the woman she assumed to be her mother-in-law winding a few straying clematis stems around a wooden frame. Then she unclipped her seatbelt.

'Where are you going?' said Kelly.

'Over to talk to her.'

'No, you can't!'

'I can't sit here and do nothing!'

'But you might upset her! And it's not her fault.'

'For all I know, she could be part of the scam.'

'What scam?' Kelly looked over at the woman and then back to

Josie. 'You've lost me. Is there something that you haven't told me?'

Josie floundered. 'No, but you have to admit, something weird is going on.'

'Yes, but she might *not* know anything. Imagine how upset she'll be then. She probably thinks Stewart's a devoted son. God knows how she'll feel when you tell her he's married to you. Even worse, he's been lying to you both for years.'

Josie stared through the windscreen. Mrs Mellor was standing up now, rubbing at her back. It made Josie realise that, although age must have shrunken her slightly, she was still tall. Like Stewart.

She reached for the door handle. 'I've got to find out the truth.'

Kelly unclipped the buckle on her seat-belt. 'Then let me come with you.'

'No. Don't worry, I won't say anything to upset her, but I do need to know.'

Josie crossed the road and stopped in front of a neat privet hedge. Her heart was beating so loud she thought everyone would be able to hear it. The woman was bending over, tending to a rhododendron bush this time. Josie watched her as she carefully dead-headed the stems, tenderly moving each branch to stop it from bouncing back to damage another.

'Excuse me?' Josie started. 'I'm sorry to trouble you, but I think I'm lost. I was wondering if you know of a Sue and Stewart Smith who live in this road.'

The woman turned towards Josie with a frown. Then she shook her head. 'I don't think I do. My son's name is Stewart but he isn't married. And our surname is Mellor – Smith, did you say?'

It took all of Josie's strength to nod her head. While the elderly lady continued to talk, surreptitiously she studied her smart appearance, hair and make-up used to enhance rather than detract from her age. But apart from that, there was no mistaking it. Josie could see Stewart's nose, his dark eyes, his long arms and fingers.

'No, I'm sorry,' the woman added, after naming most of the families in the surrounding houses. 'I don't think it's this road. Are you sure you've got the right address?'

Josie gathered herself together and smiled politely. 'I thought I had. Perhaps I'll give them a quick ring to make sure. Thank you for your time.'

Josie got back into her car, drove to the next street out of view and parked up again.

'Aaaaarrrrrrggggggghhhhhhhhhh!' She banged her fists on the steering wheel. 'Oh, Kelly, I've been so stupid!'

Kelly looked as shocked as Josie. 'I thought it would be a rumour,' she said. 'It seemed too far-fetched, too nasty, to be true. But –'

'It's her.'

'– it is her? Shit!'

Josie couldn't believe it. Stewart Mellor's mum was alive, which meant that Stewart Mellor was a lying, two-faced bastard. Josie felt sick to the pit of her stomach. How could he have done that? And not just to her, but to his mother. All in the name of money – for that's the conclusion she had drawn from this. There could be no other reason but greed.

'At least you found out now before parting with any of your money,' Kelly tried to soften the blow.

Josie nodded, tears welling in her eyes. 'You've just read my mind.'

'What are you going do now?'

'I'm not sure.' Josie started the engine again. 'But if Stewart Mellor thinks he's getting as much as a penny from me now, then he's very much mistaken.'

Subj: Home Sweet Home
Date: 05/06/2013 11:00
From: Americanboy@bluememory.com
To: J.Mellor@MitchellHousingAssociation.co.uk

Hi Josie,
Well, it had to happen. I've been here, what, weeks, and I'm... homesick. I can't tell you how much I miss baked beans, mugs of coffee without labels of 'extra skinny' or 'decaf' attached to them, Eastenders *and good old fish and chips. Even though I hardly*

ever eat them, I'm craving them! Talking about cravings, I can't wait to meet my new nephew, too. Hell, I'm even fed up of the sun, although I know you're having a run of hot weather over there.
I'm fed up of being with people most of the time. I'd like some space of my own. Ah well, at least it's only a short contract and then it's back to good old Blighty.
I haven't heard from you so I can only presume things are hectic. Either that or I'm boring you with all of my photos. I'd love to hear from you.
Tata for now, James.

Subj: Hello
Date: 05/06/2013 17:28
From: J.Mellor@MitchellHousingAssociation.co.uk
To: Americanboy@bluememory.com

Hello James,
I'm sorry it's been such a long time before I've been able to reply. I've had a lot to deal with, on a personal and professional level. The Workshop deadline date for opening is still on target for the first week in July. Things are running smoothly, so I guess something will go wrong soon! That's usually the case, isn't it? I hope you're doing well with your project.
I loved your photos. You're right, New York looks so inviting.
Bye for now, Josie.

Josie wasn't even sure if she should be replying to James' emails or not, but she didn't want him to think she was deliberately ignoring him. Besides, it had been nice to receive them, and if it took her mind off thinking about Stewart for a moment, it was worth it.

But as Stewart's face kept pushing its way to the front of her mind, still she couldn't get over what he'd done. She wanted to smash her fist right into it, make him hurt, make him bleed; make him cry out in pain. She hated him, hated everything about him.

She was annoyed with herself too, the way she'd been so

gullible, the way she'd been tricked. Then again, Stewart Mellor was a con-man. He'd used her. He'd probably never loved her.

But Stewart Mellor was going to get his come-uppance... if she could hold her nerve. She knew what she had to do.

CHAPTER TWENTY-NINE

Before heading over to The Workshop on Friday morning, Josie made her first port of call the office. Noticing Debbie wasn't in the main room, she found her eventually in the staff room.

'You still on for our visits this afternoon?' she asked, as she rummaged in the cupboard for her mug.

'Yeah.' Debbie pulled a sandwich box out of the fridge and sat down at the table. 'What time will we be back, though? I'd like to leave at four tonight.'

'Well, I might need to do a bit of detective work on Mrs Marley. She should have moved into Ryan Place by now but when I called to check, the bungalow was still empty. She's moved some of her stuff in but it's all on bloody show because there are no curtains up yet. Actually,' she turned to Debbie, praying that her face wouldn't redden too much, 'would you do me a favour and look up her daughter's phone number? If the place still looks the same when we visit, I'll give her a ring.'

'Will do.' Debbie nodded.

Josie sighed, thankful that it seemed to have gone as planned. Sadly, she knew full well that the next thing she had to do wasn't going to be easy at all.

After work that evening, Josie switched off the car engine and sat in silence as she looked across the road towards Sarah Mellor's house. Stewart's car was squashed onto the driveway. She could imagine him now, his scrawny body flat out on the settee, mug of tea by his side after a home-cooked meal with his mum. Before she could change her mind, she took out her phone.

'We need to talk,' she told him.

'I've got nothing to say. My solicitor said not to –'

'But things have changed since we last met, dear husband. I'm in my car across from your mum's house. I suggest you come out to me, unless you want me to knock on the door and introduce myself.'

She ended the call and got out of the car.

Stewart appeared in seconds. 'What the fuck are you doing here?' he cried as he crossed the road towards her. Then, 'Your hair! I –'

'– not so much of a dowdy bitch now, huh?' Josie said calmly, recalling his spiteful words. She was glad she had her new clothes on. She'd swapped her work boots for higher shoes too. 'High heels, red lipstick and a push-up bra,' Livvy had told her. 'Forget diamonds: those are a girl's best friends, by far.'

'No wonder you've stayed away from me a lot more than I thought you would since I told you to leave,' she added. 'And now it makes perfect sense why, when we met, you never took me to your place. You said you were embarrassed of it, when actually you wanted to keep everything secret.'

'How did you find out?' He reached her side of the pavement.

'About the twenty-three grand in your mum's bank account? Or the fact that she was alive and well and not dead and buried like you'd told me?' She prodded him in his chest. 'You piece of shit.'

'Keep your voice down!' Stewart looked up and down the street furtively.

'Or that no one at the factory knows of my existence and they think you live at home with your mother?' she added. "Mummy's Boy', isn't that what they call you at work?'

He grabbed her arm. 'How?'

'It doesn't matter how. I just want to know why.'

'Why what?'

'Why you hid me away, why you never told anyone you were married and why you were so ashamed of me.'

'You, you, you, it's always you, isn't it?' Stewart pointed a finger close to her face. 'What about me?'

'What about you? I'm not interested in you anymore.'

'I'm still your husband.'

Josie frowned in disbelief. 'You still have the audacity to call yourself that?'

'It's true and I have rights!'

She shrugged her arm but he held her steadfast.

'You think you're such a clever bitch working it all out, don't you?' he seethed. 'But I've still been married to you for five years and I want my reward. I haven't done anything wrong to stop me getting it, either. If you don't cough up, I'll sue you for every penny.'

'Fine, I'll go and chat to your mum,' Josie snapped. 'I'll tell her what an evil, selfish bastard she raised as a son. Sarah, that's her name, isn't it? Mrs Sarah Mellor.'

'You wouldn't do that.'

'Let go of me.'

'You wouldn't do that!' he repeated.

'Take your hands off me.'

Josie shrugged her shoulder but Stewart dug his fingers in deeper. Using all the force she could muster, she recalled what she'd been shown on a self-assertiveness course last year, caught hold of his free hand and yanked back his fingers.

Stewart yelped. His grip tightened on her arm.

Josie bent his fingers back until the tips were nearly touching his wrist.

'Let go, you mad bitch!'

'Okay.' She did as he asked – but then she brought up her hand and swiped the back of it across his face.

Taken by surprise, Stewart stumbled and fell to the pavement. He pressed his fingers to his lips and lowered his eyes to see blood.

Josie didn't stick around to see his reaction. She was halfway into her car when he caught hold of her again and swung her round to face him. Her body rigid, she waited for him to hit her but he never moved. Seconds passed before she realised he wasn't going to do anything.

From the corner of her eye, she saw Mrs Mellor rushing up her driveway.

'Stewart?' she shouted. 'What's going on across there?'

'Nothing, Mum,' he shouted back to her, having the decency to look embarrassed. 'Go on in, I'll be across in a minute.'

Josie felt her chest rising and falling rapidly. Had she really drawn blood? She had! Feeling braver now, she challenged him one last time.

'I don't think I'll ever understand why you did what you did. Staying in a marriage for five years just for convenience is weird – it's beyond belief, really. It's also devious and calculating when all the time you knew you were going to inherit money and a house from your mum. And to tell me that she had died? I wonder what she'd think about it all.'

'She won't disown me, if that's your plan.'

'I'm sure she won't. But if you don't want her to find out, then you'd better do things on my say-so.'

'What are you going to do?'

'I want a divorce – you can pay for that – and I'll decide, with the advice from my solicitor, on a figure that you may be entitled to. One that I think will be reasonable for five years of marriage – perhaps on the basis of how much you paid towards the running of the house.'

'But –'

Josie held up her hand to stop him.

'Take it or leave it,' she said calmly, 'or I will tell her everything. You have my word on that.'

Once she was safely back at home with the door locked to the world, Josie sunk into her settee and sobbed. She wondered if it was really over now that she'd had the courage to face Stewart, or whether it would all kick off again. Was she mad to have reacted in that way? But she couldn't let him get away with it, and going to his mother's house was the only shock tactic she could think of.

She glanced around the living room, wondering if she would ever recognise this house as her home. She cast her mind back to distant memories, long before Stewart had arrived on the scene – like the time her mother had surprised her with a birthday party when she'd been ten. The time when she'd fallen off her bike and landed in the ornamental pond at the bottom of the garden – it had been filled in shortly afterwards. She remembered coming home with a prize for being the best history student that year in junior school. She'd been as proud as punch, even if she had already read the book twice.

But then she remembered the constant whining, the moaning as she tried to reach out for her independence. Brenda had been livid the first time she'd worn make up, stating that no daughter of hers was wearing lipstick and mascara that made her look like a prostitute rather than a fourteen-year-old girl. Unlike most of the pupils at her school, Josie was never given pocket money to spend as she wished. A trip to the local library had to suffice for her Saturday morning jaunts.

Yet sitting here, Josie felt calm, peaceful even. She sensed a huge weight being lifted from her shoulders as she looked ahead towards a brighter future. She had some challenging days ahead – especially when sorting out the fiasco with Debbie – but, right then, she knew the new Josie could cope. The Workshop was on schedule to open in two weeks and she knew that would mean extra duties for her, which she was looking forward to, even if they would also challenge her current workload.

When she went to bed that night, Josie felt her fears and anxiety float away into the warmth of the night. Maybe she was free of Stewart at last.

Subj: Hello
Date: 14/06/2013 15:01
From: Americanboy@bluememory.com
To: J.Mellor@MitchellHousingAssociation.co.uk

Hey, not to worry. It's just great that you found the time to reply eventually. I saw an article about it in your local news online last night. You look like you have a mammoth task on your hands! I wish you luck. It's a pity I won't be back until after it has opened. PS You look like a million dollars (no pun intended).

Subj: Hello
Date: 14/06/2013 20:03
From: J.Mellor@MitchellHousingAssociation.co.uk
To: Americanboy@bluememory.com

Why thank you, kind Englishman. I hate having my photo taken but I suppose it is in the name of advertising. We have over sixty percent of the units filled now – only another forty percent to go. And guess who's left doing all the grant applications?
PS. Surely you like the new Josie better than the old one?

Subj: Re: Hello
Date: 14/06/2013 15:05
From: Americanboy@bluememory.com
To: J.Mellor@MitchellHousingAssociation.co.uk

Are you flirting with me, Ms Josie?

Subj: Re: Hello
Date: 14/06/2013 20:05
From: J.Mellor@MitchellHousingAssociation.co.uk
To: Americanboy@bluememory.com

Are you flirting with me, Mr James?

Subj: Re: Re: Hello
Date: 14/06/2013 15:06
From: Americanboy@bluememory.com
To: J.Mellor@MitchellHousingAssocition.co.uk

I might be.

Subj: Re: Re: Hello
Date: 14/06/2013 20:06
From: J.Mellor@MitchellHousingAssociation.co.uk
To: Americanboy@bluememory.com

Well, I might be then, too. Goodnight James.

Subj: Re: Re: Re: Hello
Date: 14/06/2013 15:07
From: Americanboy@bluememory.com

To: J.Mellor@MitchellHousingAssociation.co.uk

Goodnight? It's three o' clock in the afternoon here! So I'll leave you with a message for tomorrow:
Have a nice day. I'll be thinking of you.

All that weekend, Josie kept her phone on, waiting for a call or a text from Andy. He said he'd ring her if anything happened as soon as he could. When she arrived at the office on Monday morning having heard nothing from him, the first thing she checked was the weekend call-log to see if anything untoward had been reported. But there was nothing apart from one entry about the kids playing football over on Vincent Square. Debbie's desk was empty, too.

She'd just sat down at her own desk when her phone rang.

'Please tell me it worked,' she said – caller ID told her it was Andy. 'I've hardly slept this weekend.'

'It worked,' Andy told her. 'We got him.'

'I can hear you smiling down the phone.'

'Can you talk?'

'Yes, there's only me and Ray in at the minute. He's gone to make a drink.'

'No sign of Debbie?'

'No.'

'Good, I'm heading over to there soon. But there's something else. We got Scott Johnstone too.'

'What?' Josie cried, and then lowered her voice. 'At the bungalow?'

'Yes, they've been in on it together. Johnstone's admitting his part right now.'

'Bloody typical of him,' Josie retorted without thinking. 'Grass everyone else up to save his own skin.'

'Josie, we want him to cough.'

'I know, but you'd think he'd have some sort of respect or honour amongst thieves or what have you.' Then, knowing how it sounded she added, 'oh, you know what I mean.'

'I have to go. They're still questioning them both but Johnstone has mentioned something else that needs checking out. I've been asked to go along.'

'What do you mean?'

'I can't say yet but it might become clearer soon. If it does, I promise you'll be among the first to know. Are you still there?'

Josie had gone quiet because she didn't believe what she was seeing.

'Yes, I'm still here,' she whispered. 'But Debbie's walked in.'

'Keep cool! Don't do anything that might make her suspicious. It'll be better for us with her out of the picture anyway. Does she look any different?'

'In what way?'

'Worried? Nervous? Does she look as if she suspects anything?'

Debbie was checking her mobile phone as she waited for her computer to load up. She smiled as she caught Josie's eye.

Josie smiled back. 'I don't think so,' she whispered to Andy. 'But I'd better go in case she comes over to me.'

'Okay, but remember what I said. Keep cool. Oh, and keep her there if you can. If she does do a runner, then ring me straight away.'

For the next hour or so, Josie observed Debbie furtively while trying to keep her happy demeanour. She wished she had a bit more fight in her, as she wanted to march right across there and slap her hard. Maybe then she would get rid of this rage burning inside. Debbie was being her usual chatty self. The only thing Josie particularly noticed was that she was checking her mobile phone constantly to see if she had any messages.

Finding out that Scott Johnstone was involved in the burglaries had blown Josie's mind. It was going to be hard to break that to Kelly too. Josie was certain that she had no idea what had been going on, but she also realised that she'd be mortified that she had been lied to about something else.

She picked up her pen and glanced across at Debbie again. She had her head down, working on something or other. She didn't seem to be bothered about anything.

Unable to concentrate, Josie was thankful when Andy finally

walked in, along with Mark.

Andy came across to Josie first. 'You won't believe what we've found,' he said. 'I can't wait to get her into custody.'

Confused by his remark, Josie quickly followed him and Mark across to Debbie's desk. It took a few moments before Debbie looked up. Her eyes ran over the three of them suspiciously.

'Debbie Wilkins,' said Andy, 'I'm arresting you on suspicion of obtaining information under false pretences and aiding and abetting a known criminal. You do not have to say anything, but it may harm your defence if you do not mention when questioned something which you later rely on in court. Anything you do say may be given in evidence.'

A silence fell across the room.

Debbie stood up. 'You can't arrest me,' she said defiantly. 'You don't have anything on me. I might live with him but I had no idea what he was doing and that's my final word on the matter.' She folded her arms.

Josie half admired Debbie's stance. She hadn't even questioned the whys and wherefores.

'What's going on?' Irene asked. She'd been joined by Ray; Doug wasn't too far behind him. Sonia and Craig were already close by.

'She's involved with Philip Matson and she's been passing on addresses for him to burgle,' Josie told everyone.

'I never did!' cried Debbie.

'You used me to get information – you used us all for your own means. Have you any idea how much damage you've caused? How long it takes for the victims to get back on their feet, if they ever do?'

'I told you,' said Debbie. 'It's got nothing to do with me.'

'Save it,' said Mark. 'We have bigger fish to fry.'

For a split second Debbie froze, but then she regained her composure. 'You can't prove anything.'

'So you haven't been supplying Matson with addresses of vulnerable people?' said Andy.

'No, I haven't been supplying *Phil* with anything.'

'You had no idea that he's a thief and a murderer?' said Mark.

Debbie sighed dramatically. 'No, I had no idea that he was a thief and a....'

Andy reached into his pocket and pulled out a small evidence bag. He held it up to Josie.

'I need you to verify this for me until I can check with the family.'

Josie gasped as she spotted the pearl necklace with its unique butterfly clasp. She held onto the desk for support.

'What's that?' asked Debbie.

'You bitch!' Josie seethed. 'That necklace belonged to Edie Rutter.'

Debbie frowned. 'But what's that got to do with me?'

'It was found at your house less than an hour ago,' said Andy.

'But that was missing from –' Debbie paled as she worked out its significance. 'You don't think that Phil did... no, he wouldn't do that.'

'Scott Johnstone reckoned he did,' said Mark. 'He told us where to look for it, inside the rose of the light in the hallway. Not every thief goes to so much trouble to hide things and we would have found it eventually, but it was great to know where to go.'

'No.' Debbie shook her head vehemently. 'He wouldn't do that. He wouldn't!'

'Don't give me that,' said Josie. 'You knew perfectly well what he'd done. He left Edie Rutter to die in a pool of blood. You might as well have been there with him.'

'Josie's right,' said Ray. 'How could you do that? We trusted you.'

'But I wasn't involved in her murder. I wasn't there!'

'You set her up though, didn't you?'

'No... please!' Debbie faltered. 'I didn't know he'd left her there to... to...'

Josie moved past everyone to stand in front of her. 'And to think that I helped you out when you first started here,' she hissed, prodding her in the chest. 'I could slap your face for what you've done. But that would make me just as bad as you.'

'I didn't know!'

Not a sound was heard but a ringing phone as Debbie Wilkins was handcuffed and escorted off the premises.

CHAPTER THIRTY

Andy was ensconced on one of three new settees in the reception area at The Workshop while Josie tried out the coffee machine again. She was so looking forward to the opening next week, but dreaded the pace upping further as the day drew nearer. Still, Andy turning up made her find time for a break: any excuse to rest her legs at the moment.

'Who would have thought it, though?' Andy shook his head yet again. 'Debbie Wilkins giving out inside information to that creep Matson so he could then go and rob them all blind.'

'Yep, she conned me good and proper,' Josie replied. She handed him a plastic cup and sat down beside him. 'And I thought I'd exorcised vulnerable Josie over the past few months.'

Andy stretched out his legs as his radio crackled in the background. 'It wasn't your fault. She seemed so nice every time I saw her. I would have done the same things in your position.'

Josie sighed. 'I suppose so, but when I look back I wonder how it went on for so long. She was always so keen to learn anything about my job. I just thought she aspired to be a housing officer. But all the time she was gleaning information from me, using me to scope out which tenants to rob. And because of that, I told her everything *and* took her into their homes.'

'But you would have done that with any housing assistant, wouldn't you?' Andy tried to ease her conscience.

Josie nodded. 'If they expressed an interest, yes. Not everyone wants to do this job – and who can blame them? Sometimes I wonder why I've done it for so long.'

'Because you're good at it. And because you care.'

'And look where that got me.' Josie snorted.

'I hope they throw the book at her when she's up in court again next month.'

'I reckon that's why she was so keen to go on his eviction, too,' Josie acknowledged, going off at an angle slightly. 'She thought it'd take the scent off her.'

'I bet she didn't think the greedy prick would register for benefits from there afterwards,' Andy added. 'Which indirectly linked us to her.'

'And directly linked her to him,' Josie noted.

'But if he hadn't registered to claim his benefits, you might never have twigged what was happening, unless he really did slip up.'

'I'm glad that he did. It was his downfall after all.'

'That and the fact that Johnstone grassed him up.'

'Hmm.' Josie thought back to the time she'd seen Debbie across the shops talking to Scott Johnstone. She'd thought Debbie had been taking grief for doing her job when she was probably handing out addresses of vulnerable tenants that she'd been to visit.

'And with Matson and Johnstone on remand,' she added, 'the Mitchell Estate is that little bit safer.'

Andy laughed. 'The Mitchell Estate will never be safe.'

Josie smiled. 'What I can't work out, though, is why she turned up for work that last morning. I know if it was me and my boyfriend hadn't come home from the take the night before, I would have gone on the run immediately. Where to, I don't know, but I wouldn't have come into work.'

'She denied everything on the day, though didn't she? And Johnstone told us that Matson often stayed with him after a robbery, to take the heat off Debbie if they did get caught. So she had no idea we had him in custody.'

'That's why she was constantly checking her phone,' Josie nodded again. 'She must have been waiting for him to text her.'

'Yep,' said Andy. 'And if Johnstone hadn't come forward with that little gem – or rather, necklace – we would have been none the wiser for Edie Rutter's murder.'

Josie involuntarily shuddered. 'I still can't believe he left Edie to die. I mean, why didn't he call an ambulance after he'd left the property?'

'Perhaps she could identify him?'

'Sadly, we will never know,' Josie said. 'I still miss calling round there for a cuppa.'

Andy pointed to the room. 'But you have this place to concentrate on now. It looks amazing, by the way.'

Kelly had decided to take a few days off between leaving her job at Miles' Factory and the opening of The Workshop. Now on her last shift, she was helping Sally to remove the wrappings around the many plates laid out in the staff canteen. As a leaving gift, everyone had provided an item of food for a buffet. About a dozen people had come into the room so far.

'I can't believe you're leaving today,' Sally moaned.

'Well, I can't believe all the fantastic presents I've had,' said Kelly, eyeing the flowers she'd received along with other personal gifts. 'I feel like I've only been working her for five minutes.'

Sally gave her a hug. 'I'm going to miss you so much, but I know you'll do okay with Office Options. If anyone deserves to, it's you.'

'Are you going to miss me as well?' Leah swapped places with Sally, not to be outdone.

'Like a hole in the head,' muttered Sally, then looked away all innocent. Leah frowned at her for a moment before grinning.

'Course I'll miss you, you big nerd,' Kelly told her. 'I'll miss you both. And you can always pop over and see me.'

'You'll be too arty-farty-in-your-new-office for us, won't she, Sal?'

As Robbie was warming up, threatening to sing another cover version from the real Robbie Williams, Stewart walked in. Kelly took immense pleasure in the fact that 'Mummy's Boy' looked miserable. It was laughable really, but it still shocked her to think that he could have been so cruel.

She couldn't help herself when she beckoned him over to join them.

'I think you're in need of some cake to cheer you up,' Kelly said, handing him a plate. As he was about to take a bite, she turned down the radio and spoke again. 'Does your wife bake cakes?'

Stewart's fork hung in mid-air. Everyone stopped what they were doing amidst the silence.

'It was you!' Stewart slatted the plate and its contents down onto the table.

'Christ, Kel,' said Robbie. 'Have you been upsetting our Mummy's Boy?'

'He's not a mummy's boy,' Kelly remarked. 'Until last month, he lived with his *wife*. This snide creep has been married to my friend for years.'

There was a gasp around the room.

Stewart launched himself at her. Kelly stood her ground but Robbie and some of the other male workers watched her back regardless, blocking him access to her.

'He told her that his mother was dead,' she continued. 'He never told his mother he was married, either. I reckon he was waiting to inherit all of her money, live with my friend rent free and then do a runner when his mum really died.'

'You sneaky bastard!' Leah was the first one to speak out.

'What does she mean, you're married?'

'When did this happen?'

'That can't be true! It's like something from Jeremy Kyle.'

'Why didn't you say anything?'

'You've ruined everything, you stupid bitch!' Stewart pushed into Robbie but was held back again.

'Back off!' he was told.

'Or fuck off,' said Robbie. 'We don't want you in here. You're not invited to this party.'

Knowing he was beat, Stewart stormed off.

'And don't come back, you sneaky prick!' one of the packers shouted after him.

Sally gave Kelly a hug. 'Well done, girl. You certainly put him in his place.'

'Yeah,' said Leah. 'I bet he'll be looking for another job soon. Those boys can be bullies when they all gang up on someone. You make his life hell, Robbie,' she shouted over to him.

The lively atmosphere of the party soon came back again and, with the undercurrents of the rumour spreading like wild fire, everyone had a good time. Sally changed the music from radio to a CD and turned the volume up again.

'Let's make a toast: to Kelly!'

'To Kelly!' cried everyone.

'To Office Options,' added Kelly.

With one week to go, all stops were pulled out to get The Workshop ready to face its public. On Monday, Josie and Kelly returned after the weekend to a burst pipe. Two of the rooms had been completely flooded; carpeting had to be ripped up and replaced. Luckily, the water had been dripping rather than gushing, so the walls had been spared.

On Wednesday, the caterers turned up. Great news – but they weren't due until Friday, the scheduled date for opening. Even though it was clearly written on Josie's confirmation order, the woman had gone off in a tizzy, insisting the date was correct. But when Josie had checked with the owner of the business, she hadn't been able to apologise enough. As it had been their mistake, she said everything would be redone on Friday without a further charge.

Even their last day had its moments, with items going missing and turning up unannounced, but by five o'clock everything was in its rightful place. Now they were sitting on the chairs behind the reception desk. The last workman had gone roughly an hour ago and, after checking every room was exactly how they wanted it to be for the big unveiling tomorrow, they'd opened a bottle of wine to celebrate before going home.

'Here's to The Workshop. I can't believe it was finished on target!' Josie chinked her wine glass with Kelly's. 'And here's to our futures in it, too.'

'Did you ever think we'd get this far?'

'Are you referring to the building or us?'

Kelly grinned. 'I suppose I mean both.'

'Things have certainly changed since the beginning of the year,' Josie acknowledged.

'For me too,' said Kelly. 'I lost my home – which, while we're on the subject, you forced me out of –'

'For a very good reason.'

'– I survived on my own in Clarence Avenue, found a job to tide me over, passed a secretarial course, sacked a loser, applied for a grant and got ready to set up my own business – that goes live tomorrow.'

'Yes, and once it does, maybe you and Jay could share some quality time together afterwards. You've worked so hard lately.'

Kelly blushed. 'I don't know about that.'

'You've a lot of catching up to do.'

'I... maybe –' Kelly didn't want to say anything aloud in case it all went wrong. Jay had been shocked when she'd told him about Scott, even more shocked when he realised how guilty she'd felt.

'What?'

'I think it's too late.'

'It isn't! You're mad about him, anyone can see that. And you know how he feels about you, don't you? Lord knows, he ribs you about it often enough.'

Kelly puffed out her cheeks and then blew out her breath. 'Would it sound stupid if I think that he's too perfect?'

Josie shook her head. 'Not at all.'

'I knew Scott wasn't right for me but it was only when he went inside that I realised exactly how much.' Kelly began to tick things off with her fingers. 'He blamed me for everything. Then there was all that business with Anne-Marie. And then to find out that he was involved in all of those robberies makes me wonder exactly what he was capable of. I suppose until he threatened me, I thought he'd never lay a finger on me.'

'But Jay's not like that,' insisted Josie.

'I know.' Kelly's face lit up as she thought of him. Sweet, loyal Jay, who'd become her saviour over the past few months; loving Jay who she realised she loved back with every atom of her being. He'd stood by her through everything, even when she didn't think she'd deserved it.

'I still think that too much has happened,' she added.

Josie disagreed. 'He knows Scott's an idiot and he doesn't blame you. And he adores Em. That's something extra special.'

'But when things seem too good to be true, they usually are.' Kelly's face crumpled. She'd been an idiot letting Scott do what he wanted, but maybe she did have time to put it right now.

She twirled her chair round to face Josie more and rested one elbow on the desk. 'I hope Scott goes down for years rather than months this time. I can't believe the amount of times I covered for him! I hate him more now. He'll never change.'

They heard a car horn beep.

Josie drained her glass and got to her feet. 'Are you going to give him the grand tour or let him wait until tomorrow?'

'Tomorrow will do,' said Kelly, anxious to get home now that he was here.

'Come on, then, let's lock up and go.' Josie smiled. 'I suppose neither of us will get much sleep tonight.'

In the middle of the room, Kelly and Josie hugged each other. There was no need for words. Both women realised how far they had come.

Once back at the flat, Kelly couldn't stop thinking about Josie's advice. They'd dropped Emily off at her mum's so that they could go out for something to eat. She was staying overnight.

'I fancy a red hot curry to celebrate the opening of Office Options. What do you reckon?' Jay asked as he walked into the living room behind her.

Kelly turned to face him, reached for his hand and drew him close. 'I thought we could stay in and celebrate, seeing as we have the place to ourselves.' Smiling shyly, she slipped her hand inside his jumper and ran it over the length of his back, nervous at the feel of his skin for the first time.

Jay grinned, his eyes darkening with lust. 'And what did you have in mind to get the party started?'

Kelly held up her other hand. In it was a DVD.

'It's a girlie flick,' she said. Then she threw it onto the settee. 'But first, there's something we need to clear up.'

Before she could say anything else, Jay cupped her face and kissed her lightly on the lips. 'I don't give a flying fuck about anything right now. I just want to get inside your knickers.'

Kelly giggled. 'You don't understand, do you? That's exactly what I want to clear up. Now get your kit off, Jay Kirkwell.'

Jay's jumper was over his head in a flash.

CHAPTER THIRTY-ONE

Subj: Good Luck
Date: 05/07/2013 02:05
From: Americanboy@bluememory.com
To: J.Mellor@MitchellHousingAssociation.co.uk

Hi Josie, I just wanted to say all the very best for your big day. I'm sorry I can't be with you. I would have loved to have seen everything as you've planned it.
I'll be thinking of you when I get up (only because you'll be getting ready to open the doors when I am eating my breakfast..!)
Tata for now,
James x

Josie was awake earlier than the birds the following morning. She'd been mentally going over her to-do list all night. There was so much to think about if the day was going to go as planned.

She propped up her head with a pillow in order to see her clothes laid out on the chair: plum-coloured jacket and matching pencil skirt, black sling-backs that instantly seemed to lengthen her legs, cream short-sleeved blouse with a low neck line. On the chest of drawers, a beaded necklace that Livvy had brought as a good luck present and a bottle of new perfume that she'd treated herself to.

She hoped today was going to be a new beginning for her. She had so much to be thankful for recently. Despite everything that had happened with Stewart, she'd found a good friend in Kelly and hooked up with Livvy again, so she wouldn't be lonely – and maybe, in time, she'd get to know James better. That might be nice.

She stretched out every muscle in her body. Then she threw back the covers. Today was going to be so special that she didn't want to waste a moment of it. Within forty minutes, she was heading out of the door.

'Wake up, sleepyhead,' Jay whispered into Kelly's ear. He slid a tray towards her. On it was a bowl of cereal, a boiled egg complete with toast soldiers, and a mug of coffee. A pink flower Kelly recognised from her garden stood proud in a half pint glass of water.

Kelly's smile widened. Jay gave her a lingering kiss before pulling back the duvet and climbing in beside her. Once he'd settled, Kelly picked up her mug – then put it down again.

'God, I'm so excited, Jay.' She clapped her hands like a toddler. 'Today I am going to open my own business.'

Jay's torso disappeared down the side of the bed. From underneath it, he pulled out a large pink envelope and sat up straight again.

'I hadn't realised Em wouldn't be here, this morning – not that I'm complaining after last night.' He raised his eyebrows lasciviously. 'So I'd better give you this anyway.'

The envelope contained a handmade card. The words good luck had been outlined and filled with silver glitter.

'We made it yesterday,' Jay explained.

To Mummy, it read inside. *Good luck tomorrow. Love from Emily and Jay.* Hearts and flowers had been drawn everywhere and a shape which Kelly later found out to be a horseshoe. A lump came to her throat.

'It's lovely.' Kelly put it down on the bedside table. Then she moved aside the tray. 'And so are you.'

Jay drew her into his arms, where she now understood she truly belonged. She kissed him long and hard. Thank God he'd waited for her.

At ten thirty, on a fairly dull, yet extremely dry day at the beginning of July, The Workshop was officially opened by The Lord Mayoress, her consort, and two local businessmen.

Rapturous applause and short speeches were followed by a surge of people through the doors.

Josie posed for numerous photographs, dragging Kelly and some of the other unit holders into most of them with her. Kelly became Josie's unofficial deputy, showing everyone around the building, remarking when appropriate on what a massive team effort it had all been. Josie worried that they'd cope: Kelly told her she worried too much.

By lunch time, the place resembled one of Josie's garden complaints. Discarded leaflets were scattered over table tops and chairs, at least four helium balloons had floated up to the ceiling, and people young and old stood around in groups. Some of the dignitaries were hanging around, waiting for the buffet to be unwrapped.

Kay, the office manager who was never there to manage the office, stopped by with Ray and a new girl who had yet to learn the joys of housing. Andy rushed in and out, due to a call coming through just as he was about to sample a cake that Dot had made for Kelly to bring along.

Livvy showed up around two thirty, closely followed by James. Josie's eyes nearly popped out of her head. He looked relaxed, if a little jetlagged, in jeans and designer T-shirt. His hair had lightened slightly: his skin had tanned dramatically.

'Hi,' he waved.

'Hi! You were the last person I expected to turn up,' Josie said. 'I thought you weren't back until next week.'

'I thought I'd surprise you,' he smiled warmly.

'But the email...'

'I asked someone to send it for me this morning.'

'Oh, I...' Consciously, she ran a hand through her hair, remembering her tumble in the bouncy castle earlier with Emily.

After introductions, Livvy went to grab a cup of tea.

'This place looks great,' James enthused as he skimmed the room before quickly tuning to her.

'Yes, it's been a lot of work but well worth the effort.'

'Maybe... maybe I could take you out for something to eat this evening and celebrate your success?'

Josie smiled shyly. 'Yes, I'd like that very much.'

She heard a giggle behind her and realised that Kelly and Livvy had obviously been listening. As James wandered off to fetch coffee and Livvy moved to talk to one of the councillors, Kelly whispered to her.

'He's a nice dude. Where have you been hiding him?'

'Nowhere,' said Josie in her own defence. She watched as James added milk to her drink and chatted to everyone around him. 'He's my neighbour's brother and has just come back from America.'

Josie smiled, then turned abruptly. Kelly had gone. She realised she'd been left on her own again as James walked back to her. Nerves fizzled up in her stomach – or was it a tiny bit of excitement?

James moved closer and spoke to her in a whisper. 'So, tell me, Ms Josie, how do you like your eggs in the morning?'

'In the words of Dean Martin,' she replied cheekily, 'I like mine with a kiss.'

'Hmm, Ms Josie,' he wagged a finger at her and grinned. 'Now you're definitely flirting with me.'

Once everyone had helped themselves to lunch, Josie moved over to where Kelly was sitting with Jay. James and Livvy had left half an hour earlier. Emily had gone back onto the bouncy castle with some of the other children.

'I've got something to show you.' Josie handed an envelope to Kelly. 'It's yours if you want it.'

Kelly flicked through the photographs of a semi-detached house. Her hand rose to her mouth and she gasped. It looked a bit tatty, but it was huge. And the living room was big too, not to mention the kitchen that looked onto the garden. She knew she could do so much to improve it.

From the last shot, she recognised where it was.

'It's in Norman Street!' She handed the photos to Jay.

Josie nodded. 'That's right. You won't be 'living on the hell' anymore. You'll be on The Mitch, the *better* half of the estate, and around the corner from Jay. I take it that won't be a problem?'

Kelly looked at the photographs again. 'Why didn't you tell me last night?'

'I wanted to wait until today, make it more special. And I can certainly vouch for you in saying that you've been a model tenant.'

'I'm hoping that the tenancy might become a joint one soon,' Jay broke in. He slung an arm around Kelly's shoulders.

'Oh my god!' Josie's eyes widened as she looked from one to the other and back again. 'Don't tell me that you two have finally got it together?'

Kelly smiled and nodded.

Josie clapped her hands in glee. 'Wow, I can finally say, 'case closed'.'

Jay grinned. 'I couldn't let this one get away now, could I? You're a right pair of clever broads. And this place is amazing. But if you're looking after it, won't you miss working on the streets, Josie? All that crime and grime?'

'Oh, I'm sure I'll get to hear about everything, one way or another.' Josie smiled. 'Besides, I've got loads of unfinished cases to keep an eye on. You know as much as I do that there's never a dull moment on the Mitchell Estate.'

ABOUT THE AUTHOR

Mel Sherratt has been a self-described "meddler of words" ever since she can remember. After winning her first writing competition at the age of 11, she has rarely been without a pen in her hand or her nose in a book. Since successfully self-publishing Taunting the Dead and seeing it soar to the rank of number one best-selling police procedural in the Amazon Kindle store in 2012, Mel has gone on to publish three more books in the critically acclaimed The Estate Series.

Mel has written feature articles for The Guardian, the Writers and Artists website, and Writers Forum Magazine, to name just a few, and regularly speaks at conferences, event and talks. She lives in Stoke-on-Trent, Staffordshire, with her husband and her terrier, Dexter (named after the TV serial killer, with some help from her Twitter fans), and makes liberal use of her hometown as a backdrop for her writing.

Mel's website is www.melsherratt.co.uk and you can find her on Twitter at @writermels